BITTER CRY

Also by S.L. Stoner
in the
Sage Adair Historical Mystery Series
of the Pacific Northwest

Timber Beasts
Land Sharks
Dry Rot
Black Drop
Dead Line
The Mangle
Slow Burn

BITTER CRY

**A Sage Adair Historical Mystery
of the Pacific Northwest**

S. L. Stoner

Yamhill Press
www.yamhillpress.net

Bitter Cry

A Sage Adair Historical Mystery of the Pacific Northwest

Bitter Cry is a work of fiction. Names, characters, places and incidents are the products of the author's imagination or are used fictitiously. Any resemblance to actual events, locales, or person, living or dead, is entirely coincidental unless specifically noted otherwise.

A Yamhill Press Book

Cover Design by Vladimir Stefanovic based on the original series' design by Alec "Icky" Dunn

Interior Design by Slaven Kovačević

Printed in the United States. This book may not be reproduced in whole or in part, by any means, without written permission. For information contact: Yamhill Press at www.yamhillpress.net.

Edition ISBNs
Softcover ISBN 978-1-7320066-2-1
EBook   ISBN 978-1-7320066-3-8

Library of Congress Control Number:2019911427

Publishers Cataloguing in Publication

Bitter Cry / S.L. Stoner.

214 pages cm – (A Sage Adair historical mystery of the Pacific Northwest) 1. Northwest, Pacific—History—early 20th century—Fiction, 2. Detective and Mystery Fiction, 3. Action and Adventure—Fiction, 4. Progressive History—Fiction, 5. Child Labor—Fiction, 6. Poverty—Fiction, 7. Newsboys—Fiction, 8. Messenger Boys—Fiction, 9. Historical Fiction

For
George Slanina, Jr.
Always and Forever the Absolute Best!

And

For My Siblings: Dennis, Sally, and K'Lynn
Who Have Always Been Just Plain Wonderful
and Inspirational In So Many Ways

ONE

•

THE BOY SLIPPED INTO THE saloon on the heels of a stumbling drunk. Squaring bony shoulders beneath a dirty canvas jacket, he headed for the bar, scuffing across the uneven plank floor in too-large boots. Shin-length knickers and woolen socks covered spindly legs. The tattered cap riding low on his forehead didn't hide the bright, appraising eye he cast over the saloon's patrons.

He clomped around the room offering his newspapers, a wide smile on his thin face. The smile didn't work. No one bought a paper. The reasons were obvious: stale news and drunken patrons, most of them likely couldn't read. Not their fault. They probably had gone to work at an early age when schooling was rare and not compulsory. So, one after another, heads shook and grimy hands shooed the newsboy away.

Then it was Sage's turn. The serial rejections had dimmed the boy's smile. "Please, Mister. How about you buy a paper? I only got but a few 'afore I can head home. I've been on the streets since early this morning." He thrust the stack forward, his eyes as imploring as his words.

Memory punched Sage's gut, stopping his breath. It was an elfin face with peaked eyebrows, pointed nose and chin. A tentative smile exposed those same bucked and gapped front teeth.

This boy isn't Mickey. Mickey is long dead, he reminded himself. He switched his attention to the boy before him. What to do? He was here to meet up with someone to discuss confidential matters. Still, Meachum was already an hour late so it was unlikely he'd show up at all.

"Go ahead, take a seat," Sage said, gesturing at the chair across the table.

The dark, slightly slanted eyes narrowed as the boy studied the stranger. He was no innocent street urchin ignorant of predators. The boy glanced at the barkeep that was busy elsewhere. Calculation raced across his face. Curiosity or the hope of earning a few coins won out. Besides, the people in the saloon would stop the dark-haired, mustachioed man from trying anything peculiar. The foggy streets and inky alleys outside held more danger.

The boy pulled out the chair but perched on its edge with his feet barely touching the floor and his body tense and ready to flee.

'So, what's your name?" Sage asked, settling farther back in his own chair to give the boy more space.

Pride raised the pointed chin. "William Gladney Tobias," the kid said. "But, the other fellas call me, 'Glad,'" he said, raising a hand to smooth his hair and exposing an inexpensive copper wrist band. Sage momentarily wondered if it had been a gift.

"My name's John Miner," Sage said. "How old are you, Glad?"

"I'm fourteen," he said and added as his eyes flicked sideways, "but small for my age."

More like ten, if even that, Sage thought. But, no point in challenging the boy. "How about a sausage and sarsaparilla?" he asked instead.

Once again suspicion narrowed the boy's eyes and he stiffened in his chair. "What 'xactly will you be wanting in exchange?" he asked.

Sorrow was Sage's first reaction. What had this child suffered from the adults in his world? Glancing around he noted no one was looking in their direction. Nobody cared what happened between the child and the stranger who wore drab canvas and a weathered hat. More's the pity, he thought.

"Only a little conversation, Glad. Nothing else. My friend never turned up so some friendly company would be welcome while I finish my beer," he said matter-of-factly.

At the boy's nodded agreement, Sage strode to the bar and returned with a bread-wrapped sausage, large dill pickle and mug of foamy sarsaparilla.

Glad's first bite was tentative but that soon gave way to ravenous swallows of pickle, sausage and drink, each in turn. A smile tugged at Sage's lips—he liked to eat the same way. He never understood why some people would eat all of one thing before moving on to the next. After all, it was a meal, meant to be savored as a palette of complementary bites—one after the other.

There was time for such idle pondering because Sage wanted the boy to satisfy his hunger without interruption. While he waited, his gaze turned inward, mulling over those long-buried memories triggered by Mickey's spitting-image sitting across from him.

Sage had been younger, only eight, the first time he'd climbed up beside the conveyor belt that carried chunks of coal and rock toward the crusher. His arms had grown long enough to grab and toss aside the rocks passing between the belt's edge and its center. Mickey had stood across from him doing the same job. The work had been hard and dirty but they still managed to exchange grins.

He'd been lucky. His mother worked in the same coal shed, close enough to countermand the foreman's order to put a knee on the belt if there were rocks just beyond Sage's reach. She'd tried to do the same for all the boys but Mickey was across the belt and she didn't hear the foreman's order to Sage's friend.

Though he was now a grown man and sitting in a saloon clear across the country, Sage still tensed at the memory of what happened next. His mother's shout jerked Sage's eyes from the belt just in time to see Mickey clamber onto it, face tense with fear that he tried to overcome with a carefree shrug. That shrug cost him his balance. Sage yelled but no one moved fast enough. Mickey screamed as he tumbled down the fast-moving belt and disappeared into the crusher.

A sheen of sweat coated Sage's face at that memory. He noticed Glad had finished eating and was eyeing his benefactor, a furrow of concern between his brows.

"You okay, Mister?" he asked. "You're looking kinda peaky."

"Yeah, just remembering something that happened when I was about your age," Sage said before quickly changing the subject. "How long you been peddling newspapers?"

"Going on two years now. Ever since us kids and ma got here from Missouri."

"Ever since you were eight, then?"

The boy's agreeing nod froze the instant he realized Sage had just caught him in a lie. He didn't bother trying to wriggle out of it. Just shrugged and gave a lopsided smile that made Sage like him all the more.

"So, do you have brothers and sisters?" Sage asked.

This time the nod was definite and the eyes held steady. "Yup. Got me an older brother and two sisters. My brother works nights as a messenger. Carrie Lynne mostly works at home taking care of Ma and baby Emma. She earns us a bit of money watching after neighbor kids and by helping Ma make artificial flowers."

"What's wrong with your mother?"

A look of helplessness washed across the boy's face. "She's took ill with that consumption. Always coughing and spitting up blood. She can't work no more. But she tries real hard, anyway. Does piece work at home for the paper flower company when she can sit up. Don't know how long that's gonna last 'cause she just keeps getting sicker. All night long—cough, cough, cough." The words trailed off into heavy silence and the boy looked down at his hands on the table.

"What about your pa?"

Sage's question brought a grimace and for a beat, Glad said nothing before answering reluctantly, "We done left him in Missouri. The drink got him and he took to hitting us when he wasn't off throwing all our money at some saloonkeeper."

It was a familiar story. Every day countless men, lost to drink's temporary oblivion, abandoned their wives and children. Sage thought alcohol in moderation acceptable. In fact, his business sold it. Still, encounters with families made destitute by drink made him wonder whether those ax-wielding temperance women had a point.

The boy stirred and continued, "So's we came here and Ma got a job and things were looking pretty good until she got sick."

Glad didn't need to give further explanation. When the only parent was unable to work, it became the children's job to keep the family afloat. Earning enough for food and housing became their daily task. Dreams of anything beyond that were just that—dreams.

"You going to school tomorrow?"

The boy shrugged. "Maybe. Depends on how late I get back. Since I paid a half-cent for each paper, I got to sell them all 'afore I'm done." He straightened. "You want to buy a paper, Mister Miner? Only one cent."

Sage fished in his pocket for a dollar. "Well, Mr. Tobias, I think I'll just buy them all."

Glad's eyes fixed eagerly on the coin. "I don't have change for a whole dollar but I bet the barkeep does."

He started to rise but Sage grabbed his elbow. "Hold up, Glad. You can keep the whole dollar if you will promise me one thing."

Glad sank back on the chair, suspicion darkening his face. "What do you want me to promise?" he said, with a hint of glum resignation.

"That you'll go straight home and that you'll go to school tomorrow. A fellow's got to learn to read and write and calculate if he wants to get anywhere in this world. You don't want to be selling newspapers forever do you?"

Relief brought an emphatic shake of the head. "I'm going to college when I get a bit older," Glad said and added proudly, "I can read pretty good already. Mama taught me and every day I read the newspaper from cover to cover."

Sage sat back in surprise. "How do you plan on paying for college?" he asked.

Glad's eyes brightened and he leaned forward, eagerness vibrating in his spare body. "I got me a bank account. Every week I put in a few cents. The rest I give to Ma. I don't have nothing to do with playing craps or wasting money on the nickelodeons like the other newsboys. Anyway, next fall, I'll have enough saved so's I can buy a delivery route up there in the West Hills. Them rich folks like having the paper with their breakfast. It'll be a steady bit of cash and I'll have my route done before school. Then, starting at 4:30 in the afternoon, I'll sell rush hour papers—that's the best money," he confided.

"How long have you had this plan of yours?"

"Oh, I started thinking on it awhile back," Glad said, sitting back and crossing his arms across his chest. A worried look crossed his face and he leaned forward again to say, "'Course, first off we got to find a better place to live. That dampness ain't helpin' Ma's breathing none."

"Where is it that you live?"

There was a slight hesitation. Sage waited for the hasty lie only to realize that it was embarrassment holding Glad's tongue because the boy flushed as he said, "We got us a one-room place down there in Sullivan's Gulch."

Sage knew where he meant. Only the destitute and crazed lived in the shacks that squatted on the ravine's bottom beside a spring-fed Tanner creek.

"I've heard there's fish in that creek. You ever fish it?" Sage asked, and was gratified to see the question ease the boy's embarrassment.

Glad nodded eagerly. "I surely do and I've caught some good ones. But my brother, Terrance, is even better at catching them."

Seeing that the boy was again on firm footing, Sage said, "Well, you best head home. I'm sure your ma's worried." Sage handed Glad the dollar coin and received the boy's remaining papers in return.

Pocketing the coin, Glad's face turned solemn as he said, "I thank you kindly, Mr. Miner, for the sausage and the pickle and the sarsaparilla. And the dollar," he added hastily. He stood, leaving his papers on the table. Sticking out his hand he said earnestly, "You ever need anything, anything at all, you can always find me down here late evenings 'cause I stop here to Slap Jacks on my way to home."

Sage smiled, his mind fixing momentarily on the fictional Sherlock Holmes and his army of helpful street urchins the author called, "the Baker Street Irregulars."

"I'll keep that in mind, Mr. Tobias. It's been a pleasure," he answered solemnly as he shook the boy's hand.

As Glad turned to go, Sage couldn't resist cautioning him, "And, you take care going home."

"I will." Glad gave his gap-toothed grin. "I surely will, especially tonight," he repeated as he patted the pocket holding the coin.

After the boy slipped out the saloon doors, Sage pulled his tin watch from his pocket. Almost eleven. Definitely too late for Meachum to turn up. The last freight train from the south would have pulled in an hour ago.

Stepping out onto the boardwalk, he paused when an odd noise, about half a block away, caught his attention. The street was partially obscured by thinning fog so Sage stepped in that direction and squinted to see better. Sure enough, there was Glad; a stack of newspapers draped over one arm. He was running toward a cab that had pulled to the curb.

"The little imp," Sage muttered, realizing Glad must have stashed some papers outside the saloon. As it was, he'd been taken in by that newsboy ploy, "Gee, Mister. These are my last papers to sell before I can go home to bed." He smiled and felt a bit of admiration for the enterprising youngster.

Sage watched two men dismount from the cab. The driver stayed on his rooftop perch, holding the horse in place. Suddenly, Glad gave a cry of alarm, dropped his papers, backed away and turned to flee.

"Hey!" Sage shouted and began to run.

His shout didn't divert the men. One of them, the biggest fellow, snatched the boy, turned him upside down and shook him like a pepper shaker. Sage heard coins raining onto the boardwalk. The two attackers didn't pause to pick them up. Instead, the second man opened the cab door and tossed Glad inside like a bag of laundry. Then both men jumped in after him and the cab rattled away at a fast trot.

Outrage powered Sage's legs. Over the thudding of his feet, he heard Glad shriek. Sage ran until his lungs started heaving. Still, the cab drew even further away. Finally, after three blocks, it turned a corner, leaving him so winded that he had to stop, hands on thighs, to catch his breath, stale beer forming a nasty bubble in his throat. Seconds later, he ran on but, rounding the corner he saw only an empty street. The cab's red tail lantern had vanished.

Defeated, Sage headed back to the scene of the attack despite knowing nothing there could explain what he'd just seen happen. A slight breeze began dispersing the fog and fluttering Glad's dropped newspapers. He leaned against a darkened storefront and pondered the scattered copper pennies and the silver dollar in their midst. Rain began pattering the newspapers, a dismal accompaniment to the despair washing over him. If it wasn't a robbery, what the hell was it?

TWO

"Hey, Lazy Bones, we could use your help downstairs this mor—" The chiding cut off as she took in the unused bed and her son, sitting slumped in a chair, staring out the window.

"What's wrong? Did something happen to Meachum? Is he hurt?" Alarm sharpened her words. Mae Clemens liked the Flying Squad's leader. Like them, Meachum was one of St. Alban's undercover operatives. But Meachum's role was more dangerous. He and his small group of men rode the rails, confronting the violent railroad bulls who beat, robbed and killed the thousands of homeless men forced to hop boxcars as they searched for work. Meachum and his Flying Squadron never killed the bulls. Instead, they tossed them off the trains on slow curves—usually without their boots.

Sage straightened in his chair and scrubbed his face with his hands. "No, Ma, far's I know, Meachum is just fine. At least, I haven't heard otherwise. His schedule is always kind of iffy."

She pointedly looked at the bed and at her son in his chair. "Well, something sure the heck happened. Did you catch any sleep last night?"

He heaved a sigh. "No. And, yes, something happened." He told her about his encounter with William Gladney Tobias and how he'd seen the boy snatched off the street.

"The poor child. What do you suppose they wanted with him?"

Sage grimaced. "I hate to think." Then he added, knowing what he said next would be a blow to her heart. "Ma," he began gently, "he was the spitting image of Mickey—right down to the gap between his front teeth."

She sagged down onto a chair, the searing memory weakening her knees. "I see," she said. Looking at her son, her dark blue eyes, so like his own, were sympathetic as she added, "Maybe the boy is why Sergeant Hanke is sitting at the kitchen table downstairs."

Sage lurched to his feet. "Why didn't you say so in the first place? I filed a police report. Maybe they've found Glad."

As he hurried to the door her dry voice stopped him in his tracks. "Surely, you're not going to walk through Mozart's dining room as John Miner?"

She was right. Many considered Mozart's Table the second most elegant restaurant in Portland. Only the Portland Hotel's dining room ranked higher. Ironically, their restaurant was merely a cover for their labor union work. Sage, disguised as John Miner, moved around the city in workingman's clothes when he was on one of St. Alban's missions. But in his role of Mozart's well-to-do proprietor, John Adair, he wore only silk, linen, gabardine, and fine worsted wool. It was in that role that he was able to mingle with and, gather information about, the shenanigans of the city's wealthy elite.

So, she was right. He couldn't mix the two personas. "Will you ask him to wait while I change?" he asked her.

"I'll ask but, from the look of him, I don't think he's planning to go anytime soon."

"Oh. So, he's got his feed bag on?" Sage guessed. Hanke started partaking of their cook's culinary delights when he worked as a beat patrolman. Even after his sergeant's promotion, Hanke still dropped into Mozart's kitchen now and again.

Mae shook her head. "Fact is, that's what's got me worried. He turned down food and he's not smiling."

"Damn," Sage said. He snatched clothes from the wardrobe and headed for the bathroom down the hall.

Ten minutes later, with mustache ends waxed, hair pomaded, an expensive suit and vest donned, and accessorized by a gold watch chain, Sage stepped into Mozart's kitchen where the big policeman sat waiting for him. After taking a seat and gratefully accepting a mug of coffee from Ida, Sage asked, "Is this about the report I filed last night? Did you find the boy?"

Hanke stared into his coffee mug before looking at Sage. "Maybe. We found a boy's body. It's with the coroner over at Crofton's funeral home. He looks about the right age and all."

Sage groaned and felt his mother squeeze his shoulder. He hadn't realized that she stood behind him. He reached up and put his hand atop her's.

Hanke said, "I was hoping you'd take a gander—see if it's the Tobias kid. We need to find and tell his folks if it is. If not—" Hanke's shrug finished his sentence. The police would try to find the dead boy's family but, with so many children working and living on the streets, they might never identify the body.

Crofton's funeral home was also the City morgue. That's how it worked in Portland. The chosen funeral home's director also served as the coroner and pronounced the cause of death. Crofton's narrow, pale face was glum when he opened the door.

"Sergeant, given the circumstances of the child, I thought it prudent to call in Dr. Harry Lane to consult. Just to make sure there wasn't foul play," he said, before leading them down the basement stairs.

Sure enough, the doctor awaited them, smoke from a briar root pipe wreathing his head. His strong chin jutted forward and his gray eyes coolly scrutinized Sage from head to toe. "You're that John Adair fellow. You run that fancy restaurant," he announced in an accusatory tone.

Momentarily taken aback by the man's unfriendly attitude, Sage said nothing. Lane kept talking. "Been there. Good food but don't particularly like the company. Too many self-satisfied nabobs. I prefer rubbing elbows with the plain folk."

Sage couldn't disagree but this was neither the time nor place to voice his opinion. Lane turned his attention to Sergeant Hanke. "Let's get a move-on. I have patients waiting."

Peering over Lane's shoulder, Sage was relieved to see that only one small, sheet-covered body lay on a zinc-covered table. The rest of the tables stood empty. Even so, the room with its medicinal and other scents gave him the willies.

The four of them crossed the room to stand around the body. Saying nothing, Lane drew the sheet off the face. Sage's heart stopped and then stuttered back to beating. The little face had a red puckered scar on one side and the hair was dirty yellow.

"It's not him. It's not Glad Tobias." Hearing the relief in his own voice, Sage felt shame. After all, a boy was dead. One about Glad's age. He rushed to ask, "What killed him, doctor?"

The lines around Lane's tight-lipped mouth deepened. Despite his cranky attitude, Sage knew the doctor cared. He'd never met the man but he'd heard of him. Born the grandson of Oregon's first territorial governor and senator, Lane had thrown social prestige aside to become a physician who treated the poor without charge. In fact, he was known, locally, as, "The Poor People's Doctor."

Lately, Lane had been raising a ruckus over the City's failure to inspect butcher shops. Before that, he'd fussed over human waste fertilizing the city's vegetable gardens. When no one listened, he stopped the practice by shooting the urns used to hold the stuff. Lane was a man with causes who also took action. Had to admire that.

Lane gently pulled the sheet down to the boy's waist. It was a painful sight. Every single rib in the boy's sutured chest protruded. He was so underfed that his collarbones nearly pierced his thin pale skin. Lane gently pulled an arm from beneath the sheet. It was sticklike and sprinkled with other red scars, some old some new. The doctor turned the wrist so that they could see the calluses on the boy's fingers and palms. Tenderly, Lane returned the hand to the body's side. "His lungs are also scarred."

"Scarred?" Sage repeated.

The doctor nodded. "He was in some place where he breathed in harmful particles for a considerable time. That's what did the scarring."

The doctor drew the sheet back over the body. "I found no broken bones, no evidence of strangulation. I don't think he was murdered. I think he was starved and worked to death or, at least near enough to death, that he couldn't survive last night's cold."

Hanke cleared his throat. "A patrolman found him early this morning, wrapped in a blanket, lying behind a row of dust bins. At first, he thought the child was just sleeping."

The doctor nodded. "That's why he looks so peaceful. Probably died in his sleep from hypothermia. There's not an ounce of fat on his frame. The blanket wasn't enough."

"What are those scars on his body?" Sage asked.

"Burns. Some old, some relatively new. Whatever work they had him doing involved fire."

They stood around the covered body, each one contemplating the horror that had been the child's life until Hanke finally asked, "How old is he, do you think?"

Lane waved his pipe in the air, sending out a trail of smoke. "Hard telling. He's been worked hard and starved, so his growth is stunted. That's always the case with these factory children. I'd guess somewhere between nine and twelve. Can't tell you anything more."

With that, Lane nodded at them, tapped the brim of his hat and headed toward the doorway. When he reached it, he turned, removed his pipe and pointed its stem at Hanke as he said, "I'm counting on you to find the bastards who did this." His lips twisted before he added, "Unless some damn politician tells you to back off, of course." There was no mistaking the contempt he gave the word, "politician."

They trudged back to the police station in silence beneath a heavy blanket of gray clouds. As the station came in sight, Hanke stirred himself to say, "The boy had a few other belongings with him. You want to see?"

The possessions lay on Hanke's desk: A shirt that looked far too large, a penknife with a broken tip, a creased photograph of a grim woman and a kerchief, bright red against the faded blue of the shirt. Profound sadness washed through Sage.

Hanke seemed to feel it too, because he dropped into his chair behind the desk with a heavy sigh. "He'd wrapped himself in that big shirt to keep warm. I'm guessing he's a runaway. Given how skinny he is, I'm also thinking he might be one of them orphan slaves."

Sage sat down across from the police sergeant as he echoed, "Orphan slave?"

Hanke nodded. "I've been knowing about them. They've too many orphans back east so they ship them west on trains. Folks actually go to the train stations, pick out the one they want, pay for their fare and take them home. For the lucky children, it means hard work but a good home. For others—" here he shrugged, leaving the rest to Sage's imagination.

"You don't think he had a family, then?"

"Well, of course, there are some families, especially those without a father, that have no choice but to have everybody out earning money as best they can. And, I've seen where some folks send their little kids out to work so they don't have to or because they want the family to get ahead at any cost."

Hanke heaved a sigh before saying, "But, a family seems unlikely since his folks would have at least fed him just to keep him working. Looks like nobody cared whether our young fellow got enough food. Orphan slaves, they're treated like they're replaceable. I've seen it before."

"Here? In Portland?" Appalled didn't begin to describe what Sage felt. "We have orphan slaves here in Portland?"

Hanke shrugged. "I don't know. I hope not. I saw lots in Chicago when I was growing up. At first, I just thought they were sick kids because they were so little, pale and skinny. Later on, I learned about orphan slaves. I've also seen burn marks like his before."

"You know how he got burned?"

Hanke's lips were tight as he said, "Yup. Pretty darn sure it was molten glass. I'm thinking the poor kid ran away from a glass factory. They've got tons of them in Illinois. Not that many around here and I've never heard of them using kids.

"So, I'm thinking maybe he rode a freight train in from somewhere. God only knows where he came from. I hate to think it was all the way from Chicago. Though, I suppose the hobos could have looked after him. Lots of them would try to help a kid that young."

Mae met him at Mozart's front door. The noon dinner hour was in full swing but she walked right past waiting customers to take his hat and coat and hang them on the hall tree. Her face was set and ready for bad news. Sage didn't keep her waiting. He shook his head. "It wasn't him. It wasn't Glad," he said, and watched as her face reflected the same train of thought that his own had traveled upon first seeing the dead boy's face—first relief, then shame, and finally, sadness.

He glanced behind her. The dining room was full, the ever-dependable Homer was rushing to and fro, as was the second waiter they'd just hired. "Where's Mr. Fong?"

She said, "I told him to go home. Kum Ho is very sick. He was too worried to work."

That news gave Sage pause. Kum Ho would have to be very sick indeed if she'd let Fong stay home with her. The two of them owned a small provision store that catered to the city's Chinese. She usually ran the store while Fong worked at Mozart's, and sometimes slept there in his third-floor room. Originally, Fong wanted to work at Mozart's Table so he could learn how to run a fancy restaurant. His plan had been to open one that served Chinese food. No one would call the town's nondescript Chinese cafés, "elegant." Fong had meant to open the first upscale one catering to whites as well as Chinese.

But everything had changed when Fong used martial arts to repel an attack against Sage. In the aftermath of that attack, he and Mae had told Fong the truth about their mission in Portland and he'd wanted to help. Now the three of them carried out St. Alban's assignments and Fong taught Sage the snake and crane martial art. He'd also become Sage's closest friend.

Sage periodically offered to fund Fong's Chinese restaurant only to have Fong wave a dismissive hand as he said, "When I get old and tired, then I run restaurant."

Sage looked around the crowded dining room. "Do you want me to take over the podium or the busboy job?"

"Podium," she answered without hesitation. "You aren't exactly dressed for hauling dirty dishes. Besides, we're about to get several more customers. A new lawyer in town, Ambrose Abernathy, has reserved a table for twenty people. Apparently, it's his wife's birthday."

"He must have come to town with heavy pockets," Sage said drily, as his inner voice sarcastically observed that yet another rich lawyer was just what the town didn't need.

"Where do you suppose Glad is?" she mused, once the restaurant was closed and the two waiters were in the kitchen prepping for the four o'clock tea hour.

"That's what's nagging at me. That and wondering about that little fellow who died." Sage was sipping whiskey, hoping it would slow his thinking enough that he could sleep for a few hours. "Children of that age shouldn't have to—" he began until he remembered who was sitting across from him.

Unshed tears glittered in her eyes. "You go ahead and say it, Sage. Say that 'children that age shouldn't have to work'. I agree with you. You know I do."

"You had no choice."

She shrugged and he knew his words failed to lessen her guilt. Still, she agreed, "No, I didn't have a choice. Your uncle had that black lung. It was only a matter of months before he coughed himself out of work. And, I couldn't earn enough to feed the three of us. Still, I nearly lost you."

They didn't often talk about Sage's year spent as a breaker boy or his subsequent descent into the mine at the age of nine. Nor did they talk of the mine explosion and Sage's rescue of the mine owner's grandson. They also avoided talking about their twelve years apart when he was fostered and educated by that same mine owner.

Those memories pained them both. For her, it was a revisiting of the sorrow she'd felt every day for his lost childhood and long absence. For him, it was twelve years of bitterness—of enduring the mine owner's resentment that the explosion had killed his only son instead of the "hillbilly", Sage. It had been a life of luxury awash with undercurrents of contempt and anger.

He reached across and squeezed her hand. "But you didn't, you didn't lose me. I'm right here."

She dabbed at her eyes with the corner of her apron before straightening in her chair. Her face turned resolute and strong. It was a look that always reminded him of a ship's figurehead, one proudly leading the ship into the unknown.

"Anyways, come tomorrow, how do we find out what happened to Glad and that poor dead boy?" she asked.

THREE

"Let me take your coat, Sir. My, you've brought her a lovely bouquet today." Elvira's formal tone signaled that strangers were about the house.

After taking the roses, she ushered him into the second parlor where heat radiated from a tall coal-burning stove. It was his second favorite room in the house. He smiled. His liking for his favorite room had little to do with its décor.

The best thing about the second parlor was that it contained little of the bric-a-brac so popular with the day's Victorian sensibilities. Most of its too-busy wallpaper was hidden behind framed landscapes and mirrors. The room's corners each had a purpose. One held a whiskey table and another sported a potted rubber tree. In the third corner, a folding screen concealed a lounging divan while the fourth corner held a walnut gramophone with its huge brass horn.

Along the two side walls stood four hard-backed, green velvet chairs facing a matching two-person settee. The red Oriental rug lying between them got rolled up whenever the customers wanted to drink and dance before heading upstairs. There'd been no changes since he'd last been in the room except for the newly installed electric sconces and floor lamps. She entered as he was pulling the chain on one of the latter, switching the light off and on.

"Do you like them?" she asked.

Turning, his mind momentarily froze as it always did when he first saw Lucinda Collins. He smiled wryly and shrugged. "Well, the light is less harsh than I expected. Guess I'm used to saloons with their ugly dangling wires and bare bulbs."

"Does that mean you might reconsider and electrify Mozart's dining room?" she said with a grin only to hurry on before he answered. "Can I be the one to tell Mae? She'll be so delighted." Her teasing referred to an on-going dispute between Sage and his mother. So far, only the restaurant's kitchen was electrified and then, only with a single bare bulb.

In a more sober tone and with odd intensity, Lucinda added, "I'm told the electricity adds to the house's resale value."

Before he could reply, Elvira poked her head around the door frame and raised her eyebrows dramatically.

"Oops, be back in a minute," Lucinda said and strode from the parlor.

Sage's eye roamed over the caramel-colored glass shades covering the electric sconces and the brass floor lamps sporting matching magenta silk and gold-tasseled shades. Maybe the time had come to make the switch from gas to electricity like his mother wanted. According to his recently acquired firefighting friends, the city's new electrical code made fires less likely.

When Lucinda returned she was shaking her head. "One of our newer patrons. I just banned him from returning. Not exactly our kind of clientele." Her lips twisted in disgust. "You'd think a lawyer would know better."

Lucinda ran the city's most exclusive parlor house. She expected her visitors to act like gentlemen and her girls to act like ladies otherwise, she threw them out.

She gestured toward the settee. "Take a seat, Sage," she said, and sat beside him. "What have you been doing with yourself? Any more adventures in the offing?" There was a chill in her question. He thought he knew why. He'd been busy and not seen her for a week.

At least, he could answer her honestly. She was one of the very few who knew Sage was St. Alban's undercover operative. And, she was also one of a hand full of people who called him "Sage"—a diminutive of his middle name, "Sagacity". He never thought of himself as "John" though all but his most trusted friends did.

He shook his head. "No. At least, I don't think so. But something strange happened the night before last." He shifted uncomfortably in his seat. "Look, I'm sorry you haven't seen me lately. Things got busy and—" He caught her skeptical look and shut up with his excuses, saying, "'Anyways,' as Ma would say, I need your help."

She said nothing so he held her hand and launched into his story. "The other night I met this young boy, he reminded me of—"

She made no comment until he had finished telling her about Glad and Mickey and the kidnapping. "What can I do to help you find Glad?" she asked, to his relief. The melancholy in her voice meant his tale had stirred up sad memories for her as well. He'd long ago told her about the mine, the explosion and his subsequent fostering with the rich mine owner, but he knew nothing about her childhood. All she ever said was that there'd been monsters, "real" monsters.

"Maybe. God, Lucinda, I just don't know. You don't think. I mean, we stopped the sale of children from the Boy's Christian Society and closed down that one house in Lair Hill—"

She withdrew her hand from his and spoke in a tone that chilled the warmth between them. "You are a fool to think we can stop the trade in children. As long as there are customers, someone will provide the service. So, it's possible they sold your Glad to a house. But, I doubt it."

"Really? Why?"

"Selling a child who has family in Portland is riskier than just snatching one of the homeless street orphans who've just arrived from someplace else. A child who's lived here for a while knows the city, knows people who might help. It's far easier to entice and trap a child new to the city."

Her explanation made sense. Still, he had to ask. "Is there any way you can confirm that's not what happened to him?"

Her lips pressed tightly together and he feared she was angry at the request. Sometimes she turned prickly when he alluded to the prostitution business. But, she sighed and spoke as if she'd read his thoughts. "I don't harbor illusions about the things that go on in the sex trade. While this house might be posh, it's still the same business. That means I do talk with the other madams. And, like people everywhere, we gossip. I'm sure I can find out whether a new pedophile house has opened and where it is. It will be harder to learn whether Glad's there. I can't promise to find that out. But, I'll try."

"Thank you, Lucinda. I wouldn't ask but I hate the idea of him—" He stopped when she held up a hand.

"Sage, I know. Better than you realize. If that's what happened to your young friend, we need to find him fast."

He said nothing, thinking as he always did how lovely she was with her honey-colored hair, corn-flower blue eyes, dainty nose, and generous mouth. In that high-necked dress and with her regal bearing she was the equal of any society matron in the City.

"You are doing it again," she said, startling him out of his contemplation. "What are you thinking?"

He shifted uncomfortably. "You need to be careful, Lucinda. We don't know who or what is behind Glad's kidnapping. Those men looked rough."

His answer seemed to sadden her but all she said was, "I will have my driver with me. Where will you be looking for him while I'm off sleuthing?"

He fingered his mustache thoughtfully. "I guess I better try to find his family. I know the general area where they live. Who knows, maybe Glad's safe at home. Or, maybe I misinterpreted what I saw."

Abruptly she stood up from the settee. "I have an idea," she said and left the room.

Returning, she handed him a scrawled name and address.

"Millie Trumbull," he read aloud. "Who's she?"

"A customer was complaining about her. What caught my ear was him har-haring and bawling, over and over, 'Put on your hat Willie! Here comes Millie!' as if it was the funniest thing."

Sage arched an eyebrow but said nothing.

Lucinda lifted and dropped a shoulder in response to his unspoken question. "He was laughing a bit too loud for his mirth to be genuine. He was worried and so were his buddies. I figured it might come in handy to get this 'Millie's' full name."

"But who is she?"

"Near as I could tell, she's one of those do-gooder women. But she must do more than meet for tea and tittle-tattle." Sage had to smile. Lucinda rarely bypassed an opportunity to deride the judgmental wives of her wealthy patrons.

She smirked again, as if he'd read her mind, and then continued, "'Anyways,' as Mae would say, this Millie person helps children. That's the most I could tell."

He shook his head.

"What?" she demanded.

"I don't know why I bother to read Johnston's *Daily Journal.* All I have to do is visit you. You keep up on everything."

She looked gratified by his observation. "Given our clientele, we women need to stay current on events. Who's in, who's out. Who is doing what to whom," she said.

Of course. Her customers expected the women of the house to offer intelligent conversation as well as the traditional service. But not Lucinda, he told himself. She offered the conversation but did not provide the service. At least, that's what Elvira had told him once in confidence. And, as for him, well, their relationship was not commercial.

He reached out and gently traced her cheek with his fingers and leaned toward her.

She pulled back with a regretful sigh. "Sorry, Sage. Better not to start something we can't finish. I am expecting a guest."

It was as he descended the front steps that her words made him pause. "Guest? What guest? Whose guest? What kind of guest?" Reaching the sidewalk, he fought the temptation to enter the park across the street. From there, he could stand behind a tree and watch her front door. He made himself keep going.

"Damned if I'll skulk around like some jealous lover," he muttered. Then he ruefully added, "Face it, Sage. You're afraid she'd catch you."

It was only when he was halfway back to Mozart's that he remembered her earlier, more disturbing, comment. "Resale value." What the hell was that about?

"Millie Trumbull?" Mae started to shake her head and then stopped. "Well, come to think of it, maybe I do know her. She rarely comes in and, when she does, she's all business. Not one of those la-di-dah ladies wanting afternoon tea and gossip."

Sage gave a mental chuckle. No wonder his Appalachian mother and Lucinda liked each other—'two peas in a pod' as his mother would say. "Do you think Trumbull would remember you?" he asked.

She pursed her lips, thought, then said, "Who knows? We always visit a bit while she waits for her teacher friend, Valentine Pritchard. That gal is never on time."

These were names Sage had never heard. Sometimes he forgot that Mae was also making friends in this new city. No wonder, really. She was someone people trusted—dignified and reserved about personal matters but quick to smile and do a kindness.

"What exactly do you ladies chat about?"

"Mostly, she talks and I listen. The two of them are doing things for poor children—orphans and the like. Millie's some kind of factory inspector. But she does a lot more. Once she told me she was on the board of at least ten charities— and she acts as the secretary or some such officer in each of them."

"All of them about children?"

Mae considered that in silence before saying, "I recollect her saying that she and that Rabbi Wise have started a TB sanatorium."

"You have any idea what she thinks about unions?" His was not an idle question. They often worked with and helped people who were not in unions. But, the question's answer revealed something fundamental about a person's world view.

"Well, we've never talked specifically about it. But, she did say that when her inspection group was picking its office location she insisted that it be in the State Federation of Labor building at Second and Washington."

Sage smiled. "That's a good sign. Do you think she'd help us?"

"'Help,' seems to be her middle name. I could tell her I want to volunteer."

He shook his head. "She'd expect you to keep doing it long term. The last thing you need is more work. Maybe you could say that you heard Glad's mother has TB and no money and you want to help."

Mae nodded. "I like that better because it's the truth with a bit left out. For sure, that poor family needs help. Maybe Millie Trumbull can suggest ways to do right by Mrs. Tobias and her kids."

After a thoughtful lull, Sage asked, "Any chance of Herman turning up sometime soon?" He grinned at her sudden flushing. Mae Clemens and the ragpicker poet had become quite friendly ever since an arsonist locked them inside a burning building. Something had certainly happened between the two of them.

Not that he disapproved. She'd been alone far too long. And, the ragpicker poet had substance way beyond how he made his livelihood. Thoughtful, kind, educated and intelligent—and, most important, Herman Eich clearly held Mae Clemens in high regard. All of that and, there was the added bonus that he readily assisted in their secret endeavors, putting his life on the line more than once.

"Stop grinning like a jackass chomping a carrot," she ordered and asked, "Why do you want to see him?"

"You can't approach the Trumbull woman until we find Glad's family and figure out their situation. Since Herman roams the city with his cart, I'm thinking he might be just the person to find them."

"I'll send Matthew to his place with a note right now," she said. She got to her feet, patted him on the shoulder and headed downstairs to the restaurant.

FOUR

"HERMAN, I DON'T KNOW IF there's anything to worry about. Maybe Glad's already back with his family. I've looked for him on the streets and asked at Slap Jacks. No one has seen him since we met last Friday night," Sage said, as he added sugar to his coffee and stirred.

"We are in luck. I know Sullivan's Gulch well. It is on one of my routes." Eich was referring to the fact that he and his pushcart ranged citywide, rummaging through people's dust bins for usable or repairable items. Whatever he found, he sold back to those of limited means.

"You do business in Sullivan's Gulch? I wouldn't think those folks had useable things to throw away, let alone money to buy anything." Sage paused upon noting that his words made Eich uncomfortable. He noticed something else as well. The ragpicker poet had trimmed his beard. Sage knew Eich frequently visited the public baths and his clothes, though shabby, were always clean. But, a trimmed beard? Mae was probably the inspiration, he thought with an inward smile.

Eich shifted uneasily, fiddled with his coffee mug and at last said, "Some people, you can't take their money." He gazed out the café window.

The distant look in those dark brown eyes told Sage what was coming. Sure enough, Eich's warm voice recited,

> If any sue for pity –
> Though he be friend or foe—
> I'll whisper to my soul,
> "He goes the road I go."

"You wrote that?" Sage asked.

Eich shook his head. "No, a woman friend of mine named Mary Sinton. She helps prisoners and writes poetry."

Sage pondered the poem's meaning and asked, "You're saying sometimes the Sullivan Gulch people pay nothing for what you give them?"

Eich shrugged, "They are among the poorest of the poor." He straightened, signaling the end of his musing. "I visit each shack so I've come to know them all. From what Mae told me, I'm fairly certain I know Glad's mother and siblings."

"Do you think you could discover whether Glad's made it home?"

Eich nodded. "I assume you don't wish to draw attention to your interest at this point?"

"That's right. Until we figure out why those men snatched Glad off the street, I'd rather no one know of my interest. It would be best to get the information without being obvious. That'll leave us with more options if we need to get more involved."

Eich again nodded. "Usually, I start at the beginning of the gulch where Tanner Creek empties into the Willamette. I recall that the Tobias family has a one-room shack about halfway in. If I just do my regular route, stopping at each shack, it will take me about three hours. Do you want to meet back here then?"

"If you don't mind, I'd rather come to your place. The less we're seen together, the better. At least until we know what's happened to the boy."

The path alongside the creek was muddy and Eich had to wrestle the cart forward with the little bell on the cart's side announcing his approach. Men and women emerged blurry-eyed from ramshackle huts to make their requests—a chipped cup here, a dented pot there, a patched coat or blanket. If he had what they needed, he gave it to them, accepting what little they could pay with a smile and a, "thank you."

"Mr. Eich, please come inside for a bit of tea," one old crone urged. He accepted her offer, after resting his cart handles atop two rocks sticking out of the mud. He didn't worry about thieves. The people of the Gulch would watch out for their benefactor.

Her name was Maisie Duncan and her age was old enough for her to have lost most of her teeth and seen her hair turn gray. A wood round destined for the corner stove served as his stool. While she bustled about, pouring hot water into a chipped pot, he studied her tiny space. This shack, built of castaway lumber, held so little and provided inadequate shelter. The wadded paper stuffed into gaps struggled to hold in the stove's heat. Scattered tin cans caught raindrops in an attempt to keep the dirt floor from becoming mud with only partial success. In the corners and along the wall the tin cans had failed in their mission. Drips had turned the dirt black.

She handed him a cup and sat down on the cot's edge, her grimy hands wrapped around a cup of her own. "I was digging in the garbage pail of one of them homes up on the bluff and darned if someone hadn't thrown out a whole box of tea. Must have thought it went stale. I think it's still pretty good, don't you?" she asked, eager for a positive word.

He sipped the tea. It was weaker than what he'd drank when growing up in New York, those many decades long ago. But, it was still recognizable as tea. "It is mighty fine, Mrs. Duncan," he assured her. "Far better than some I've had in fancy restaurants."

She smiled a gap-toothed grin and mimed a ladylike gesture by raising a pinky in the air while the rest of her fingers firmly gripped her handle-less cup.

"How are things going down here in the Gulch?" he asked.

"We feared there'd be a flood last week with all that rain. Everybody cleared out and hunkered under the bridges just in case. Luckily it stopped raining, though it sure did turn our path into a sea of mud. Course, we don't have to worry about tracking none in," her tone was rueful as she gestured to the shack's dirt floor.

"Mrs. Duncan, why don't you move onto that poor farm out Jefferson way? Or, there's the Patton Home right near here in Albina village. At least you'd be dry and warm."

Her head shake was adamant. "No siree, bob. I ain't never going back to no poor farm. I grew up in one. It's hard work, lottsa stupid rules that you can't say nothing about least they boot you out. Besides, that poor farm is too far out. I can't be traipsing up and down Jefferson road every time I want to come to town. And, the Patton place, why it's just a bunch of old folks sitting around talking about all them that's dead and gone."

She has a point, Eich thought, and changed the subject. "How's your neighbor, Mrs. Tobias faring? Last time I passed through, she was looking poorly."

Maisie shook her head sadly. "She's mighty sick. I don't think she's going to make it to the spring. Those poor kids."

"There's how many of them?" Eich asked.

"She's got four—two girls and two boys. The boys are the oldest. They all try to help out, except the baby."

"How?"

"Well, the girl stays home but she looks after the kids of folks off working during the day. She and her mom turn out some of those paper flowers but that don't get them but a few cents. The two boys do a bit better. The younger one sells newspapers and the older one works as a messenger."

"The boys are gone a lot?"

"Yup, I see the older one fishing the creek sometimes, late afternoon. He works nights. Comes and goes mostly in the dark now it's gone winter."

"I suppose the younger one works just the opposite hours?" Eich asked, hoping to spur her into talking about Glad. It worked.

"Yeah, 'cept I haven't seen him the last few days. It's kinda funny because he's a kid that's real regular. He leaves way early to pick up and sell his papers. About noontime, he comes back with food for the rest of them. After that, he sometimes goes to school. He says he loves school. Late afternoon, he goes out again selling to folks wanting evening papers and comes back around ten. Regular as clockwork, he is. Bright little fellow, too."

"But not lately, huh?"

"Ain't seen him. I finally asked his mother about him but she mumbled something about a pot burning on the stove 'afore she scooted back inside like a bunny rabbit." Her lips twisted and she confided, "That were a lie."

"How do you know that?"

"No smoke coming out her chimney. Can't nobody burn food on a cold stove," Maisie said, crossing her arms across her chest to emphasize her point.

Eich shook his cart bell vigorously until the door finally inched open to reveal a wan face peeking out from around the weathered boards.

"Why, hello there, Carrie Lynne, is everything all right?" Eich's voice was hearty and his smile wide. "Will you tell your mama that I have some very nice blankets on the cart today?"

She nodded solemnly before closing the door. He listened and could hear the sound of voices, the high one of the little girl and the murmurs of the ill woman.

The door opened once again. "Mama says she ain't got but one penny to spare so we'll have to pass on the blanket today." Regret lowered the girl's brows and set her lips to quivering. Eich glanced upward. No smoke drifted into the cloudy sky from the rusted stove pipe.

"Well, isn't that just great," he said, making Carrie Lynne's' pale forehead wrinkle while she tried to comprehend why having only a penny was "great."

"It just so happens that I have two blankets that I can let you have for a single penny."

Skepticism filled the small face. "How come you're giving us such a good deal?" she asked, putting her thought into words.

"The thing is, little lady, blankets take up too much room on the cart. And right now, I've got too many of them. I need to get rid of a few so I have space for other things."

He could tell his explanation hadn't eased her doubts. Sure enough, she said, "I'll have to go ask mama," and banged the door shut once again.

When she returned it was to hold out a single tarnished penny. "Please, Mr. Eich, we'd like to buy those blankets." The exchange made, Eich dug around in the cart and turned to her, a book in hand. "Last time I came through here I spoke to your brother, Glad. He said he liked to read. I found this book I thought he might enjoy. Is he maybe here so that I can give it to him personally?"

To his dismay, tears flooded her pale eyes and she clutched the blankets so tightly that her fingers turned white. "No. Glad ain't here."

"Maybe I can come back with the book later today when he's home?" he prodded.

She mutely shook her head and backed away. "Glad ain't coming back today," she said, as the tears began rolling down her cheeks.

"Maybe I can just leave it with you to give to him when he returns?" he suggested gently, stepping forward. Either his question or his step forward drove her back into the house. Once she and the blankets were inside, she shook her head and said softly, "Thank you for the blankets, Mr. Eich," before she closed the door, leaving Herman Eich standing on the muddy path, the well-worn book in his outstretched hand.

❀ ❀ ❀

They met up in the snug lean-to attached to the back of a small house beside another ravine, this one on the Willamette River's west side. Eich's home was smaller than the shacks in Sullivan's Gulch but had a plank floor underfoot. Tightly chinked walls and a solid tin roof kept the heat from his pot-bellied stove inside. Sage had seen to the roofing and chinking while Eich was away recovering from nearly dying during one of their adventures.

From his perch on a small stool, Sage studied the workbench where Eich repaired porcelain dishes, containers and figurines. Everything was tidy and in its place. A chipped and garishly painted chamber pot, standing front and center, was the ragpicker's current project.

"So, the boy, Glad, is not with his family?" Sage asked.

Eich spoke with regret, "I'm afraid not. The family is desperately upset given what I saw of Carrie Lynne. I am sure they miss both him and his financial contribution."

"Well, now that we know he's truly missing we can have Ma go a 'visiting. You know her. Once she lands in their midst, things will be set right pretty quick."

Eich laughed. "She is a formidable woman, your mother," he said with warm admiration.

Mozart's Table was quiet during the few hours between the end of the noontime meal and the beginning of teatime. "Okay then, I'll skedaddle over to Millie Trumbull's and find out what she can do to help. And, I'll need to pick up some things before I head out to Sullivan's Gulch," Mae said. She started to stand up.

"Whoa, Ma," Sage said, putting a restraining hand on her forearm. "Let's take this a step at a time. Go ahead and see Trumbull today. But wait until tomorrow for your visit to Sullivan's Gulch. Herman insists he has to be there."

She bristled. "I can take care of myself! I've done so for many a year, if you recall."

He raised a calming hand and wasn't surprised when she batted it away. He persisted with an explanation. "Herman has to point out which shack is theirs. We're trying to keep our interest quiet. You can't go knocking on doors asking where they are. Besides, he says it can be a rough place for strangers."

The fire in her eyes dimmed a bit but all she said was, "I guess I do need to know where to go."

"What do you plan on saying to Mrs. Trumbull?"

She leaned forward, her irritation forgotten. "I'm going to tell her that I bought a paper from young Glad and he told me about how hard up his family was. I plan on saying the same thing to Mrs. Tobias when I give her the food. If she's as sick as Glad told you, I figure she won't have the strength to argue. Besides, she's a mother. She'll accept what's best for her children even if it means putting up with a nosy stranger."

FIVE

"My Lord, Ida! What in tarnation's got you so upset?" Mae Clemens dropped her handbag and squatted beside Mozart's cook. She put an arm around the small rotund woman who had her face buried in her hands as sobs shook her shoulders. Since Ida was always cheerful, this distress was alarming.

Ida started and wiped her eyes with an apron corner before glancing at Mae with teary eyes. "It's Matthew. I don't know what's got into him."

Matthew was Ida's nephew. He lived with Ida and her husband, Knute, in the second-floor apartment. Ida's double chin wobbled and she wailed, "He yelled at me!"

Suppressing a groan and with loud knee cracks, Mae stood and took the seat across from Ida. Though it was early, a glance around the kitchen assured Mae that the pies were cooling and all was readied for the supper hour that was just hours away. Mae wouldn't have to postpone her visit to Millie Trumbull though time remained tight. Still, she needed to find out why Ida was so distressed.

"You go ahead and tell me what happened," she said, reaching across the table to touch the other's woman's hand.

Ida sniffed and said, "He came in real late last night. He's been doing that. And he won't say where he's been. If I ask, he tells me he's been with his friends. And, I know that's not true."

"You think he's lying?"

"I know he is because I saw his printer friend, Jimmy at the market. He told me that he hasn't seen Matthew in days. And, he's Matthew's best friend. The poor boy's feelings are hurt."

Ida straightened in her chair, her mouth a grim line before she said, "And, last night, Matthew came home with a bruise on his cheek and his shirt torn. When I asked what happened, he said he'd fallen off his bike." She sniffed her disbelief.

"Well, maybe he did fall."

The cook shook her head vigorously. "The shirt was torn at the buttons—like someone grabbed its front. His clothes on the side with the bruise were clean. It was raining last night. If he'd fallen, he'd have muddied up his clothes."

She drew a shuddering breath and looked about to burst into tears once again. "And then, this morning, when I asked him to be honest with me, he told me to mind my own business!" Her chins started wobbling but she gulped down the sob and said earnestly, "Mae, that's not Matthew. He's a sweet, sweet boy. Even during that terrible time, he was always kind and well-mannered."

Mae knew what time Ida meant. They all did. Matthew's entry into their lives came about when he and his brother hitched a ride north on a train from their coastal town. Their adventure turned horrific when a brutal railroad bull killed Matthew's brother. When someone stabbed the bull to death, the police charged Matthew with the murder. They'd finally straightened it all out but it had taken Matthew months to recover from the experience.

But this last year had been better. The sixteen-year-old was attending school, and doing well. After school he made money delivering messages using a bicycle Sage had bought for him.

"Has Knute tried talking to him?" Mae asked.

Ida dismissed that idea with a wave of her hand. "Same thing, Matthew just mumbles some dumb excuse and goes into his room. Knute's as worried as I am."

Ida's Swedish husband was a kindly man who didn't need distractions given his job. Knute made shingles which meant he fed cedar bolts through two saw blades at the same time. A single moment of inattention would mean disaster.

Mae slapped her palms on the table and stood up. "Okay then. We'll ask Mr. Adair to have a talk with him. You know how much Matthew admires him. He'll get to the bottom of whatever's troubling the boy.

But, Mr. Adair's headed out and about. I'll tell him about it when he gets back. Don't you worry, Ida. He'll get this straightened out right quick."

Ida sucked in a deep breath and stood up. "Thank you, Mae. You and Mr. Adair are so good to us." She smoothed down her apron and when she next spoke her tone was decisive. "Well, I best get busy. Those peas aren't going to shuck themselves." She tightened her apron strings and looked at Mae. "Thank you," she said again, and stepped over to the stove.

Mae stood, grabbed her handbag, slipped into her coat, slapped on her hat and headed out the kitchen door into the day's watery sunlight. Ida wasn't the only one running behind.

No one can claim this building is fancy, Mae thought as she climbed the grubby linoleum-covered stairs to the second floor. She wandered down the hallway with only a dim gray light from an overhead skylight lighting her way. Discrete plaques displayed the names of labor unions until she reached a sign announcing the "Child Labor Commission."

"Sounds close enough," Mae said aloud, and turned the doorknob. She stepped into a small room with filing cabinets on one side and a couple of hard-backed chairs on the other. A doorway opened into a small room lit by a single window. Through that open door, Mae saw a woman sitting in a chair facing a desk, her body craning forward even as her arms encircled two toddlers who leaned against her, one on each side.

Mae couldn't see who sat behind the desk but she recognized Millie Trumbull's Midwest voice. So, she took a seat in the waiting room, hoping the lady's business wouldn't take long. She had to be back at Mozart's before the five o'clock supper hour.

On the walk over, she'd thought long and hard about Matthew's strange behavior and reached the same conclusion. If anyone could get to the bottom of things, it was Sage, even if he had to trail the boy. Fong could help, too, once Kum Ho recovered. Fong's note had said she had pneumonia. That was worrisome.

The woman in the next room stood up, putting an end to Mae's musing. As she and the kids passed by, Mae noted her raggedly thin coat and broken boots even though her children wore heavy coats and new galoshes. That woman's sacrifice is plain to see, Mae thought approvingly.

The large figure of Millie Trumbull appeared in the open doorway. A perplexed look crossed her broad face followed by one of recall.

"Why, it's Mrs. Clemens from Mozart's isn't it? It took me a minute to recognize you outside your element."

Mae stood and they shook hands. No one would call Millie Trumbull beautiful or pretty. Even handsome might be a stretch. But there was strength of character in her firm chin, the promise of intelligence in her wide forehead, and most of all, compassion in her large brown eyes.

Mae laughed. "True, I don't get out much." Then she added soberly, "Mrs. Trumbull, I have a problem and was hoping you could advise me on how to solve it."

The broad forehead wrinkled and Trumbull said, "First of all, dear woman, call me, 'Millie.' Secondly, I have to be somewhere right now. Truthfully, I'm running late. Do you think you could tell me about it while we're walking?"

"I can come back."

"No, no. Actually, you can lend me a hand, if you will." Even as she spoke, Millie was removing her coat and hat from a wall hook and donning them. Opening the door, she gestured Mae into the corridor and locked the door behind them.

Upon reaching the street, Trumbull turned north and started walking as she said, "I'm inspecting workplaces for children. Ever since the law passed last year, I've been trying to make sure no children are working when they should be in school."

Mae had heard of the law, "Children under fourteen, isn't it?"

Millie nodded grimly, "We tried for sixteen but had to compromise to get the law passed. Still, employers try to sneak youngsters in. That's where I am hoping you can help, Mrs. Clemens."

"I'd be happy to, Millie. But, please, call me, 'Mae.'"

"Well, then, Mae. I got a report that at least three children are working in the Renfrow Crackers factory when they should be in school. That devil of an owner knows me by sight. I'm sure he's having someone hide the children while he stalls me in the front office. He's got an ad in today's paper for a lady worker. If you could go in asking about the job and maybe get a tour of the factory, you could come out and tell me if he has kids working there. Then, when I go in, I'll know just how pushy to get and maybe where to look."

Mae rapidly calculated the time she had remaining. Millie misinterpreted her hesitation. "Oh my, what am I thinking? You come for help and the next thing you know, I'm asking you to partake in skullduggery. I do apologize. I can do the inspection and probably find the kids on my own."

Mae grabbed Millie's forearm to bring her to a halt. As the woman turned toward her, Mae said, "Millie, I'd be honored to help you with this. I was hesitating only because I need to be back to Mozart's before five o'clock. But, I think there's enough time to engage in a little 'skullduggery.'" She grinned, released Millie's arm and the two started walking again.

"Thank you, Mae," Millie said. Taking a deep breath she continued, "Okay, suppose you tell me about your problem while we walk—we have a few blocks."

So Mae explained that a good friend had learned of Mrs. Tobias being sick and how three of her four children were supporting the whole family. Mae said one of the sons was a newsboy but she didn't say the boy was missing.

Millie was silent for at least half a block, then she began, "One of my big frustrations is that newsboys aren't covered under the new law—they are 'independent contractors' according to the newspaper companies' testimony before the legislature."

She walked a few more paces before saying thoughtfully, "There are things we can do for this lady, once you verify what you've heard. We just opened a TB sanatorium, south of Milwaukie Village. Dr. Lane is on our board. He could examine the lady with an eye to admitting her to the sanatorium. But, the problem is, the care costs $6 a week."

"The fees will not be a problem. I know someone who will donate the money. But, what's it like there?"

"We house the patients in canvas tents during the late spring through early fall. Once it gets cold, like now, there are little cabins for them to stay in. We have nurses on staff and visiting doctors. Our goal is to make sure they get good food and fresh air at all times," Millie said.

Mae pondered that idea before asking, "She has those four children. What happens to them? Can they live at the sanatorium with her?" Mae asked.

Millie shook her head. "No, that's not healthy for them. But I'm also secretary for the Boys and Girls Aid Society. The Society can house the children or maybe place them in foster homes until their mother is well enough to care for them."

Mae didn't say anything. She wondered if Mrs. Tobias would agree to enter the sanatorium if it meant leaving her four children in the hands of strangers. The thought of that choice sent dread ice picking into Mae's heart. Still,— "How long would they be separated do you think?" she asked.

Millie raised both hands, palms up. "Who knows? Some people come out of the sanatorium after two months, some after six months and some die there. Until Dr. Lane examines this woman, we won't know how sick she is. And, really, it's up to God how long it will take for her to get well."

This time it was Millie's hand on Mae's arm that brought them to a halt. "The cracker factory is in the next block. All you have to do is get the owner to show you around."

"I don't know. I was getting six a week for laundry work. Dropping down to five dollars don't make much sense."

"Like I said, this work is easier and the conditions are much better," he assured her. The man was short and stocky with a nose that tried to touch his upper lip.

Mae's expression was skeptical. "You say that, but I like to see things for myself."

Heaving a sigh, the man raised his bulk from the chair and gestured for her to follow. The room behind the closed door had a high, girdered ceiling but was still stifling hot from the ovens that stood against an inside wall. Men stirred huge kettles of cracker dough that women spread on conveyor belts and sent through rollers. From there, the thin sheets of dough moved into a side room and past women who stamped out rounds that other women put onto metal trays. This is where the children stepped up. They took the trays and slid them into a wheeled tray rack that they pushed to the ovens once the trays were stacked a good two feet above their heads.

There was no mistaking that these were children. The youngest looked about ten, the oldest no more than twelve or thirteen. They were skinny, pale, and ill-clothed.

"Why aren't the windows open? It's nearly hot as a laundry in here." Mae asked, deliberately making her voice sound judgmental.

"We need an even temperature for baking. No drafts," the manager said. He frowned at her before abruptly grabbing her elbow and pulling her toward the front office. He'd noticed her intently studying the children.

"Everyone is working a twelve-hour, six-day week?" Mae persisted.

"That's what I already told you." Now there was no mistaking his hostility. He steered her so she was in front of him and then stayed close on her heels as they headed back to the office. Once they'd entered it and, with the closed door muting the factory's noise, he turned to her, a pursed scowl raising his lips even closer to his nose. "I'm afraid that you are not the kind of employee who'll find success in our factory," he said, and again seized her elbow to herd her toward the outer door. Once she'd crossed the threshold he gave her a little shove and banged the door shut behind her without saying another word.

"So, aren't you going in?" asked Mae.

"Oh, you can bet I am," said Millie. "But he'll be suspicious right now. I'm going to sit right here in this café and watch his front door. The minute he leaves for lunch, I'll head in. You saw about eight children working in there?"

"That's what I counted. When one leaves the conveyor belt to push the rack to the ovens, another is just returning and steps into his or her place. Two kids work on each side of the belts at all times. He's running two conveyor belts."

"Like I told you, I've tried getting in there before. I suspect he has a buzzer in that front office that sounds in the factory. Once it goes off, I think the kids are supposed to run for the back door or somewhere else to hide."

"Can't you just run around the building and catch them that way?"

Millie's headshake was adamant. "They have a solid eight-foot fence back there that I can't see over or get through. The man's not stupid. But you've been a tremendous help because I know for certain that they are in there today. If I do it right, I'll be able to find the children.

Mae finished her coffee and set her mug down with a thump. "I'd sure like to see that but I'm afraid I can't stay and wait with you. I've got to get back to Mozart's. Are you sure you'll be safe—going in all by yourself?" Mae asked worriedly, the space between her shoulder blades still feeling the anger behind that final shove out the door.

SIX

"Hello there, young lady. I spoke to your brother, Glad, and—" That's all Mae got out before the blue eyes in the sallow face widened and the door banged shut. Through the flimsy door she heard the girl holler, "Ma, the lady outside says she's talked to Glad!" There was a joyful cry, the clatter of something falling over and footsteps. When the door swung open, a frail, pale woman stood in the threshold. The joy in her face hit Mae's heart like a spear.

"Glad? You've talked to our Glad? Is he alright? Where is he?"

Mae took a deep breath. "Maybe I better come inside," she said gently.

The light in the woman's face died sure as water doused fire. She mutely gestured Mae inside.

Mae was a bit taller than most women. Sage's six-foot height came from her Irish side of the family, not from his Welsh father's shorter line. So, she towered over the tiny woman who hurried to set a fallen stool upright.

"Please sit down, ma'am," said Mrs. Tobias, gesturing to the stool. "Carrie Lynne, take the kids out to play. Mind you, play upslope, away from the creek."

For the first time, Mae noticed the three toddlers and one infant sitting on the edge of a mattress pile that filled one corner of the shack. The older child, Carrie Lynne, was maybe six or seven. Her too-small, faded, pink gingham dress was covered by a too-large, dingy, white apron. After nodding to her mother, she herded her charges out the door, carrying the infant on her tiny hip.

"All yours?" Mae asked her hostess.

The question brought a tired chuckle. "No, just Carrie Lynne and the baby are mine. The rest are neighbor kids we take care of." The woman paused, gasped and began to cough, spasms shaking her whole body. Mae glanced around and saw a pail with a dipper sitting on a crude counter. Crossing to it, she selected a canning jar that looked clean and filled it with water. When she brought it back, the woman choked back a cough, accepted the jar and took a sip.

"You said you talked to Glad? When?"

"It was about six days ago on Friday. He was selling papers. We got to talking. He told me about your troubles. I thought maybe I could help a bit."

"Six days ago." The woman sighed, sat on the room's other stool, and with her elbows on the rickety table, hid her face in her hands.

Mae surveyed the table. It was piled high with paper petals and stem wires. They'd been making artificial flowers. The wires were very thin and the light from the single, oilskin-covered window was dim. No wonder both mother and child look a tad squinty-eyed, Mae thought.

The one-room shack was as tidy as possible. Looking at the ill woman across from her, Mae wondered how much of the neatness was due to the efforts of little Carrie Lynne—a child with no childhood.

"Look," she began, "I don't mean to butt my nose in where it doesn't belong. But I liked your little son. He told me you're sick but doing everything you can to keep the family together. That's why I came. But, something's wrong, isn't it? Has Glad gone missing?"

"No, no. He's fine. Just visiting, um, visiting my sister. I was just surprised to hear that you'd seen him since she lives way off in Oregon City."

Mae fought the urge to tell the woman her lie was about as believable as a trotting trout but she hesitated. It wouldn't do to make her mad. Why was the woman hiding the fact her son was missing? If it'd been her, she'd be hollering from the rooftops. Something strange was going on and, for sure, this woman was not going to spit it out. So Mae said instead, "Well, like I said, I took a real liking to your boy and wanted to help you all."

She reached down for the drawstring bag at her feet. "Anyways, I brought you some eggs and flour and such. It ain't much but I was hopeful you'd accept it."

Glad's mother lifted her face from her hands and stared. "I don't understand. You're a stranger. Why would you help us, right out of the blue?" There was no hostility in the woman's question, just dull puzzlement.

"I had a boy. He was a lot like your Glad. Many a day we had trouble finding enough to eat. And then it got worse." The pain in Mae's voice was genuine.

Mae reached across the table to touch the woman's hand. "I'm sorry. Don't know where my manners run off to. My name is Mae Clemens. Please call me, 'Mae.'"

The woman gave a weak smile. "Mary Tobias. Mary," she said in return.

"I just want you to know, I'm not here just because you think you're somebody important, Miss High and Mighty."

The other women shifted uncomfortably until one said, "We know, Vera. It's Lucy's offer of a free feedbag that got you here." Derisive chuckles followed this remark.

Lucinda considered the six other women sitting around the table. There were at least four hundred houses of prostitution in the city. Unlike Lucinda's sophisticated establishment, the ones these women ran were either boarding house brothels or collections of stall-like cribs sprinkled throughout the North End. She resolved to ignore Vera's hostility. Taking a deep breath, she said, "Thank you all for coming. I appreciate your time."

"Cut the crap. What is it you want?" snarled Vera. Evidently, the other woman's defense of Lucinda had only fueled Vera's ire. She was relatively new in town. One of the other women had brought her without asking Lucinda.

Before Lucinda could respond, Madge stepped in. "Vera, it seems to me you sing a different tune whenever Lucy helps one of us out. Whatcha gonna do if you need some quick cash to bail out your girls? Who will you go to if not Lucy?"

Louise Rumbold jumped in before Vera could reply. "How can we help, Lucy?" she asked Lucinda, her deft subject change sending Vera into a silent, cross-armed glare.

"A friend of mine saw a little newsboy snatched off the street the other night. We wondered whether they grabbed him for a house or for something else. After the Lair Hill house was raided and closed last year, I haven't heard whether there's another one up and running."

The women shifted uncomfortably—except for the stony-faced Vera who continued to fume, arms folded. Louise cleared her throat, "I don't hold with selling kids and I know none of you do either." She looked at the other women, all of whom nodded—except for Vera.

Louise continued thoughtfully, "I recall hearing about a new place opening up somewhere on the eastside. What's the boy's name?"

Lucinda told them and then asked, "Can you think of any other reason why he might have been kidnapped? Have you heard anything about snatching kids?"

Vera scraped her chair back and stood. Contempt dripping from her words, she said, "You parade all over town in that fancy carriage of yours, showing off your gals like they were something other than common whores. Now you have to come to us because you're too good to run a bawdy house like us or know about kid-selling houses. Well, I've had enough of this bullshit. You want something from me, you pay for it just like any other customer!" With that, Vera turned her back on the table and left the restaurant. The other women exchanged raised eyebrows and shrugs but otherwise ignored her exit.

As Lucinda rode home in her "fancy" carriage, she concluded that her foray had met with limited success. Louise thought she'd be able to get the address of the new pedophile house on the eastside. With that information, Sage and Mr. Fong could check to see if Glad was inside. But, other than that, the other women were as mystified as she was about the reason behind the little newsboy's kidnapping.

Gazing out the window, she felt weighed down by a melancholy that seemed to fill the carriage. Part of it was Vera's words. Was she fooling herself that, somehow, she'd made the best of a bad situation? Was it a comforting delusion that her ladies were reasonably content, safe, and working their way out of the life—unlike the other prostitutes in town?

She sighed heavily at the thought of the missing boy. She felt certain that they wouldn't find Glad in that house. And, unfortunately, the other madams could offer no other explanation for his kidnapping.

She knew exactly how it felt to be small, alone, and at the mercy of cruel adults. She took a deep breath to force her emotions under control and unknot her stomach.

As they rolled up before her mansion a vague recollection slid into her thoughts. There'd been a brief moment when fear flickered in Vera's pebble-brown eyes. Why? Lucinda tried but couldn't remember which words had triggered that reaction.

Sage hung around outside the Newsboys Benevolent Association's hole-in-the-wall office until the boys began to trickle in. It was time for the afternoon papers delivery. The dry and unseasonably warm mid-February day kept some of the boys outside, tossing dice against the building's wall.

After watching the game for a while, Sage said, "I'm looking for William Gladney Tobias. He calls himself, 'Glad,'" he said to the small group crouched at his feet.

They paused, glanced up, exchanged looks and then went back to their game except for one older boy who rose to face Sage. "What is it that you want with him?"

"He's my nephew. My sister's his ma. I just got to town but I don't have their address. I know he's a newsboy and thought you fellows might know where he lives or sells his papers," Sage told him.

For a moment their eyes locked and then the boy's shoulders dropped and his face relaxed. "They live in Sullivan's Gulch across the river. To tell the truth, Mister, I'm worried about him. We ain't seen him for almost a week on his regular corner." The kids crouched at their feet were completely still, and obviously listening.

"Is he sick?"

A voice from below piped up, "Can't be home sick if his brother Terry is out looking for him, can he?"

The standing boy retorted, "Ralph, his brother was only looking that one day—right after we last saw Glad. We ain't seen Terry since, have we?"

"Maybe Glad's dead," said Ralph at their feet.

"Nah," said another, "if you could read Ralph, you'd know that there weren't nothing in the newspaper about Glad dying. They found a dead boy but the paper said he had old burn marks all over his body. That ain't our Glad."

As one, the other boys rose to their feet. Sage looked down into their young faces and at their scrawny little bodies. "So, when's the last time anyone saw him?" he asked.

"We done talked about that," said a kid who'd been quiet up to that point, "We figure it was when he was heading home last Friday night."

Sage felt the last vestige of hope trickle out. That was the night he'd met the boy. "But not since that night, huh?"

"Ain't a one of us seen him nowhere since," the first boy said, sweeping his arm in an arc that took in the whole city. "Awhile back, I ran into Glad's brother but when I asked him, where was Glad, he told me to 'mind my own cotton-picking business'. For a minute, I thought he was going to punch me."

Sage was in a foul mood when he reached Eich's little lean-to. The ragpicker took one look at him before directing him toward a recently acquired, slightly faded, upholstered armchair. Seeing Sage's questioning look, Eich explained, "A West Hills lady is redecorating. Thought I'd wallow in a little luxury before selling it on."

"It certainly is more comfortable than the wood round you usually offer me," Sage said with a smile as he relaxed into the soft cushions.

Eich laughed before turning away to fiddle with a pot and cups.

Minutes later, Sage was sipping the tea and feeling the tightness in his shoulders ease. "I can't find anyone who's seen Glad. From what the newsboys say, I was the last to see him—other than his kidnappers," he said.

Eich sat on the edge of his cot, took a sip of tea, and said, "Have you spoken to Mae since she's come back from visiting Mrs. Tobias? I watched out for her from the top of the ravine but when she left, she climbed up and out the other side so I've had no opportunity to confer with her."

Sage shrugged. "I haven't had a chance to talk to her either. She's probably at Mozart's for the noon dinner. Mr. Fong is staying home with his sick wife so we're shorthanded."

The two men sat in silence as rain pattered against the tin roof. A distant, steady roar came from the rushing stream at the ravine's bottom.

"Interesting that Glad's still not at home, yet, his brother stopped looking for him so quick," Eich observed.

"Good observation. Though, if he's staying with relatives, it could explain why the brother gave up looking. Maybe Glad ran away from home," Sage suggested though he thought that unlikely given the boy's obvious devotion to his family. "I never imagined I'd be relieved to find a child in a house of prostitution but that'd be a hell of a lot better than finding his body in the Crofton funeral home's basement."

Eich nodded thoughtfully, "You are right, as long as there is life, there's a chance things will improve for the boy. I doubt he ran away to a relative. It doesn't fit with his little sister's reaction when I asked for him. If he's safe with a relative, why did she cry? And what you saw on the street that night was a kidnapping. Maybe he escaped and then ran away and hid?"

Sage shook his head. "No, that doesn't fit the facts. Even if he ran and hid, he'd find some way of getting word to his family."

"Going back to what we know," Eich said as he raised a hand, straightening out each finger as he counted out his points. "First he's snatched off the street. Second, the following day his brother searches for him. Third, the day after that, the brother stops looking. And finally, four days after the kidnapping, the sister bursts into tears and tells me he's not expected back."

"Maybe Mrs. Tobias confided in Mother," Sage said.

Eich shrugged. "Maybe. But we better plan our next step in case she did not."

Sage straightened. "I'm thinking Glad's brother might have some answers."

SEVEN

Halfway through the snake and crane's one hundred and eight movements, Sage sensed Fong stepping into the attic behind him. He wanted to stop to greet his friend but knew he'd only get a scolding look. So he kept moving, acutely aware of Fong shedding his shoes and stepping into a position slightly to his side and rear. Forcing himself to focus on the movements and ignore the welcome but scrutinizing presence of his teacher, Sage finally reached the end. He turned, put knuckles to palm and bowed to his teacher. Fong grinned in response.

"Kum Ho is alright?" Sage asked.

"She say she 'right as rain.' Funny. Rain may be good if you are bush," Fong said and shrugged, though his relief was evident in his easy smile.

Sage knew Ida had been sending soup and other healing vittles to the Fong's provision shop. The last message she'd gotten back said that Fong's wife had turned the corner and was on the mend. Still, pneumonia was nothing to fool with.

"Mr. Fong, are you sure it's okay to leave her? It's been tough without you around but she's more important."

Fong nodded and held up a hand. "No problem, Mr. Sage. I hire young fellow to watch shop and Kum Ho. She not happy but that too bad."

Sage laughed. Fong's wife was the tiniest woman Sage had ever met but her iron will countered any size disadvantage. For much of her difficult life, she'd needed that strength.

"In that case, you got here just in time. We have a problem," Sage began and told Fong about the Gladney Tobias situation. "So, Eich and I think we need to learn more about the brother. If you could follow him, find out who he works for, that would help. Eich can't do it, his pushcart is too noticeable and he can't move as fast as a young boy. As for me, at this point, I don't want Terry Tobias to know I'm involved because something's fishy about all this. Depending on what we learn, I may need to get close to him as a stranger, not as someone hunting for his brother."

"You say he live in Sullivan's Gulch? How do I find him to follow?"

"Eich says if we send word, he can point out the Tobias shack from the top of the ravine."

"Okay. I send word right away. Maybe start trailing him tonight. Lady wife tell me she not want to see me until tomorrow. Right now, I'm out on ear because I hire helper."

Since Fong had a room next to Mae's on Mozart's third floor, his banishment was harmless. He often stayed at Mozart's while his wife ran their provision store. Regardless, Fong's sojourn in the dog house would be short-lived. Sage had seen Kum Ho's affectionate looks at her husband. She probably just wanted Fong to end his sick room duty without guilt.

Fong turned toward the steep stairs to Mozart's third floor. "We go down now. Lady Mother said she meet us in your room."

Sure enough, Mae sat at the small table in his bedroom's bay window, a coffee pot and biscuit plate awaiting them.

"What happened at Glad's house, yesterday?" Sage asked her without preamble.

"The boy isn't there, just like Herman said. And the family's mighty upset about it. For some reason, his mother is keeping secret that he's gone or why he's gone. I sure don't understand it."

Sage repeated what he'd learned from the newsboys and what he and Eich thought should be their next step. "What we want to know is—why did the brother stop searching for him? Fong's going to tail him tonight. Hopefully, he'll turn something up."

She agreed with their plan to have Fong shadow the brother. Switching topics she asked, "What are you going to do about the dead boy, the one that doesn't have a name? There's another article in the newspaper again today. They still don't know who he was."

"I've been thinking on that. Hanke thinks the boy ran away from a glass factory. We don't have one in Portland, though I heard the Kerr brothers are building a canning jar factory. That means it's likely the little fellow rode the rails into town."

"Meachum," she said.

"Yup, that's what I was thinking. He's best situated to learn whether the boy got here by boxcar and where he might have come from. Meach knows more people riding the rails than ten hobos put together. If the kid traveled that way, someone will remember him."

"So, have you heard from Meachum? Is he in town?"

"While I was looking for Glad, I went into Slap Jacks. There was a message for me, saying he'll arrive tonight. I figured I'd describe the kid and ask if he can find something out about him. With that god awful burn on his face, someone should remember him."

Mae nodded in satisfaction and stood. "Okay then, I want to talk to Millie Trumbull now that I know more about the family's situation." She put their dirty cups on a tray and headed for the door until Sage asked a question that stopped her.

"Hey, Ma, what's going on with Ida? I couldn't coax even a little smile out of her this morning."

Mae stopped in her tracks and turned back to them, guilt flushing her face. "Oh, my Lord. I forgot." She put the tray down on the walnut bureau and returned to the table. Quickly she told them about Matthew's transformation from sweet boy to surly teenager. "And, I promised her, the day before yesterday that you'd talk to him. What must she think of me?"

Seeing her distress, Sage patted her hand. "Don't worry. I'll take care of it. If she asks, I'll tell her that you told me but I couldn't break away before now."

Mae nodded briskly and rose again. "Good. See that you do." Seconds later she and the tray were gone. Although her words lacked gratitude, the squeeze she gave his shoulder told him she was grateful. He exchanged looks with Fong and they both chuckled.

Sage was leaning against a fir tree across from the West Side High School, waiting to do what he'd promised Ida—talk to Matthew. He didn't have to worry about the boy peddling off on his beloved Blue Beauty. Matthew had banished the bicycle to the cellar. That stored bicycle was worrisome in itself. Matthew loved it. He rode it all over town carrying messages, determined to earn enough for his college tuition.

The school doors slammed open just as the clouds parted and students poured out. Matthew's auburn hair shone like a bright beacon in the fitful sunlight but otherwise, he was a picture of gloom, descending the stairs alone and slowly, his shoulders slumped as if carrying a heavy weight.

Sage hurried to intercept the boy. "Matthew!" he called and saw the boy start only to relax at seeing Sage. Then concern quickly replaced his relief.

"Mr. Adair, what are you doing—" but he didn't finish the question. "Oh no!" he exclaimed. "Has something happened to Uncle Knute, to Aunt Ida, to Mozart's?" Alarm turned the boy's face white, making his freckles stand out like cinnamon sprinkled on milk.

Sage raised a calming hand, "No, everybody is just fine. No problems with them or the restaurant." He searched Matthew's face. "Why did you think something might be wrong, Matthew?"

Red overcast the freckles and Matthew's lips tightened. He looked away and mumbled, "No reason."

Taking hold of the boy's elbow Sage said, "Come on. You and I have to talk. Let's get some hot chocolate." He didn't wait for Matthew to agree before steering the boy down the sidewalk toward the corner café.

Once inside and sitting at a back table with hot chocolate before them, Sage got to the point. "Okay, Matthew. Something is clearly wrong. What is it? You've got everyone worried about you."

Matthew didn't answer. Instead, he lifted the cup to his lips and swallowed. Sage noticed the boy's hand shook.

"You might as well tell me. You know I'll find out eventually. You've got your Aunt so upset she's burning things. Our customers don't particularly relish charcoaled food," he said, trying for a little humor.

That effort failed. Matthew still said nothing, only looked down into the mug he was now turning round and round.

"Is someone threatening you? Have you gotten into a fight with one of the other messengers? With one of your friends?"

That question brought first a hesitation, followed by a vehement shake of his head. Matthew cleared his throat, "I just decided I didn't want to be a messenger anymore. Thought I'd concentrate on my school work instead."

"That's not a bad idea but it doesn't explain the fight or your foul mood lately." Sage decided tough talk was called for. "You know I'm happy to pay for your college but quite frankly, this sudden dislike of messenger work is puzzling."

Matthew shrugged, drained his cup and stood up. "Sorry, Mr. Adair, but I got to get going. I promised a friend I'd study with him this afternoon. Thank you for the hot chocolate." Matthew left the café without a backward glance.

"Well, damn," Sage said to himself.

When the door opened soft piano music drifted out. "Miss Lucinda is in the front parlor. Go on in," Elvira said to Sage as she took his coat and hat. He slipped into the room and saw Lucinda sitting at the piano, with her back to the door, and playing the wildly popular "Sweet Adeline." He slipped into a chair to listen. She was singing the words softly to herself in her sweet soprano.

He clapped when the song reached its end and she whirled around on the piano stool, looking flustered. "Nice playing," he told her, "Though I don't like the song, all that much. It's one long howl at the moon."

When he saw the hurt reaction in her face he rushed to say. "You played and sang it beautifully. I guess I'm tired of hearing it. Last count, there were a hundred versions of it. Anywhere there's a piano somebody's plunking it out."

"I suppose 'Uncle Josh and the Insurance Company' is more your taste," she said before turning around to drop the cover down over the keyboard. She didn't drop it gently. Sage sighed. He'd stepped in it once again.

When she turned back toward him her face was bland. She rose, tugged the call ribbon and when Elvira appeared, ordered coffee. Still saying nothing, she gestured him to a chair and took the one next to it.

No canoodling on the sofa, he thought ruefully. Well, if she wanted their meeting to be all business, so be it. "So, is there a new pedophile house in town?" he asked her.

"Getting right to it, Sage? No 'hello' or, 'how are you'?"

"Did seem like you were in that kind of mood," he said.

She shrugged and let it drop. "To answer your question, I think there may be. But the women I met with don't think we'll find Glad there. He isn't the type of boy they want—because he has family here. Still, one of the women is going to try to find the address of the new house. Once she does, she'll send it to me."

As if summoned by the words, Elvira stepped into the room with the coffee and announced, "One of Louise Rumbold's girls is here. She says she needs to talk to you right away."

When the young woman stepped into the room, her hat was askew and her stockings sagging. She was breathing hard.

She didn't wait but rushed into speaking, "Miss Collins, Mrs. Rumbold said I should come to warn you. Some men just came to our house and said she better stop helping you or else she was going to be sorry. They pushed her around. Even slapped her."

Lucinda jumped to her feet. "Is she alright?"

The young woman nodded vigorously. "They only got but the one slap in and Mrs. Rumbold dodged too fast for it to hit hard. Us girls drove them out of the house. Our cook brained one of them with her iron skillet. But Mrs. Rumbold wanted you to know right quick in case they aim to visit you next."

Sage butted in, "How many of them were there?"

"Four big fellows," she answered.

After a beat, during which Lucinda and Sage exchanged worried glances, Lucinda said, "Tell her I am very grateful for the warning and to let me know if there is anything I can do." Then she added, "And, please tell her I am very sorry for the trouble I've caused her and her ladies."

The girl turned to go then whirled back to Lucinda and extended a piece of paper. "I almost forgot. Mrs. Rumbold also asked me to give this to you."

Lucinda took the paper and waited until the girl was out the door before reading it.

Sage jumped up, impatient. "What is it?" he demanded.

"It appears to be the address you wanted," she said holding it out to him. He noticed her hand was shaking.

He glanced at the writing, shoved it in his pocket and headed for the door. Glancing back he was alarmed to see her eyes filling with sudden tears. Surely she can't be that scared, she's too tough. Then he realized what the problem might be instead. "Hell, Lucinda. I'm not leaving. I'm going to ask Elvira to send a message to get us some help."

Lucinda reached behind her for the chair arm and lowered herself down, the tears now spilling in earnest. He fought the urge to cross the room to comfort her. There wasn't time. The thugs could be already heading their way. He sped from the room.

EIGHT

A rapidly diminishing twilight lit the transom window above Lucinda's front door. They were ready. Elvira was at her post, peering out a small window. She was to inform arriving customers the house was closed and give warning when the thugs showed up.

Sage shifted on the bottom step of the staircase and checked his watch again. If they were coming, it'd be soon. Otherwise, they'd risk running into the last people in the city they'd want to offend—Portland's powerful, monied, elite men. He glanced around the entry hall. They'd stripped it of furniture, pictures and mirrors and knickknacks and locked every door off it. A barricade of wooden boxes blocked the corridor leading to the kitchen. The house's other outside doors were also locked and barricaded. That left the front door as the only way in.

Sage shifted again. He hated waiting. He glanced up at his companions who sat on the stair treads above him. The scarred knuckles on Lucinda's new driver, Bernard, indicated this wouldn't be his first dustup. Fong was relaxed, sitting quietly on his step, thinking who knew what. Lucinda was there too. She had insisted on being present but had agreed to stay farthest from the action on the topmost step. He'd grinned as she'd climbed past him carrying a heavy iron skillet.

Elvira tensed. "I think they're here," she said. Everyone stood.

"You be careful. Jump out of the way if they push their way in," Sage told Elvira, just as the brass knocker clanged.

Elvira took a deep breath, glanced at them all and reached for the door handle. She eased the door open only a few feet. "May I help—" were the only words she got out before the door was shoved wider, knocking her backward. She quickly scuttled behind the door and beneath the wide leaves of a potted rubber tree.

Four rough-looking fellows filled the entryway. One of them was holding a length of wood. He glanced around as if seeking something to hit. His forehead wrinkled at the sight of the stripped-down entryway.

"What exactly do you men want?" Sage asked, stepping onto the floor. Behind him, he heard Bernard and Fong descending the stairs to stand at his back.

"We want to speak private-like to the Collins woman. That her up there?" asked one of them.

"Sorry, gentlemen, but I am afraid Miss Collins is not available for a conference at present."

"'Not available for a conference'?" mimicked the man in front just before he and the other three charged forward and Lucinda's defenders stepped to meet them.

Sage dropped into a bow stance with his feet rooted, hands raised, his body centered and sideways to the leader who got within striking distance and threw a punch. Before it could connect, Sage stepped forward, his raised right hand rolling around the man's wrist, grabbing it, and yanking. The man fell forward, off-balance, bringing his chest close to Sage's left side. Sage drove a sharp elbow into the man's rib cage. Then he released the man's wrist while simultaneously delivering a right-handed open punch that sent the man stumbling backward a good six feet.

Nice beginning, Sage thought and saw that Fong was dealing with two of the attackers while Bernard was fully engaged in a one-on-one bare-knuckle fight. He glanced over his shoulder. Lucinda stood halfway down the stairs, gripping the black skillet. She was ready. He shook his head at her, saw alarm widen her eyes which snapped his attention forward.

His man had pulled a knife. "I really wish you hadn't done that," Sage calmly remarked to his attacker. The man barred his grimy teeth and charged forward, leading with the knife.

"Evade, bump, strike." The three words streamed through Sage's mind as he focused on the man's body movement, ignoring the knife. Twisting to the side Sage used his left forearm to deliver a sharp bump beneath the attacker's arm that deflected the knife sideways. This left the attacker's right temple exposed to Sage's single knuckle jab and he struck with his full force. The man's eyes rolled back in his head and he dropped to the floor, out cold.

Glancing around, Sage saw that Bernard had also knocked out his guy. Only Fong was still facing both his attackers. As Bernard moved to help, Sage grabbed his arm and pulled him away. "Fong doesn't need help. He's just been playing with them. Just watch. I give him sixty seconds to end it."

Fong overhead and threw a grin their way. He drew himself up and, with his face a serene mask, he bowed slightly to his attackers. That flummoxed them into immobility. "Bad mistake, they should have run," Sage muttered.

But they didn't run. Noses bloodied, lips split, the two exchanged looks and moved forward, each grabbing one of Fong's arms. He didn't resist. Instead, he looked grateful, like they were doing him a favor. The two thugs exchanged puzzled looks.

That is when Fong exploded into action, sinking down while stepping to one side and pulling his two arms together. This brought the two attackers crashing into each other just as Fong raised his arms, breaking both their holds. He moved forward, pushed one into the other, and they both crashed to the floor.

They clambered to their feet and, though both were panting, they charged again. This time Fong merely twisted, grabbed an arm and slung one into the path of the other. The collision sent them to the wall and then onto the floor again.

Their next effort was a pincer attack. One charged Fong's front while the other lumbered around to Fong's rear. Fong turned his back on the slower fellow, grabbed the first attacker's wrist and forearm and dropped into a very low snake creeps down position, his one leg stretched its full length out to the side. With an almost imperceptible tug, Fong sent the first attacker flying over the outstretched leg and into the second attacker who was charging from Fong's rear. The two bodies, moving fast in opposite directions, cracked heads. Both fell to the floor.

This time when they got up, they staggered toward the door. Elvira jumped forward and opened it for them. They stumbled down the steep steps to the sidewalk and soon were out of sight.

Sage turned to Bernard. "I was right. One minute."

Lucinda came slowly down the stairs. "Are they dead?" she asked, gesturing with her skillet toward the two men on her entryway floor.

Sage stepped forward, put a finger to each neck and said, with some relief, "They both have a pulse. Come on Bernard, let's dump them in the street."

Minutes later the front door was locked tight and Elvira began re-hanging pictures and otherwise putting the entryway "to rights" while the four of them trooped into the parlor.

"I doubt they'll come back," Lucinda said. "The three of you hurt them pretty badly."

Sage and Fong exchanged a look. "You're probably right," Sage said, "but it would be better if Bernard stays inside the house for the next few days, just in case." He looked at the driver who nodded eagerly, even as he flexed his hands. The smirk on his face said he'd relished his successful bout of fisticuffs.

Lucinda heaved a sigh. "I suppose you're right." She strode over to the door, opened it and they heard her say, "Elvira, kindly show Bernard the attic bedroom. He's going to be staying with us for a while."

Elvira promptly appeared in the doorway and beckoned Bernard to follow her. As they climbed the stairs, Lucinda came back into the room, closing the door behind her.

"Who sent men?" Fong asked her.

"Well, I asked a few madams if there's a new pedophile house in town. And, I asked whether anyone had seen the boy, Glad," Lucinda told them. "I know Louise Rumbold very well. She would have been discreet when obtaining the address of the new house. I know she must have gotten it without anyone knowing she'd asked."

"So, how did they know about her inquiries? And, how did they know she was helping you?" Sage asked.

Lucinda was nodding her head. "I've been thinking on that ever since we heard about the attack on Louise. When I met with the ladies, one of them, Vera Clark, was very hostile. At the time, I thought she was jealous of me. But, now I'm thinking there could have been another reason. Maybe she's mixed up in something. And, just maybe, she told whoever she's involved with about my questions."

"If so, that's the person we'd like to talk to since they sent goons to shut you and Mrs. Rumbold up," Sage mused aloud.

"Where is Vera person's business?" Fong asked.

"She runs a brothel in three wood-frame houses sitting side-by-side in the North End. They're right near Erickson's Saloon on Third, just north of Couch Street. You can't miss them. They have the same red window curtains. Real dumps," Lucinda said with a hint of satisfaction.

❀   ❀   ❀

"Somebody roughed Matthew up pretty good. He's got a black eye and a split lip," were the words that greeted Sage when he stepped into his bedroom shortly after six.

"How can that be? I just saw him at three o'clock and he was fine. He said he was going to study with a friend."

Mae shrugged. "Don't know. He wouldn't say. Just mumbled something about falling down before he headed to Ida and Knute's apartment. Brushed right past Ida, he did. Poor woman. She's fit to be tied."

"Damn. He wouldn't tell me anything. But listen, right now we've got more serious problems than some schoolboy tussle. Four men attacked Lucinda today. Someone warned us they were coming and we were able to toss them out. It seems her questions about Glad stirred something up. So, I don't know when I'll be able to get to the bottom of what's bothering Matthew. And, we can't ask Fong to follow him because Fong's busy following Glad's brother right now."

He stepped to the wardrobe and began tossing clothes on the bed. "I have to help you with the supper hour and then I have to change and head out to watch a brothel run by the woman Lucinda thinks triggered the attack. Then I have to meet Meachum and ask him to find someone who knows about the dead boy with the burns. God help us if Meach is bringing us a new assignment from St. Alban. I don't think we can take on anything more." As he talked, Sage was hurriedly donning his restaurateur outfit.

"Well, Glad's still missing. I went back to Sullivan's Gulch today. Millie's a board member of the Visiting Nurses' Association. When I told her about Mary's frailty and coughing, she got hold of a nurse and the three of us went to the Tobias shack."

Mae took a deep breath. "Mary was a little flustered and not happy to see us but Millie talked her around. She let the nurse examine her and Glad was right. She has TB. The nurse said that Mary needs good food, rest and a warmer, drier place to live. Millie will be asking Doc Lane to see if he'll admit Mary to that new sanatorium. Millie's on that board, too, and so is the doctor, so chances are good he'll approve her admission."

"Sounds like you had a busy day."

She shrugged. "I didn't do much. It was all Millie and the nurse. I did manage to ask about Glad again. Mary claimed that he's still off visiting that relative only this time she said it's a cousin. Yesterday, she said it was an aunt. The dear woman can't keep her lies straight. And that poor little Carry Anne starts blubbering every time someone mentions Glad's name. It breaks my heart." Mae's face was bleak.

Sage was standing before the mirror but he kept his eyes on his mother as he said, "We could rent the family a better house but if Mrs. Tobias goes into a sanatorium the kids can't stay alone, they're not old enough. What will happen to them?" He couldn't see how they could take care of three children in addition to everything else they were doing. Besides, where would they sleep?

Mae brightened. "When I saw her this morning, Millie said she can help place the kids. She says there are shelters where they can stay while their mother's getting better. Millie is happy to help. She says she 'owes' me."

"Why's that?"

"According to her, the inspection of the cracker factory was successful because I'd confirmed she'd find kids there if she just barged onto the factory floor. So that's exactly what she did. She zoomed past the receptionist, into the factory and straight into the side room where she caught the foreman ordering the kids down into a concealed cellar. Millie says she fined the owner and the kids no longer work there." Mae's words held pride and satisfaction. She was proud to have helped rescue the children from their factory labor.

"Jeez, she works fast."

"She's the kind of woman who charges ahead. She raided the factory while the owner was at lunch—just like she said she would." Mae clearly admired Mrs. Millie Trumbull. When the hullabaloo over Glad was done, he suspected he'd be hearing more about Mrs. "Grab your hat, Willie, here comes Millie" Trumbull.

"A burn you say? Which side of his face?" Meachum asked. The two of them were drinking whiskey. Meachum had said he was just passing through town on his way to Boise. As it was still freezing in the mountain passes, the Flying Squadron's leader had luxuriated in riding the cushions to Portland instead of hopping onto a boxcar. He had brought Sage a new assignment from St. Alban.

"It was a nasty scar on his left side," Sage said. He leaned over the table and asked earnestly. "Meach, are you sure you don't mind taking over St. Alban's Seattle assignment for me?" The labor leader had wanted Sage to check out the newly-formed Women's Trade Union League in Seattle. The organization's stated purpose was to support labor union women, especially those working in the garment trade. But, according to Meachum, one of St. Alban's concerns was that the organization was a mix of working and well-to-do women. Because of the latter, St. Alban wanted to make sure it wasn't a front for employers.

When Sage explained the problems he was trying to solve, Meachum offered to take on St. Alban's assignment. "We both know that's what the Saint would want me to do," he assured Sage.

Meachum tossed back the whiskey in his glass and pushed the bottle cork home. "If you don't mind, I'll take what's left of this to the camp. Might free up some talk about your dead boy.

"As for going to Seattle, riding the cushions inside a warm rail coach is like taking a vacation. I'll also get to sleep in a nice bed, instead of on the ground in the hobo camp. Pure luxury."

When he saw Sage's skeptical look he added, "Besides, I can ask the fellows about the dead kid while I'm up there. That way, I'll cover the camps here, in Seattle and in Boise once I get there. I'm more likely to get information since I know just about every regular 'bo on the west coast."

He squinted at Sage, saying, "You look tired. I hope you're heading home to bed."

Sage sighed. "I should but not just yet. I want to go back to Vera Clark's whorehouses and see if I recognize anyone. I was there for a couple of hours before I met you and mostly it looks like she caters to the timber workers living it up during their downtime."

Two hours later Sage was finally heading home. He'd seen a few men enter Clark's houses but none looked familiar. One man, though, had snagged his attention when he came up the boardwalk and crossed the porch with a purposeful stride. Clearly, he wants something other than a roll in the sheets, Sage thought. His supposition was borne out when, only a few minutes later, the door opened and the man came out. He clapped on his hat and headed south toward the business district.

Sage decided to follow and trailed the man to the doors of the Romanesque Imperial Hotel. Unfortunately, Sage's John Miner clothes barred him from entering since the Imperial was one of the city's most expensive hostelries. That left Sage with the man's height, profile and walk—tall, hook-nosed, and slightly pigeon-toed. That's all he'd seen in the dark.

NINE

"Up all night, huh?" Sage said more as a statement than a question. Fong couldn't deny it since his near-black eyes had equally dark smudges beneath them.

Fong nodded wearily. "I up all night because Glad's brother Terry work all night." There was a grim note to Fong's words.

"What did you learn?" Sage prodded.

"Boy has no more than twelve years. He go to Speedy Messenger Service, on First Street near rail station. I wait outside in dark. Man drags Terry boy out of office, pushes him against building. Waving hands and shouting. I ready to jump in but he only yell, no hitting.

"What did Glad's brother do?"

"He shake head 'no' bunch of times. Like he refusing. Man get more angry. Terry act like he afraid he get hit and finally nod, 'okay.'"

"Then what?"

"They go back in office. Later boy come back out and I follow. He go to Erickson saloon come out with bottle in sack then goes to close-by house. I think it that Clark woman's—red curtains in windows."

"They sent a twelve-year-old into a saloon and a whorehouse?"

Fong's nod was sad as he said, "All night long, that where they send him—brothels, restaurants, saloons, opium dens, gambling houses. He fetch and carry."

"You know anything about the Speedy Messenger Service?"

"Only know it new in town," Fong answered and yawned. "Has hire sign in window."

"You think you want to be a messenger? I can just see you in one of those little caps."

This time Fong's smile was sardonic, as if he knew the quandary he was about to deliver. "Sign also say, 'White Only.'"

Sage thought for a minute. "I'm too old to be a messenger boy," he said dismissively, putting an end to that idea.

"So sorry, Mr. Sage. Must tell you. Speedy messengers, some older than you." This time Fong's eyes twinkled before he yawned again.

"You better get some sleep," Sage told him.

Fong got up but, before leaving, said, "You remember men who take Glad?"

"It was foggy and dark. I only saw vague outlines."

"Was one very big man?"

Sage thought back. He pictured Glad being turned upside down and shook until all his money fell onto the boardwalk. The boy's feet had been high in the air. "I know one of them was really tall. Taller than me by at least three inches, maybe more," he told Fong.

His answer made Fong smile. "Man who yell at brother Terry also very tall," he said as he headed to his room down the hall.

Sage pondered Fong's information and then made a decision. He had no choice. They needed to talk to Glad's brother without scaring him off.

"Do you think Mrs. Trumbull could help?" Sage asked his mother. "After all, both the messenger services and newspapers employ a lot of kids."

Mae looked dubious. "You realize she'll know exactly who you are."

"You don't trust her to keep that secret?" he asked and saw her denial on her face before she spoke a word.

"I'd trust that woman with my life!" Mae exclaimed. "It's just I know how fussy you are about not letting people know about your secret doings outside of the restaurant."

They didn't have a choice, Sage thought later as they climbed the staircase to Trumbull's office. If he wanted to go undercover in a messenger service, he had to learn something about the business.

Millie Trumbull was in her office and alone. She came to her office door and raised an eyebrow when she spotted Sage beside Mae. "Mr.

Adair, I must say, I am surprised to see you here." Her deep brown eyes twinkled as she said, "Is it too much to hope that you are here to offer a donation?" She laughed before he could answer and asked them both to step into her office. Once they were inside and seated, she closed the hallway door and locked it.

She looked at Mae. "I take it this is your friend, the one who told you about the Tobias family?"

Mae nodded as Sage said, "Mrs. Clemens said you are intelligent. She didn't tell me you are also exceedingly quick off the mark."

Millie laughed heartily. "Not really. I put two and two together. Mae seemed to have your approval to be absent from work, so I'd already wondered. I could also tell there was more to the story." She sent an apologetic smile toward Mae. "I didn't think you lied, just that you withheld a bit. I figured that was on orders."

Sage jumped in before Mae could. "You're right. And, it is because Mrs. Clemens thinks so highly of you that we are here. Let me tell you what triggered everything." With that, he told of meeting Glad and the subsequent kidnapping, though he didn't mention the fact that he'd been in disguise at the time.

After Sage's factual recitation, Millie said. "It sounds like you plan to become a messenger so you can see if the brother knows anything."

"That's exactly right. I was hoping you could tell me something about the business in advance. I use messengers of course. Our cook's nephew, until very recently, was one. But he was freelance. He didn't work for a company. So, he can't tell me anything about how these places work."

Millie heaved a sigh. "Newsboys and messengers. Those are my two big defeats."

Mae jumped in, "Are messengers legally considered contractors as well—like the newsboys?"

"No, but that doesn't solve the problem. The statute forbids employing youngsters under fourteen in the messenger service but some of the companies get around it. They work them at night and they falsify their papers."

Sage scooted forward in his chair. "All of them?"

"No, thank God. Only a few at this point. Western Union and ADT abide by the new law. So does the Hasty Messenger Service." As she said this, a speculative look came into her eyes. "You said the Tobias boy works for the Speedy Messenger Service?"

Sage nodded. "Yes, so that's the one I'd be applying to."

Trumbull sat back in her chair and gazed out the rain-streaked window. "You know, we can maybe help each other out. Speedy Messenger is new in town and I've heard some bad things about them, including that they work young boys at night. If you go undercover, you could confirm whether those reports are true." She stood up, slapped her palms on her desk and said, "I've got an idea. You go find a way to make yourself look less like John Adair, owner of Mozart's restaurant. Then meet me in one hour at Third and Stark Streets. There's a man you need to talk to."

"Wait, that's close to Mozart's. Even if I'm disguised he might recognize me."

Trumbull's chuckle was brief. "No chance whatsoever of that happening. But those around him might, so you need to be disguised. What name are you going to use?"

"John Miner," Sage answered.

An hour later, Sage was at Third and Stark. It was a rowdy corner lately known for too many street hawkers and idle hooligans. As he strode up, three of the latter were in the street, trying to grab bundled laundry off a hand truck. The Chinese laundryman was trying to hold onto the bundles but was no match for the three of them. One bundle was already in a puddle. Sage darted forward, caught two of the youngsters by their collars and cracked their heads together. Yowling with pain, they backed away and all three took to their heels, yelling indecipherable threats back over their shoulders.

The Chinese man plucked his bundle from the puddle and stowed it in his cart. "Thank you," he said to Sage. "Lucky, laundry already dirty," he added, before trundling down the street.

Returning to the sidewalk, he was surprised to see Millie Trumbull standing there. She had a big grin on her wide face. "Folks are saying it's messenger boys causing all the trouble on this corner but I know it's not," she told him.

"How do you know that?"

"Because the only messenger service within a block of this corner is the Hasty Messenger Service. Jeff Hayes runs it and he keeps a tight rein on his messengers. He's the fellow I want you to meet."

As they started to enter the storefront, a hawk-faced, well-dressed man exited and nearly knocked Millie down with his elbow. Apparently, with his gold watch fob and embroidered vest, he thought himself too important to apologize. Recognition flashed through Sage. It was that new lawyer, the one who'd booked his wife's birthday party at Mozart's. Fortunately, the man hadn't glanced in Sage's direction.

Inside they found a counter presided over by a bright-eyed young man. "Good afternoon, Mrs. Trumbull and Sir," he said. "Do you need to send a message?"

Millie shook her head. "No, Davey. We'd like to see Mr. Hayes if he isn't busy."

The young man disappeared and came back within a minute. "He says he'd be delighted. Come this way."

He led them through a door into a large room containing benches and chairs scattered about. A bookshelf, overflowing with books, papers and magazines stretched along one wall. There were about twelve young men present, some stretched out asleep on the benches, others reading in armchairs and still others playing cards. There was no money on the table so they weren't gambling. To Sage's eye, they all looked older than sixteen. Each wore a dark blue tunic. Matching caps hung on wall pegs.

Millie saw Sage's look and tapped a poster on the wall. It read, "Messenger Rules." There appeared to be at least ten numbered rules, but Sage only had time to read the first one that she'd tapped, "No boy under the age of sixteen will be employed by the Hasty Messenger Service."

"And, Jeff means it," Millie said before turning to follow Davey into a back corner office. After ushering them into the small space, he departed, closing the door firmly behind him. The man across the wide desk looked about fifty with gray hair, smoked eyeglasses, and an impassive face. He stood and reached out a hand, saying, "Mrs. Trumbull, how kind of you to visit. And, I understand that you have a friend with you."

That reaching hand explained it all. It was not reaching toward Millie Trumbull nor toward Sage. Instead, it was aimed midpoint between them. Jeff Hayes was blind. Sage glanced toward Millie and she gave him a raised-eyebrow-I-told-you-so look as she shook the man's hand.

"Mr. Hayes, my friend is John Miner," she nodded at Sage to also take and shake Hayes' proffered hand. Sage did so while saying, "Pleased to meet you, Sir."

Millie wasted no time getting to the point. She gave the explanation they'd agreed on. "We came to you for help. Mr. Miner here is going to work undercover for me. We need him to get a job at the Speedy Messenger Service. I've received disturbing reports on it. We hoped you would educate Mr. Miner about messenger work and maybe tell us something about the Speedy company in particular."

All was quiet in the office as Hayes considered Trumbull's request. His first words were reassuring. "You can't get no more low down than Speedy. You probably know they're new in town. Only been here for about six months. I hear tell they aren't choosy who they hire and they're undercutting the rest of us on charges. And, you are right to be concerned. One of my fellows said there's a ten-year-old working for them. So, the rest of us would be mighty glad if you were able to pull them up short."

Sage relaxed. "I've never worked as a messenger. And, we think I should try to get a night position. Can you tell me about the work and do you think a night job is possible?"

Hayes' smile was rueful "That won't be a problem. They can't keep people so they're always hiring. And, only the lowest of the low or desperate kids will work nights at those wages."

"Why's that?" Sage asked.

"First you got to understand, no child under the age of sixteen is permitted to work before 7 a.m. or after 6 p.m. Despite that law, the Speedy folks regularly have young kids whizzing around town in the wee hours, delivering and picking up messages. But think about it. What kind of businesses are open at night?"

"Uh, saloons, brothels, opium and gambling dens, a few restaurants," Sage reeled off.

"Exactly. Now the tips in those disreputable places are good. I know. I've been in the messenger business for twenty-two years. I've seen it all. And, I've seen enough to know that no child should go into such places. I never accept any delivery that would take my messengers into places like that." For the first time, Hayes' blank face showed an emotion—disgust. "I don't want them seeing what goes on in those places, not to mention the danger of them joining in those kinds of activities."

"It sounds like you care about your messengers," was all Sage could think to say.

It was the right response because for the first time, Hayes gave a genuine smile and a look of pride suffused his otherwise blank face, "During the quarter of a century that I have lived in Portland, I've worked as a Western Union manager, Postal Telegraph manager, Pacific Messenger manager, and, now, I'm owner of the Hasty Messenger Service. I've supervised thousands of boys and very few have turned out bad. The brightest man in the last Legislature is one of my former messengers and he had the pleasure of working with six other former messengers who've worked for me. We have doctors, lawyers, dentists, actors and businessmen by the score who started out working for me. And, I know of four ministers of the gospel who once 'donned the cap' of my messenger service. That's why I worked so hard to get the night school started at West Side High School. I take great pride in my former messengers' successes."

Hayes leaned forward over the desk. Despite the dark glasses covering his eyes, there was no mistaking his intense feelings as he said, "These boys must necessarily be brighter and quicker than the average youngster. And, as their business necessitates an active mentality, it means they have little time for mischief and foolishness. And I make sure of it. I forbid my boys from entering disreputable houses, drink, smoke cigarettes or use profanity. I insist that they keep themselves neat and clean and save their money. Of course, I occasionally get a bad boy, but he does not last. I usually find him out in short order."

Hayes raised a finger and wagged it in their general direction. "And I'll tell you something else; my messenger boys have courage and self-possession. They go to the farthest limits of the city at all hours of the night and in all kinds of weather. We send boys to Mount Tabor or Willamette Heights at midnight or in the early hours of the morning—when many another man would be afraid to go. That takes nerve."

Hayes sat back in his chair like someone who'd finished saying his piece and was satisfied with what he'd said. He expected no contradiction and got none.

Instead, Sage asked, "Do you know anything else about the Speedy company?"

Hayes pursed his lips and said cautiously, "I got to be careful what I say. I don't want to get sued by a competitor. My new lawyer, Mr. Abernathy, was just here cautioning me about that very thing."

TEN

Millie spoke up. "Mr. Hayes, Mr. Miner assures me that anything you say will not be repeated outside this room. You can speak freely."

Hayes' face turned in Sage's direction and he asked, "Is that true Mr. Miner? You swear to keep whatever I say in confidence?"

Sage nodded, remembered Hayes' couldn't see him, and said, "I promise that I will not mention I ever spoke to you. This meeting never happened." He hoped that evasive response would suffice because, of course, Mae and Fong would have to know everything. That's how they worked. That's why their team had been successful.

Sage's answer seemed to satisfy because Hayes again relaxed. "Okay then, mind you that what I tell you next is only rumor. Bits and pieces I've heard from my boys and others. Bottom line, Speedy plans to drive all of us out of business by undercutting our prices and by other means as well."

"They're taking on Western Union?" Incredulity sharpened Sage's tone. He couldn't believe any upstart would challenge financier Jay Gould's telegraph company with its million miles of wire and two undersea international cables.

Hayes' answer was vehement, "No, no. Not the two companies that carry the telegrams, Western Union and American District Telegraph, or ADT, as we call it. Just us smaller ones that do message delivery for local householders and businesses."

Millie jumped in. "What "other means" are they using besides undercutting your prices?" she asked and got a grateful look from Sage. He'd forgotten that comment.

"Lately, some of us have been getting bogus orders. The other night, my messenger got called to a house clear out at the city's eastside boundary. He arrived there at the time ordered, 12:30 a.m. His knocking woke up the householder who blasted the poor boy's ears for waking him up. I got to talking to other managers and they said someone called to send their messengers to the same house that same night. The last messenger said the angry man pointed a gun at him and threatened his life. That prank cost us time and money—not to mention scaring our messengers."

"Anything else Speedy might be doing?" Sage prodded.

"Well, yes. Someone's been stealing tail lanterns off my messengers' bikes. That's dangerous. Besides which, the police arrest and haul the messenger into court for riding without a light after dark. So far this week, their fines have cost me $6. And my messengers aren't the only ones. Same thing's happening all over town."

"Anything else?"

Hayes nodded. "Some of my competitors say someone's twisting their messengers' arms to work for Speedy, even threatening them and their families. But that's a rumor too. As far as I know, it hasn't happened to any of my boys, yet. But then, they're older and better able to take care of themselves.

"Besides, I think they have a different attack plan for Hasty Messenger. I am sure Speedy's behind the rowdies hanging about outside the office here. They turned up right after Speedy went into business. Their antics; yelling, fighting, gambling and the like are scaring my walk-in customers away. Who wants to walk through that mess? You saw it today. Davey said you stopped their attack on a Chinese man. He said you cracked their heads together. That must have been something to see."

"What makes you think Speedy's behind that?"

"Quite a few things. The timing's one. Also, one of the regular rowdies outside in the street used to work for me before I fired him. My fellows say he now carries messages for Speedy when he's not out front of our place raising a ruckus. And, someone told the Oregonian reporter that it's my messengers who are causing the problem. That's a bald-faced lie. I don't allow them to wait out in the street for their assignments. They have to wait in that room, right outside this office door. Those are some of the reasons why I'm sure Speedy is behind my troubles."

"The Speedy company sounds all-around nasty. You have any suggestions on what I should do if I want to get a job there?" Sage asked.

"Look desperate and like you're willing to do anything. Tell them you know the city well and that you want to work nights. They'll snatch you up," Hayes said.

As they got up to leave and were shaking hands, Hayes said, "I don't know whose money is behind the Speedy company but I do know one thing."

"What's that?" Sage said.

"You best be mighty darn careful. Cracking rowdy boys' heads together is one thing. Going up against conniving men is another thing altogether."

They'd hatched the plan in Sage's upstairs bedroom after he had said, "We don't have a lot of time to find Glad. The longer we take, the more dangerous it is for him. My gut tells me the brother knows something. And, I have to agree with Lucinda, I don't think Glad is locked away in that eastside house."

Mae cocked her head and asked, "Does it even matter whether he's there or not?"

Sage's eyebrows pulled together. "What do you mean? Sure, it matters. We're trying to find him."

He caught a look passing between Mae and Fong. "What?" he demanded, irritated at their wordless communication. They were always doing that.

Fong spoke, "Think, Mr. Sage. If Glad not in house, who is in house?"

"Other kids . . . oh heck," Sage said, finally catching Mae's point. "You're right. Last time I waited a whole year before acting and I'll always regret that delay." He had rashly promised an old man that he'd close the house only to be later overwhelmed by guilt when he learned that the old man died before Sage delivered on his promise. Not again.

"Actually," he began, "we just don't have the time to sit outside the house on the off chance Glad will step out the door. If he is being held there, they'll never let him out on his own."

"How about we be criminals?" Fong suggested.

"What do you mean?" Sage asked, though he had a good idea of where Fong was heading.

"We raid house and take kids and customers' money to feed kids."

Sage felt compelled to argue against the plan since Mae was looking interested rather than getting ready to object. "We'd get caught. Where would we take them?"

"We do it right. Wear masks. Surprise on our side. For sure, they not call police on us. Trumbull lady know where to take kids."

Sage quickly gave in. After all, sitting outside that house during wintertime was unlikely to yield anything more than pneumonia. Crashing in and searching the place was the quickest way to determine whether Glad was there. And, the bonus would be rescuing all the children.

So, here they were about to carry out the scheme. Mae had met with Millie Trumbull to figure out where to take the children. It turned out that Millie Trumbull sat on the board of the Boys and Girls Aid Society. The Society housed orphans and children sent to it by the court. Millie had agreed to arrange for the Society to receive the children.

They'd rented a covered moving van devoid of any markings. Now it was midnight and they were rolling through the moonless night behind two sturdy horses. There were just the four of them—Fong to drive and raid the house with Sage, Mae, and Lucinda riding inside the van, ready to reassure the rescued children and make them presentable for the Society. It wouldn't do for the Society's other wards to guess where these children had come from. To that end, loose pants, shirts, and sweaters were waiting for them once they climbed aboard the van.

Fong pulled to the curb half a block away from the house. It was a run-down Victorian with scalloped shingles and turned porch pillars. Sage and Fong jumped on to the boardwalk while Lucinda and Mae crawled out of the back to hold the horses. The women were unrecognizable. Poke bonnets hid their faces while long black coats did the same for their figures.

Sage and Fong's tattered black dusters reached their shins and they wore flop-brimmed hats and kerchiefs around their necks. After checking to make sure the street was empty, they strode up to the house's front door and pulled the kerchiefs up to their eyes. Fong would stay silent—his accent being too pronounced.

This time, they were the ones shoving their way inside. "What the hell—" was all the small man who opened the door got out before Sage's raised pistol silenced him.

"We don't want to hurt anyone," Sage told the man whose mouth opened and closed like a beached fish's. "But we're taking the kids. Where are they?"

The man pointed up the stairs. Sage glanced into the front parlor. Empty. He grabbed the man's arm and steered him toward the stairs. "We're keeping you with us, so don't try anything," he told the man.

The three of them climbed the narrow stairs. Only a single gas flame lit the narrow, upstairs hallway. Spaced along it were five closed doors and a sixth that opened into a bathing room.

Sage gestured with his gun at the first closed door. "Open it," he ordered. The man looked like he wanted to protest but a well-placed gun barrel prod squelched that idea. He opened the door on the expected scene.

The boy was young, somewhere around ten or so. He scrambled into a far corner and silently began pulling on his clothes—his wide-eyed stare missing nothing.

Fong slid past Sage and held out an open cloth bag to the adult male in the room.

"Put all your cash in that bag," Sage ordered. "Don't bother with your watch or other valuables. We only want your cash—coins and paper."

The man fished in the pockets of the trousers that lay pooled around his feet. Coming up with a wad of cash he dropped it in the bag. The boy remained silent. Sage looked in his direction and said, "We're here to help you. Go with my friend here. We're taking you to a safe place."

When the boy hesitated, Fong stepped to him, seized his elbow and steered him from the room. Their soft steps descended the stairs followed by the sound of the front door opening.

"Now listen here!" The man had pulled up his trousers and began to bluster.

"No, you listen," Sage snarled. "Consider yourself lucky we're not the police. All you're losing is a little money and the chance to engage in your sick pastime. You say anything more and I'll club you with this gun barrel—that's what I want to do."

The man shut up. Fong returned and nodded at Sage. They went back into the hallway, herding both men before them. In the next three rooms, they went through the same routine. Finally, they reached the last room. A key stuck out of its lock. By this point, they had five men in tow—the manager and his four customers. Sage figured that was the most he and Fong could handle should the men try resisting.

Turning the key in the lock Sage pushed the door open and was startled to see a small girl child. She looked only about eight years old. Her eyes were huge with terror. Sage shot a disgusted look at the manager as Fong slipped into the room, picked the child up in his arms and once again headed toward the outside. This little one brought the total rescued to five.

"You don't know how much I want to shoot each one of you," Sage said. "I'd say that you should be ashamed but you're long past feeling guilt. Get inside and count yourself lucky that, unlike you, I am a decent man."

The five of them stumbled inside. Sage closed and locked the door behind them. Good, he thought to himself, now I don't have to worry about them running after us. Through the door he said, "Don't try to get out. I'm going to stand in the hallway here until I'm sure the children are far away."

Having said that, he moved silently down the hallway and descended the stairs. Exiting, he left the front door ajar in the hope that an enterprising thief would spot the opportunity.

The second he clambered onto the van seat next to Fong, they began rolling away down the street. "I feel like I should go scrub in a tub of hot water," he said to Fong.

Fong nodded. "I feel same. But we have children. That is good."

Minutes later the van pulled up in front of the Boys and Girls Aid Society building. It was an imposing wood-frame structure, standing five stories high on the corner of East 29th and Irving streets. A large garden, recently donated by banker William Ladd's estate, gave the children a place to play. At the top of steep cement steps, a covered porch stretched between the building's two wings.

Millie Trumbull hurried down the stairs to intercept them.

"Do you have the children? How many?" she asked before anyone had alighted.

"Five. Four boys and one tiny girl. Are you ready for them?" Sage said.

"Yes, although he thinks it highly irregular, Mr. Gardner understands the necessity of him not knowing who is delivering the children to us. He's waiting in the vestibule to receive them."

Sage leaned over and handed the cloth bag to Millie. "There should be enough money in here to cover their board for quite a while," he told her.

Meanwhile, Mae and Lucinda had opened the van doors and were lifting the confused children down onto the sidewalk. Seeing them, Millie hurried to take the two youngest boys' hands. "Come with me, children. There's nice hot cocoa and cookies waiting for you," she told them with a warm smile.

Lucinda held the little girl tightly in her arms, whispering reassurances in the child's ears. Mae herded the two other children after Millie. Once the group reached the front door, the children were handed over to a small group of people—Lucinda doing so with obvious reluctance.

That done, the two women hurried back down the stairs and jumped into the van. Fong immediately clucked the horses into action.

"What happen to kids now?" Fong wanted to know.

"Millie told Ma that she'll take them to juvenile court tomorrow. Apparently, she also volunteers as a matron there. The judge will determine who the children are. If they have homes, Millie will investigate whether the homes are decent. If not, the people of the Society will try to find foster homes for them. If they can't do that, the Society will keep them and try to teach them a trade. If the kids don't run away, they should be safe."

Only the rattle and creak of the van traveling on the rough street made a sound until Fong broke the silence by saying, "Glad boy not in house."

"You are right. We didn't find Glad," Sage agreed. He was happy he could say that although he was less happy about what he said next. "Guess that means I'll be working as a night messenger."

"Buddha say, 'Life is suffering,'" was Fong's only comment.

Sage's glance at his friend caught Fong smiling. "Very funny," he said. "Given a choice, I'd pick a different kind of suffering, thank you very much."

ELEVEN

The mood was celebratory as they sat in Lucinda's kitchen. "I, for one, hope they stay locked up in that room for a few days," said Lucinda.

"Can you imagine? That little girl. Why, we were just in time. She said her daddy sold her for a whiskey bottle just before we rescued her," Mae said. "I hate to think what her life has been like."

Sage glanced at Lucinda and saw her eyes fill with tears. She jumped to her feet and went to the stove. She paused with her back to them before she turned and said brightly, "More coffee anyone?"

Sage wanted to go to her, to put his arms around her but knew this was a demon she wanted to fight alone. Bad memories ambushed like that. Even in a crowd they isolated, dug their invisible claws in, and only you could shake them off. He knew. He'd revisited that damn coal mine, asleep and awake, so many times that he'd lost count.

Fong spoke softly. "We did good thing tonight." He was looking at Lucinda who sent him a watery smile.

Mae slapped her hands on the table. "Anyways, that poor boy, Glad, is still missing. We best think about how we're going to find him."

"At this point, all I know to do is get next to his brother. That means getting hired by Speedy."

"Are you sure you don't want to just ask the brother straight out about Glad? Skip the messenger job altogether?" Lucinda asked.

Sage shook his head. "Better not. If Eich or I ask, and he stonewalls us, then he'll recognize us if we try anything else. Besides, given that the family is hiding Glad's absence and the fact that Terry rebuffed the newsboy's questions about Glad, I've no reason to think Terry will be forthcoming with us. Just the opposite. We're total strangers."

He caught a glimpse of a sly smile flashing across Lucinda's face and she winked at him. "What?" he asked.

"Just thinking my bedroom wardrobe is acquiring quite a collection of your disguises. Now I'll get to add a messenger boy outfit."

Fong grinned at her. "You be disappointed. Speedy messengers only wear cap. No outfits like Western Union and ADT."

"It figures," Mae said. "Scalawags always cut every corner."

It was mid-afternoon, during a rainstorm, when Sage entered the Speedy Messenger office. Mae had been right. The company did cut corners because the space was small and shabby. A rickety table and chair facing the door served as the customer counter. Behind the table sat a sagging sofa, two scarred wooden benches and a small table with mismatched chairs. Two boys dressed in ragged clothes were playing cards on the table. Another two were crouched down, tossing dice against a wall. Coins were present at both games. In the farthest corner, a boy lay curled on the floor, his rolled coat serving as a pillow.

All of them looked younger than sixteen. One looked about ten. The only adult was an unsavory type about Sage's age sitting behind the entry table and eyeing Sage with lowered brow and sullen face. His lank, greasy hair straggled to his shoulders.

"You looking to send a message, Mister?" the man asked in a tone only marginally polite.

Sage doffed his rain-soaked hat and nervously smoothed his droopy mustache. "Why, no," he said. "Fellow told me you were hiring white men and I need a job."

Now that he knew Sage was not a customer, the man dropped any pretense of civility. "Is that so?" he asked aggressively. "And just why should we hire the likes of you?"

Turning his hat brim in his hands, Sage looked down at the floor and then up to say, "Well, I know the city, I got two sturdy legs and I don't mind working nights."

The man studied him in silence, long enough for Sage to fear rejection. Letting that fear show he wheedled, "Please, Mister. I'm at the end of my rope. I'll do everything you ask without complaint."

The man lifted his shoulders and then dropped them, seemingly having made a decision. "Can you read?" At Sage's nod, he continued, "Alright then. We pay you 2 cents to deliver a message but we charge the customer 25 to 75 cents for the delivery—depending on the distance. If you have to take a trolley, there's an extra delivery charge to the customer. You get 10 percent of that charge but the cost of the trolley is taken out of your 10 percent. Is any of that going to bother you?"

Sage relaxed. "No, no. That'd be just fine and dandy," he said.

"Our best customers might have you run errands for them. Will that be a problem?"

"No, no. The fellow what told me about the job said that sometimes folks pay tips for running errands," Sage said.

"Yup, if the customers like you, you can do pretty good." The man studied Sage for a long moment and then he said, "Alright, we'll give you a try. You don't have to wear a uniform but you do have to wear a cap. Rent for the cap is ten cents a week." He gestured at the wall near the door where a line of black caps hung from wall pegs with an inked number on the wall above each one.

Sage smiled in genuine relief. He was in. "I don't have ten cents to spare right now. My landlady—"

"You don't pay now. I'll deduct it from your first week's pay," interrupted the man. He continued, "My name's Mr. Prang and I manage this place. I expect you to be here promptly at sundown today. You work until sunup. Is that a problem?"

Sage was quick to shake his head. "No, no, that's fine. I'll see you then. Thank you, mister."

Sage started to leave only to halt at Prang's next words. "What's your name?"

"I'm called, 'John Miner.'"

Prang's face was stern and his eyes steely as he looked at Sage and said, "Well, Mr. Miner, you steal from us or our customers or cause us any trouble whatsoever, we won't go to the police. We'll deal with you in our own way. Believe me, that'd be much worse than going to jail. The last fellow couldn't walk for a month."

As he exited, elation fizzed through Sage. For some unexplainable reason, he felt certain they were finally on the right track.

Sage was back at the messenger company just as the sun dropped behind the western ridge. A sour-faced man with a bald head and scraggly beard sat at the table, flipping through papers and making entries in a ledger book. Behind him lounged a crew of different messengers.

When he looked up and saw Sage he said, "My name's Kimble. You Miner?" At Sage's nod, Kimble asked, "You ever done messenger work before?" When Sage shook his head Kimble hollered, "Tobias, you got a new one to train," and went back to his paperwork.

Sage studied the boy who came forward. No question. This was Glad's brother. He had the same widow's peak above his forehead, the same elfin features. Only this boy's dark eyes were dull and his face apathetic.

"Get a move on," snapped Kimble. "Remember what Willard told you!"

From the backroom, someone mimicked Kimble in a falsetto whine, "Yeah, get a move on, Terry!" Snickers came from the group.

Kimble jumped up and turned to glare at the others, all of whom became busy doing something else or feigning sleep. "Who said that?" he demanded but silent shrugs were the only answer. "I guess some of you need another Willard lesson," he snarled and the boys seemed to shrink.

Kimble turned to Glad's brother and handing him a slip of paper he said, "Tobias, this here is John Miner. Get him outfitted with a cap and then take him with you when you run this message so he can see how to deal with our customers and fill out the paperwork. He'll shadow you for a few hours before we send him out on his own." He turned to Sage saying, "There's no pay when you're being trained."

The boy turned to the row of hats on pegs. "What's his number going to be, Mr. Kimble?" he asked.

"We'll call him, "37". That peg's empty."

Sure enough, there was an empty peg below that number. Tobias studied Sage's head and went over to a wooden crate. He raised the top to reveal a pile of caps, many of them tattered. After pawing through it, he brought up one but he didn't hand it to Sage. "Whatcha going to do with that hat on your head?" he asked.

"Roll it up and stuff it in a pocket. It's been there before," Sage said, speaking to him for the first time.

"Alright then, let's go," said Tobias without passing over the cap. Once they were on the boardwalk and a few steps past the office, the boy turned to Sage. "Keep your own hat on for today. You'll need to take this one home and boil it to kill the lice. In the meantime, we'll stuff it behind these barrels in this alley and hope nobody takes it. Though if they do, they'll surely regret it."

For the first time, Terry Tobias smiled, making his resemblance to his younger brother all the more striking.

"Thank you," was all Sage could think to say.

They traveled just a few blocks to an attorney's office, covering the distance at a near trot. Terry explained, "Prang and Kimble check the receipts to see how long it takes us to get places. They say we have to cover a block in one and a half minutes. That's pretty fast. Speedy cuts our pay if we take too long."

The attorney's secretary signed for the message, penciling in the delivery time. "That'll be a 25 cent delivery charge, Sir," Terry told the man who promptly paid, adding five cents as a tip.

After they'd left, Sage asked. "Do people usually tip you?'

Terry nodded. "Yeah. It's a good thing they do. Otherwise, we'd all starve on what Speedy pays. Some folks don't tip, though. Usually, the ones who don't tip are the ones who hardly ever use messengers."

Back at the office, an errand was waiting. Terry glanced at the paper and frowned until he noticed Kimble watching him then his face went blank. "Mind what I told you," the man called after them in a warning tone as they left.

"What'd he mean?" Sage asked.

"Nothing," Terry mumbled.

Minutes later they were climbing the steps of a crumbling wood house, the middle one of three red-curtained houses sitting a block from Erickson's saloon. Sage knew them well—they were at Vera Clark's brothel. Sage smiled in grim satisfaction. Maybe he would meet the woman who'd sent those hoodlums after Lucinda.

Terry knocked and stepped back as the opening door sent a reeking miasma into their faces: a mix of cigar and cigarette smoke, stale booze, cheap perfume, and greasy pomades. But it was the sickly, fruity, scent that made Sage want to grab Terry's shoulders and stop him from entering. Instead, Sage balled his fists and tried for deadpan.

Terry hesitated on the threshold until the slatternly woman at the door said, "What are you waiting for, boy? You think we want to heat the outdoors or sumpthin?"

"I've come from Speedy Messenger Service, ma'am," Terry said, as they both entered and she'd closed the door.

"'Course you have," she replied and turned to shout, "Vera! Messenger boy's here."

There was a faint answering call. Terry shifted uneasily. A woman appeared at the top of the stairs. Sage studied her. This was, indeed, Vera

Clark. Wearing a flimsy dressing gown, she was hag-faced and scrawny. She descended the stairs, her eyelids drooping as if she was sedated.

She studied Terry briefly before switching her attention to Sage. "Mirabelle, why are you making this customer stand in the hallway? Show him into the parlor!"

Sage rescued Mirabelle. "Sorry ma'am, I am just a messenger being trained. I'm not a customer tonight."

Clark sniffed, stepped onto the entryway rug and said to Terry, "Well, in that case, I want you to take this envelope to the address written on it. Wait there and bring back what they give you. And, no dilly-dallying."

While she was speaking, Sage glanced into the parlor and saw why Terry stood with his back to that room. Inside were women, most scantily clothed in see-through silk. One was dancing, dreamily baring legs, breasts, and other body parts customarily seen only by husbands.

Men were there, too. Some of them held women on their laps and drink glasses in hands that weren't otherwise busy on the women. Laughter, coarse and shrill, nearly drowned out a tinny gramophone.

Glancing at Terry, he saw the boy's face was crimson. Then he saw why. Clark had let her tatty dressing gown fall open, exposing an otherwise naked body. Her emaciation made it far from sexy and her smirk said she was enjoying the twelve-year old's embarrassment.

Sage had had enough. He took hold of the seemingly paralyzed boy's arm and tugged him toward the front door. "We best be going. We have another errand to run right after this one and we're running late." The excuse was clumsy and Clark's shrill, mocking laughter followed them out the door.

Once they were back on the street Sage asked, "Do you have to go into brothels like that very often?"

"Every day. I don't have a choice. I hate it. I daren't tell Ma."

"So, you can't refuse to go?"

Terry gave a short, derisive bark of laughter. "Not if I want—" His voice trailed off. He looked at the envelope and said, "This address is about six blocks away. We better hurry. That woman complains if I take too long bringing her 'medicine.'" The sarcasm lacing that last word gave Sage a good idea of what the errand was all about.

"Medicine?" Sage echoed.

"You'll see," Terry responded and picked up his pace.

TWELVE

Their pace slowed as they walked deep into the seediest part of the North End. Except for the intermittent flicker of weak gaslights, the night was black from a heavy overcast. Misty rain began soaking their clothes.

When they reached a ramshackle wood-frame building, Terry stepped onto its low stoop and knocked three times on a metal-clad door. It opened and a skeletal hand reached through the narrow opening to take the envelope Terry held out. "Wait," a husky voice commanded and the door slammed shut. Even though he knew the answer, Sage started to ask what was happening but Terry quickly interjected, "Not here."

A minute later the door opened and the hand reappeared. This time it held a small brown glass vial. Terry took it, and even before he'd stowed it in his coat pocket, the door slammed shut.

Terry turned and hurried away. It was only after they'd rounded the corner that the boy exhaled and took a gulp of air. Sage tugged at Terry's arm to slow him down and said, "What the hell was that all about?"

Terry glanced around and stepped over to stand under one of the street's few gas lamps. The light was weak but bright enough that Sage saw the boy pull out a glass vial, unscrew its top and spill two dark brown, round balls into his palm. "It's opium. She makes me fetch it all the time," he told Sage, after tipping the balls back into the vial and tucking it back into his pocket.

Terry turned and started walking. To Sage's surprise, the boy kept talking. "At night, mostly we run errands for the whorehouses. Speedy has them wired up so they can just call when they want a messenger. They send us to get opium and liquor and food and other stuff. She always asks for me." Bitter contempt coated the word "she".

"Are there a lot of those types of errands?"

"We are busier at night doing them than the day shift messengers. That's why Prang hired you. We're always short of night messengers. Nobody wants to work nights. Normally, he only uses kids like me. Guess he thinks we'll keep our traps shut."

"You know, Terry, it sounds like you hate this job."

"If my mother found out what Speedy has me doing it would break her heart." Sage sidewise glance caught the glint of unshed tears in the boy's eyes.

"Are all the messenger services like Speedy?" Sage asked.

This question brought a vehement shake of the head. "Nope. Speedy's the worst. Western Union and ADT, they do mostly telegrams and business messages. A year ago, ADT pulled all its wires out of the whorehouses. And Mr. Hayes, at Hasty Messenger, he won't have nothing to do with whorehouses or saloons."

"So why don't you get a job with one of those companies?"

Terry went silent, leaving only the sound of their boots on the boardwalk. Sage was debating whether to ask the same question again when Terry said, "I can't quit," his voice heavy with pain, frustration, and finality.

Sage glanced down at his companion. The boy's mouth was set in a narrow line. Something told Sage it would be useless to dig for more.

Back at the red-curtained whorehouse, Vera Clark swooped out of the parlor into the hallway with her hand outstretched the minute Mirabelle ushered them across the threshold. Terry handed her the vial and she handed him the 25 cents and a half dollar more for a tip. Terry doffed his cap, said, "Thank you, ma'am" and then they were heading out the door as her voice called after them, "Sure you don't want another show, my little man?" Her mocking question was accompanied by a high pitched cackle.

As they headed back to the office Sage asked, "She do that often, let her clothes fall open."

"Every time. She thinks it's funny. Some boys refused to do her errands."

"Why don't you?"

Again the silence and again, "I can't."

Vera Clark's errands signaled the end of Sage's "training." When they returned to the office all but two of the messengers were out. "It's about time," Kimble growled when they stepped through the door. "Tobias, they want you over at Florinda's for an errand."

From the look on Terry's face, it was evident Florinda's establishment was akin to Vera Clark's. Still, the boy took the message and left without a word.

Kimble turned to Sage. "You. I'm sending you out to Mount Tabor Village. You catch the trolley named "Montevilla" out to the Village but you'll have to get back best you can—since I doubt the trolley'll be running that late. Mrs. Goodsby wants you to do something for her. She says to hurry up, it's important."

The two other messengers started snickering until Kimble turned a scowl on them. "You tell Mrs. Goodsby that the charge is 75 cents plus a delivery charge of 30 cents for the trolley since she lives so far out. Be sure you get the payment before you perform the errand." Again the snickers came.

Sage caught the trolley and rode three miles to the suburban village. Once at the address, a frantic woman greeted him. "My husband's over an hour late coming home from work. I know something bad's happened to him. I need you to trace his route and find him. I'd go but I have a newborn and can't go out in the rain with her."

Sage was dumbfounded and could only repeat, "You want me to find your husband?"

"Yes, yes, and please hurry."

"My boss says I have to get the money before I do the errand." Sage felt bad asking for money from the distraught woman. Still . . .

"Here, here," she said, taking coins from her pocket and handing them over. Just as Sage reached the gate he spied a man hurrying up the dark street at a dog trot. The woman, still on her porch, also saw the man. With a cry she ran down the steps, pushing past Sage. "Verling, where were you? I've been frantic with worry."

When Verling Goodsby saw Sage in his messenger cap, he asked his wife, "You called a messenger to find me?"

She nodded and said, "I had no choice. I couldn't leave the baby and with this weather, if you were injured, laying somewhere—" her explanation trailed off.

Her husband laughed, gave her a little squeeze and then turned to Sage. "She pay the charge already?" he asked. At Sage's nod, the man pulled a dollar out of his pocket and said, "Keep it for a tip. Sorry to get you all the way out here for nothing."

Sage took the tip and departed, figuring that the beer on the husband's breath explained both his tardiness and his generosity. Given the snickers he'd heard at the office, this wasn't the first time Mrs. Goodsby had summoned a messenger to find her tarrying husband. And, it probably wouldn't be the last.

The rest of the night brought equally strange errands. One had been a stranded kitten up a tree, its mewing keeping the householder awake. She explained she was too old to climb the tree herself.

Next came a woman who also had both baby and tardy husband. In this instance, the woman wanted to go find the man herself, leaving Sage to watch the child. She carefully instructed him on what to do if the baby cried, showing him a bottle of milk with a hose attached. The infant woke up thirty minutes after the mother left. Sage confidently stuck the tube in its mouth but the kid didn't stop squalling with his mouth so wide open Sage feared a dislocated jaw.

Sage cradled the screaming infant and paced the floor. It didn't calm him. After about an hour he struck on the idea that a diaper pin might be the problem. He undressed the kid but discovered the pins were secure. Still, he wrapped the naked kid in a blanket and laid him on the bed, deciding to just let him howl.

Just then the mother walked in the door. When she saw the baby without clothes she turned mad as a hornet. "Just exactly what have you been doing to my child?" she demanded.

After Sage explained, she calmed down. "Oh! You poor man. He's had a touch of colic. Here, I'll pay you extra," she said, handing him the delivery fee and fifty cents.

The last errand of the night came near dawn and was another one of those "hurry up, it's awful important" calls. When he reached the house on Clinton Street, the woman led him through to a window overlooking its backyard. With a trembling finger, the woman pointed at a cow browsing her back garden. "Please get that dreadful cow out of my yard. She's eating up all my flowers and shrubbery. 1 tried to drive her out but she just shook her head at me and pawed the ground."

Though unfamiliar with bovines, Sage did his best and soon the cow was trotting down Clinton in mooing outrage over an interrupted breakfast.

Kimble was at his table when Sage's shift was over. "There's been no complaints. You passed the test," he said with a snicker.

"What do you mean?" Sage asked, though suspecting he knew the answer.

"I gave you the farthest and worst errands and you didn't quit or make a customer mad," Kimble answered. "You come on back this evening."

As Mae would say, Sage's tail was dragging when he left Speedy Messengers. He'd gone sleepless the day before. He dreaded the climb up Mozart's hidden staircase to the third floor. He'd gone a block when he remembered the cap. "Damn," he groaned, and turned back the way he'd come.

He entered the alley but as he reached for the cap he heard a commotion at the alley's other end. Peering down its shadowy length he saw three figures standing over another on the ground. He crept forward, stepping softly on his toes.

"Whatsa matter Terry? Cat got your tongue? Where the hell is Dougie? We thought he was your friend. Your best friend!" The declaration was punctuated by a not too gentle toeing of Terry's ribs.

"I don't know. Honest," came Terry's voice.

A second accusatory voice sounded, "You lied to us. You promised us. Now your nose is so far up Kimble's hind end that you can't see daylight."

Sage was now close enough to recognize the standing boys as Terry's co-workers. They were taking jealousy a bit too far. "Hey," he called. "What's going on here?"

All three turned toward him and Terry's face peered out from under the arm he'd curled over his head for protection. His nose was bloody.

The three strode towards him, their hands at their sides, clearly not intending to attack. Two brushed past him without speaking while the third paused to say, "Why don't you ask Terry? Maybe he'll tell you lessen shame ties his tongue." The boy stepped around Sage and all three disappeared around the corner.

Sage helped Terry to his feet. Other than a bloody nose, and a grimace that suggested bruised ribs, the boy looked to be alright. "What was that about?" Sage asked him.

Terry shook off Sage's hand, saying, "Nothing. It was about nothing." Without a further word, he stumbled away, leaving Sage alone in the alley.

What the hell is going on? Sage wondered. This time, he'd only gone a few paces up the street before he remembered the cap. Retrieving it, he made sure his two fingers held it far from his body.

Mae was waiting for him. Before she said anything he said, "Ma, I left a cap on the back stoop. It needs dunking in boiling water to kill the bugs. Could you do that for me? I'm so tired, I feel like that cow I chased must have trotted over me."

She visibly choked back her questions. For that he was grateful. Still, she did have a piece to say but she said it quietly and without demand. "Matthew didn't go to school today or yesterday. He claims he's sick but Ida says that's not true. I don't think we can put this off much longer. Last night, she scorched the potatoes and charred the beef roast."

"Later, Ma. Later," he mumbled, as he crawled into bed fully clothed.

THIRTEEN

Drizzle soaked her coat as Mae slid down the muddy trail into Sullivan's Gulch. Overhead, the early afternoon's hidden sun glowed from behind pearly gray clouds. Reaching the bottom, she carefully picked her way along the slippery path, keeping far from the edge of the roiling, brown creek. There was no one about although muted voices sounded from behind the weathered boards. The steady rain kept people hunkered down inside their shacks.

Carrie Lynne snatched the door open only to have the hope shining in her face vanish when she saw Mae. Still, she summoned a smile and politely said, "Mrs. Clemens, please come in out of the rain," as she opened the door wider. "We ate real good last night, thanks to you." This time her smile was genuine and her eyes earnest.

"Why, Carrie Lynne, how nice of you to tell me that. I am so glad," Mae said as she stepped inside to the sound of rain pinging into tin cans scattered across the dirt floor. The day's damp air seemed colder and more penetrating here than it had outside. Mary Tobias lay shivering beneath new-looking blankets.

An adolescent boy was sitting on a stool at the table. The colorful chaos of the artificial flowers before him said he'd taken over his mother's task. A wooden produce crate close by a rusty pot-bellied stove held the kicking, gurgling infant. With its fat cheeks and rosy skin, it looked to be the best fed and healthiest of the shack's inhabitants.

Mae grabbed the only empty stool and put it next to Mary's bed. Turning to Carrie Lynne she said, "I brought some tea, can you make us all a pot?" The little girl took the bag and was soon busying herself with the kettle, water, and various cups.

Mary stared at Mae with feverish eyes. Mae put a hand on the woman's arm and said, "Mary, how are you this afternoon?"

Panic seemed to fill the poor woman's face. "I'm real sick. I can't seem to get my legs to hold me up, anymore." She punctuated her statement with a long coughing spell that bloodied the rag she held against her mouth.

Mae looked away to give the woman privacy and her eyes fell on the boy. Her heart twisted at the tear tracks on his face. "You must be Terry," she said. When the boy nodded, she continued, "I came to tell you that Dr. Lane will soon be here to see your mother today. If he agrees, we'd like to take her to the new TB sanatorium.

"No, no, I have to stay here," Mary gasped. "My children need me."

Terry stood and crossed to sit on the bed beside his mother. "Ma, if you don't get help—" His voice cracked and he leaned over to bury his face in her neck. When he straightened he said, "I can look after the kids."

"But, Glad," she began, only to stop when his hand on her shoulder gave a warning squeeze.

"Glad will come back from Uncle Charlie's soon," he said soothingly.

Mae rolled her eyes but held her tongue. To hear this family tell it, Glad was spending his days flitting among a whole flock of nearby relatives. Funny how none of them were turning up to help the family out.

Clearing her throat, Mae said, "Mary, Mrs. Trumbull is also coming with Doc Lane. She knows how important your children are to you. She has some ideas on how to keep them safe while you're in the sanatorium."

Mary looked hopeful while Terry's chin jutted forward. Mae jumped in to quell his objection. "Now, Terry, you can't expect Carry Lynne to stay here all night taking care of the baby while you run messages all over town. It isn't safe. Let's hear what Mrs. Trumbull has to say before you refuse, okay?"

As though summoned by Mae's words, a knock rattled the shack's flimsy door. Again, Carrie Lynne served as the family's greeter and soon Millie Trumbull and a strange man crowded into the little shack.

Mae took a deep breath, readying herself to confront any discourtesy from the doctor. Sage had warned her about Doc Lane's gruffness. She glanced at Mary's pale face and resolved that, if she had anything to say, Lane would not worsen the poor woman's distress.

Still, she got up from the stool and gestured for the doctor to take her place. She didn't move so far away that she couldn't hear everything he said. "Hello there, Mrs. Tobias," he said, in a voice so calm and gentle that immediately reassured Mae. Maybe Lane's gruffness only surfaced when he dealt with people who weren't patients.

Mary's weak smile in greeting encouraged the doctor to continue. "I'd like to listen to your chest and take your temperature if I may?" Once she nodded, he turned around to the four of them and said, kindly, "Do you think you can give her some privacy while I listen to her chest?"

The four of them promptly retreated to the other side of the room and turned their backs to the bed. Mae was glad he hadn't sent them outside because the drizzling rain was now a tin-rattling deluge.

Soft murmuring came from the bed in the corner. That and the sound of the rain overhead gave both sides of the room some privacy. Mae decided to move things along, knowing Terry was likely to be the stumbling block when it came to the children. "Mrs. Trumbull, could you tell Terry what can be done to keep the children safe while their mother is in the sanatorium recovering?"

Millie turned her warm brown eyes on Terry who looked lost, frightened and very young. "What's the baby's name?" she asked gently.

"Emma Jane," came the somewhat grudging answer.

"Emma. I've always loved that name. I have a dear cousin with that name," she said with a smile before turning serious. "Terry, I can understand that you're worried about Carrie Lynne and Emma Jane. Am I right in thinking that the most important thing is to keep you all together and make sure that your sisters are safe, warm and fed?"

Terry's nod, though tentative, was still an assent so Millie continued, "I am not going to lie to you. Your mother is very ill. It could take her as long as six months to get better. And, Mrs. Clemens here tells me that you are the sole breadwinner these days and that you have to be gone all night. Surely you can see that your little sister shouldn't be left alone to care for the baby."

The boy's eyes filled with tears. Mae ached to put an arm around him but didn't. He was trying so hard to be brave and older than his years. Sympathy would only weaken his grasp on himself.

Millie must have realized the same thing because her tone became more business-like. "I have a lot of experience with problems like yours," she told him. "I work with an organization called the Boys and Girls Aid Society. I spoke with them about the three of you and they would like you to stay with them."

Her voice earnest, she continued, "I'll be honest with you. At first, you three will stay in the same room until they are sure you haven't caught your mother's TB. After that, you will sleep in dormitories, Carrie Lynne with the girls, you with the boys and Emma Jane with the infants."

That last bit wrinkled Terry's brow but he said nothing and Millie hurried on, "There's a playground where you can play together, you can visit Emma Jane at any time, and, of course, you will eat together." She paused, allowing that all to sink in.

It would be an exaggeration to say that Terry's reaction was positive but he didn't seem to be objecting. He looked down into Carrie Lynne's wide-eyed stare and then up at Millie. "Anything else?" he asked.

She hesitated, knowing the next condition might be the biggest stumbling block. "You and Carrie Lynne would have to go to school during the day. And, you would not be allowed to work nights because that is against the law."

Terry's head reared back. He opened his mouth but then snapped it shut. Mae saw a look of calculation cross his face. "They won't try to adopt us out?" was all he asked.

"No. There can be no adoption since you have a mother who loves you, wants you and has done her very best to give you a home." Millie's tone was firm and believable and Terry nodded. She then added. "You will be permitted to work after school until seven p.m. so you can save money for a home once your mother gets better. The Society will even help you find a job." That little snippet didn't seem to encourage Terry. Mae wondered why.

"Okay," Dr. Lane said in a louder voice that signaled his examination was over, and he wanted their attention. "Mrs. Tobias does have TB and she is eligible for admission to the sanatorium. I explained to her that someone has offered to pay the six dollars a week cost. I also told her about the Boys and Girls Aid Society. She says that she is willing to allow the children to stay there temporarily provided they will be allowed to visit her at the sanatorium."

"Where is the sanatorium?" Terry asked

Millie was the one who answered. "It's on River Road, between the villages of Milwaukie and Oak Grove. It has cottages with steam heat and hot and cold running water. When it gets warm enough, there will be a canvas tent on a platform so that your mother can live and breathe in fresh, clean air. It will help her lungs recover." Millie's enthusiasm reminded Mae that Millie was one of the sanatorium's founders.

Terry zeroed in on the biggest problem. "It's a long way out to Oak Grove. Too far for the three of us to walk and we don't have no money for a train."

The doctor raised an inquiring eyebrow in Millie's direction but it was Mae who answered, "I will escort the three of you, myself, every weekend, and pay for your train fare."

Silence fell until Terry broke it. "I need to talk to Ma," he said. "Privately."

The doctor moved away and Terry went to his mother. There followed an intense and whispered conversation. Mary kept shaking her head vehemently which set her to coughing. Terry kept whispering and finally she gave a reluctant nod to whatever he'd been proposing.

He turned to them, his face grimly resolute. "We'll have to pack our things up. How soon can you move our Ma to the sanatorium?" he asked.

Sage was mindful that the sun had dropped beneath the clouds' edge. He was heading south toward the farmers' market. Come dusk he had to be at Speedy Messenger. That gave him less than an hour. Before embarking on that great pleasure, however, he planned to question Matthew's messenger friends as to why Matthew had left their ranks.

One corner of the market building sported a wide metal awning. From what Matthew had said, this had to be where the bike messengers gathered after school. Oddly, not a single young student stood about. He ambled around the huge granite building and never saw a single messenger. Reaching the awning once more, he asked a fruit seller where the messengers were.

"I no see them some days past now," the dark-eyed man with curly black hair said in a thick Italian accent.

"You know why?"

The seller shook his head. "One day they here, next day, poof," he said, throwing his hands in the air for emphasis.

Sage trudged back to Mozart's puzzling over the messengers' absence.

As it was, he barely arrived at Speedy on time. Kimble was there and still unpleasant. Terry arrived right after Sage. Since Mae had explained the agreements reached in the Tobias shack that afternoon Sage expected to find Terry in better spirits. Instead, the boy's expression seemed a strange mix of gloom and edgy.

"Hey, Terry. How are you doing?" Sage asked, striving to sound lighthearted.

"Alright, Mr. Miner." The boy glanced at Sage, flicked a glance toward the corner by the window and stepped in that direction after making sure Kimble remained distracted by a customer.

Sage followed the boy and smiled warmly to show he had no hard feelings for Terry's abrupt departure from the alley that morning. "I boiled the heck out of this cap until the wool baa'd for mercy," he said.

The boy chuckled but his face quickly sobered. "Say," he began, "I'm awful sorry that I didn't thank you proper for helping me this morning."

"That's okay. I haven't known you long, Terry, but you seem to be a fine person. If there's anything I can do to help, I'll do it."

His somewhat stilted offer triggered a rueful shake of the boy's head. "You ever feel like every darn thing is falling on you?" he asked.

Sage smiled at the image but he knew exactly what Terry meant so he said, "Yup, more than once. You got a lot of burdens these days?"

"More of them than I can count." Terry sighed, and visibly tried to summon optimism. "Well, maybe a few of them burdens got lifted today. We'll see."

"Miner! If you're 'bout done flapping your yap, I got a message for you to take on down to Union Station. You're to meet a lady and give her this note." Kimble was waving a paper in the air.

And so his night began.

FOURTEEN

"Did you get a chance to talk to Terry Tobias? Did he tell you they're moving out today?" Mae peppered him with questions as she strode over to the bay windows and pulled the curtains aside to let in the early afternoon sunlight.

Sage heaved a sigh, flung back the bedclothes and sat on the edge of his bed. "No, Ma, to both questions. Terry was vague, he just said some things might have gotten better but he wasn't celebrating. We only had a couple of minutes to talk. Then we got busy and he was already gone when I got back from an errand to hell and gone."

Her brow wrinkled though. "Now, that is interesting" was all she said. "But, that's not why I'm getting you up. Hanke's downstairs, again."

"Oh, no. Another boy?"

She nodded, her lips pursed. "Yes, another meeting with the coroner, I'm afraid."

"You mean with Dr. Lane. Coroner Crowley just rubber stamps Lane's conclusions. That'll be a real pleasure I'm sure."

"He was right kind to Mary Tobias and the children. I can't think why you have taken against him."

"I didn't. He took against me on sight. I figured that was his normal way and thought you ought to know. Good to hear that he's nicer to his patients. Maybe he just doesn't like rich people as a rule." Sage stood up, pulled on a pair of trousers. "Tell Hanke I'll be down in five minutes," he said on his way to the bathroom.

❀   ❀   ❀

They didn't talk much on the walk to Crowley's funeral home. Hanke said the body had been found floating in the Willamette, lodged against the pilings of the Couch Street dock. Early morning stevedores shifting cargo onto a ship had spotted it and pulled the boy out of the water.

"Another kid froze to death?" Sage asked.

Hanke shook his head. "No, there was something funny about this incident. We've already called Doc Lane."

Crowley was waiting at the door, distress making him wring his hands. "Two boys in one week. What on God's green earth is going on, Sergeant?" he asked, though he didn't wait for Hanke to answer before turning on his heel and heading toward the basement stairs.

Dr. Harry Lane again met them at the entrance to the embalming room. If anything, his facial expression was sourer than the last time. So were his words. "Sergeant, I don't appreciate starting my mornings like this."

Hanke shrugged but said nothing. Lane turned toward a table where another small body lay covered by a plain white sheet. As before, Sage approached the table with trepidation. Lane seemed to sense Sage's anxiety because his voice was kind when he looked at Sage and asked, "You ready, Adair?"

At Sage's nod, the doctor pulled the sheet off the boy's face. Sage let go the breath he'd been holding. Once again, it wasn't Glad. Instead, a boy of about twelve lay on the table. His hair was carrot-colored and his face freckled. Sage shook his head and looked at Hanke saying, "He's not Glad Tobias."

Hanke turned toward Lane. "What killed him, Doc?"

Dr. Lane heaved a sighed and pulled the sheet further down, exposing hands crossed over the thin body. "Look at these marks around his wrists. Those are ligature marks. He's got the same marks around his ankles. Given the clean edges and thin lines, I'm thinking that someone used wire to tie him up.

"He was thrown into the water with his hands and feet tied?" Outrage and the urge to hit something seized Sage. After a beat, he forced himself to unclench his fists.

The doctor shook his head. "No, I don't think so. He was already dead when he went into the water. There are no signs of drowning."

"So, what killed him, then?" Hanke asked.

"His neck is broken. I can't say if it was deliberate. A bruise on the back of his head makes me think it might have happened in a fall. There's no way to tell."

"But someone had him tied up," Sage reiterated, anger clenching his jaw so tight it ached.

Lane glanced at him and pulled the sheet back over the boy's face as he said, "No doubt about it. He spent time tied up just before his death. The marks around his wrists and ankles are new. It looks like they were still tied when he threw his hands out to save himself from the fall because the outsides of both palms are skinned like his hands were pressed together."

Sadness darkened the doctor's eyes and dragged down the corners of his mouth as he laid a gentle hand on the dead boy's shoulder. "He was a cute little lad," he said, his sorrowful tone banishing any lingering animosity Sage felt toward him.

Hanke appeared to be contemplating the overhead steam pipes as if some answers perched amid their welter. Breaking his gaze, he looked at the three of them and said, "I'm going to call it murder until I learn something different."

This time, Dr. Lane exited the funeral home with them. Upon reaching the sidewalk he said to Hanke, "You'll get my report later today. I'll have it messengered over."

"Thanks, Dr. Lane. I wish—" Hanke began, only to stop when Lane raised a hand.

"Sergeant, we both wish you didn't have to call me out on this kind of duty. Just do the best you can to get the men behind this. That child couldn't have been more than twelve. Who knows what he might have accomplished in life? Who knows what we all lost with his death?"

Lane turned toward Sage. "Mr. Adair, I don't know what your interest is but I was wondering if you might have a few minutes to spare? I'd like to show you something."

"I can spare some time," Sage said, expecting the doctor to elaborate. He didn't.

Instead, his next words dismissed Hanke. "Good. Thank you, Sergeant. I'll be in touch." Sage exchanged puzzled looks with the Sergeant as Lane turned and started walking north. Hanke headed east toward the police station.

Sage caught up with the doctor who said, "I understand from Hanke that you met a newsboy who is now missing. Is that why you are coming to view the bodies?" Lane asked.

"Yes, he is a newsboy by the name of Glad Tobias. He's been missing for ten days. I saw him kidnapped off the street."

After half a block Lane said, "I see too many dead children. Disease kills most of them but I blame the poverty and hunger that makes them vulnerable. That's upsetting enough. But when they die from maltreatment it makes me especially angry."

Sage could only nod in agreement. Lane glanced at him. "I suppose you're wondering why I wanted you to come with me. I'm going to show you something in the hope you will want to help me with a special project. I won't fool you; I hope to part you from your money."

The doctor sent a pointed look at Sage's tailored suit with the gold watch chain draped across his matching vest. "But don't worry, I'm not talking about more than you can afford. Have you ever heard of a woman named Valentine Pritchard?"

That name rang a bell and Sage searched his memory until, at last, he had it. His mother had mentioned her. "Isn't she one of Millie Trumbull's friends?"

For the first time that day, Lane smiled. "She sure is," he said. "Miss Pritchard came to Portland to run our public school kindergartens. She's done a fine job—such a fine job that she's been hired as the director of the new People's Institute."

Sage vaguely recollected reading something about the organization. "Isn't that a new settlement house in the North End? I've seen the building at 4th and Burnside."

"Well, you know more than most. That's exactly what it is. And, that's where we are heading."

"So what's the project?" Sage asked.

Lane shook his head. "I think it best to let Miss Prichard explain it," was all he said.

They reached the corner across from the Institute and Lane paused. "We have ambitious plans for the whole Institute. Pretty soon, that place will be hopping. Luckily, someone's donated a large space."

Lane was right. The two-story sandstone building took up half the block. Three concrete steps led up to its corner entrance door. There were big windows on the street level with top panes that louvered inward to admit fresh air. A row of closely-spaced sash windows ran along two sides of the second floor. The Institute would be light-filled.

"What are your plans?" Sage asked.

"Health clinics and sewing classes, adult reading, and mathematics classes in conjunction with the public schools, job finding services, lectures on public health, and a kindergarten. The special project I'm talking about is for the kindergarten children."

They crossed the street and entered into a somewhat chaotic scene of people passing to and fro, mostly adults herding packs of small children.

Lane ushered Sage into an office near the front door. The minute Sage laid eyes on Valentine Pritchard, he knew he'd never seen her before. He would have remembered the dark-haired beauty, with her widely spaced, large brown eyes above delicate cheekbones and a naturally red pair of lips. His survey went unnoticed as the woman's full attention was on Harry Lane.

"Harry! How wonderful to see you! Do you have good news?" she asked him and then noticed Sage standing behind the doctor. "Oh! I'm sorry. I didn't notice that Dr. Lane had brought a friend." She held out her hand, saying, "Welcome. I'm Valentine Pritchard, the new director here at the Institute."

"The first director," Lane corrected.

Pritchard's laugh was musical. The woman had barely said a few words yet Sage knew he was wearing what his mother called his "dopey grin." He struggled to bring his features under control. "I'm John Adair and I'm pleased to meet you, ma'am," he said as he shook the slim hand and noted that it applied just the right pressure.

She smiled at him, "Ah, ha! I recognize that name." She turned to Lane, saying. "Am I right in thinking that you've roped this famous restaurateur into helping with our little project?"

Lane laughed. "Well, I've driven him into the corral. It's up to you to do the roping. I've got to take off. Patients are waiting."

She laughed and gestured Sage toward a chair in front of her desk. She took a seat herself and folded her hands atop the desk's scarred surface. She studied Sage for a moment and then said, "You look tense, Mr. Adair. Don't be afraid. I will not harangue you for thousands of dollars in donations."

Sage grinned and said, "That's a relief," when, in fact, it was his unexpected attraction to her that had made him tense.

Reassured, she launched into her pitch. "We are starting a kindergarten for poor children. The hope is that it will give the children a safe place so that their mothers can work. It'll give us a chance to provide the children with a head start on their schooling. And, there's a greater chance the parents will let them stay in school, now that Millie Trumbull's crew has made schooling compulsory. But, you never know. Lots of piece work is done in homes and other places where Millie can't inspect."

She smiled, shrugged and said ruefully, "I am afraid that's more than you want to know."

Sage was quick to shake his head and say, "No, I am interested and think that is a great approach. What can I do?"

She held up a hand and said, "Just a little more back story, if you have the time." Not waiting for his agreement she said, "The problem is our little tykes come to school too hungry to learn. It's a national problem." She took a deep breath and launched into what was obviously a set speech given many times before. "The children come to school underfed and too weak in mind and body to learn anything. They are cranky and disruptive. Those who say they've had breakfast tell us it was just coffee, because they were cold, and cheap bread. Because the North End is so poor, most of them arrive at school having eaten nothing."

Sage heard the words but it was her passion that held his attention. Her whole body seemed to vibrate with it. Still, he nodded soberly.

Pritchard continued. "We've had the visiting nurses survey the children. They report that fully 40% of our students have eaten nothing before coming to school. Another 18% ate only the poorest bread—the kind that is usually augmented with sawdust.

Our numbers here in the North End, are much higher than the national average of 23% underfed children. Like every poor neighborhood in the country, this neighborhood has more impoverished children than the City's average.

"Mr. Adair, what studies show is that all of these underfed children will grow up inches shorter and pounds lighter than other children of their age. That's how serious hunger is."

Again, Sage could only nod. He knew hunger was the poor's constant companion although the high percentage of North End children going hungry was unexpected. He'd had no idea there were so many. Then he thought of a test that might diminish her irresistible attraction.

"So, I understand that Mother Jones woman made quite a fuss over how this country treats its children." What Sage didn't say was that he knew and adored the Irish born, Mary Harris Jones. The gray-haired, sweet-faced woman had made national headlines when she organized and led a children's march from Pennsylvania to Teddy Roosevelt's front door in New York.

Pritchard's laugh was genuine. "Oh, she is one crazy lady, that Mother Jones. But, I'll tell you something. The President might have ignored her Children's Crusade but a whole lot of other people didn't. I may not agree with all her socialist solutions but I am grateful for what she did. She's forced people to acknowledge the importance of saving our children from hunger and toil."

Sage gave a mental sigh. Every word she spoke increased his admiration. He fought to keep his face showing only polite interest. He must have succeeded because there was no sign she sensed his inner turmoil. Instead, Pritchard briskly rose to her feet. "Come next door and you can see for yourself the problem we're trying to solve."

She led him into a classroom. About thirty kindergarten-aged youngsters sat on benches before long, low, roughly-made counters. A teacher was reading to them. Some of the children were alert and attentive. Others, though, sat with their heads atop pitifully thin arms and their eyes closed. Still others, equally thin, twitched atop their stools with pale blue smudges beneath eyes in heads that looked too big for their small bodies.

Pritchard gestured him toward the door and they stepped back into the hall. "What I am hoping, and Dr. Lane is hoping, is that you would be willing to donate toward our breakfast program. We want to serve the children good bread, hot porridge, and fruit when they come to school. All thirty of them. Those who aren't hungry won't have to eat but we're betting that most of these children are undernourished."

Then she answered a question Sage hadn't thought of. "This isn't just a stop-gap program. We mean it to be a pilot project. We want to show that children learn better when they are adequately nourished. We plan to compile data on how well and fast they learn now and then track how well they do after eating a decent breakfast every morning. With that data, we can go to the public schools and insist on them serving breakfast. France and England are already doing it with remarkable results. Once adequately fed, many of their undernourished children turned alert and achieved success in school and later in life."

Valentine Pritchard led Sage back to her office. Once again settled in chairs, she leaned forward over her desk and continued, "Fully thirteen percent of America's schoolchildren are labeled 'feeble-minded.' That's because their school performance is viewed as 'backward and mentally dull.'"

He startled when she slammed a fist onto the desk and said forcefully, "Any fool knows that the problem is that they are malnourished. These children become discouraged by their failure and hardened by constant rebuke and the taunts of the brighter, well-fed students."

She sighed and spoke more quietly, "Eventually, these kids become careless, defiant and altogether incorrigible students who leave school at an early age. After that, they turn to vice or eke out a bare living that's no better than their parents'. They are never given the chance to develop into the healthy, happy and educated citizens our country needs."

Her indignant sorrow made her eloquent. No question but that she meant and felt every word she spoke. He kept his face interested when what he wanted to do was agree wholeheartedly and share his personal experience with childhood hunger. But he didn't. She had to consider him a potentially helpful but, somewhat disinterested, wealthy donor to her cause.

He headed back to Mozart's, his thoughts on Valentine Pritchard. He told himself that he would have pledged the monthly fifty dollars donation no matter what. After all, it was a good cause and Doc Lane was right. Sage's money from his Klondike gold strike just kept growing without any effort on his part. I would have donated it even if Valentine Prichard wasn't so damn interesting, he assured himself. That was a step too far into self-delusion because his mind's eye momentarily flashed on the faces of his mother and Lucinda, both of whom were eying him skeptically.

Further thought of Valentine Pritchard ceased when he stepped into Mozart's kitchen and saw his mother's face. Mae Clemens was visibly upset and wasted no time in idle greetings. "Millie was just in here and she's fit to be tied," she announced. "Terry Tobias is missing."

"Missing?" Sage echoed dumbly.

"Dr. Lane sent a nurse and a wagon first thing this morning. They had to carry Mary Tobias on a litter up out of the Gulch, she was so weak. But, she's on her way to the sanatorium, safe and sound. Probably there by now."

"And, Terry?" Sage nudged her story along.

"Millie was there at the shack to escort the children to the Boys and Girls Aid Society. Once they got there, she showed Carrie Lynne and Terry where they'd sleep with the baby until Dr. Lane decides they don't have TB. She also gave them a tour of the dining room, classrooms, and the playground where they could be together during the day. Millie said Terry was very somber the whole time but praised the place. He was definitely willing to have his sisters stay there."

She paused for so long that he said, "But?" again to move her story along. He had to change his clothes and get to Speedy.

"Well! Not ten minutes later that imp ran off. He walked right out the back door and across the playground. One of the other children watched him go and went to tell the matron. By the time she got down to the playground, he was nowhere in sight. Millie waited an hour but he never came back."

"That was this morning and, he's still not back?"

She shook her head. "I asked Eich to see if the boy had returned to the shack for some reason. He went to the Gulch but says another family was already moving in. They said that they've seen neither hide nor hair of Terry. Eich believed them."

FIFTEEN

Dusk hadn't fallen when Sage strolled into Speedy Messengers that Friday night. He was lucky. Prang seemed to have no customers and a surplus of messengers. For the first time, Sage could sit and talk to his fellow messengers.

"Hey, can a guy get into your card game?" he asked the three who sat at the table, cards in their hands, coins at their elbows. One of them was the leader who'd been kicking the stuffing out of Terry a few days ago. He was the one who answered.

"You can if you got the money. We're playing penny-ante poker. You know the game?"

"Yup," Sage responded, drawing up a chair and slapping a few coins down.

As they played, Sage intentionally lost every hand. Since he'd played poker many long winter days in the Klondike, his losing was more choice than happenstance. Today, his opponents grew ever more cheerful as his coin stack shrank.

"So, who's the Dougie guy you were so het up about?" he asked.

"Why you want to know?"

"Curiosity, I suppose. Terry Tobias seems like a right enough fellow, so I figure you must have a good reason for being mad at him."

The other three exchanged looks and reached silent agreement. The leader, a boy named Christopher, answered Sage's question. "Dougie used to work here. He disappeared a few weeks ago."

"Why's that Terry's fault?"

A boy who'd been quiet up to that point, piped up, his voice as reedy as his body, "Dougie and Terry were working together to start a Messenger's Protective Association. One like the newsboys have. Prang and Kimble didn't like it none. All of a sudden Terry stopped doing anything except kissing their butts and Dougie just up and disappeared. We figure Terry's nothing but a turncoat."

They played the next two poker hands in silence. Seeing darkness outside Speedy's windows, Sage finally asked the question he dreaded asking.

"What's this Dougie fellow look like?"

Again, the smaller fellow answered, "Ah, he's right easy to spot. Dougie has orange hair and more freckles than a ladybug has spots."

"What's Dougie's last name? Does his family live near here?"

"Douglas Spencer is his full name," said Christopher, "and he's only got his pa. They live down near the railroad station. But his pa ain't seen him either and that ain't just 'cause of the whiskey he drinks."

Christopher's eyes narrowed and he asked, "How come you're asking so many questions about somebody you don't know?" At Sage's shrug, Christopher slapped down his cards and stood, saying, "Game's over, fellas."

His announcement coincided with Prang standing up so Kimble could take his place. The night shift had officially begun. Just then Terry charged in the door.

A relieved Sage crossed the room to greet him. "How are you doing, Terry?"

The boy's clothes were rumpled and his face drawn from exhaustion. "I'm alright, I guess," he said. "How'd last night go? Sorry I didn't get to talk to you this morning. Kimble kept me running all night long and I had to leave early to take care of something."

"Last night was okay. You look like you didn't get any sleep today."

"Yeah, well. I had a lot to do. Plus, I had to find a place to stay."

"Your family moved?"

Terry's lips twisted. "Yeah, but I couldn't move with them."

"Why? Did they move out of town or something?"

"Or something."

"So, did you find a place?"

Terry met that question with a frown before saying, "Sorta, but it ain't a place I want to stay too long. It's a better fit for the cockroaches and rats that live there. The best thing I can say is that it's close to work."

Near midnight, while out running one of his errands, Sage knocked on Hanke's apartment door.

"Adair! Come in, come in," said the police sergeant, who was still dressed and wide awake.

"Can't do that. I'm working and being timed," Sage said, tapping his black wool cap with a gold "Speedy" embroidered above its short bill.

"What? You're playing messenger boy now?"

"I'm still trying to find Glad. I think his brother knows more than what the family is saying about Glad's disappearance. Since the brother, Terry, works at Speedy, I'm hoping he'll confide in me as a friend."

"Any luck?"

"Well, now that I've been around him, I'm certain he knows something but he won't trust me with it as of yet."

"So, is there a reason why am I standing here letting all my household heat escape into the cold hallway?" Hanke asked with a smile.

"Unfortunately, I'm here about that boy we saw this morning. His body fits the description of a boy named Doug Spencer who worked for Speedy Messenger. He and Glad's brother, Terry, were trying to form a messengers' union and then Spencer disappeared about the same time as Glad. The Spencer boy and his father lived near the rail station. I was told that his pa likes whiskey more than he should. So, you might find him in one of the saloons around there. "

The rest of the night passed quickly and Sage was less tired than usual at the end of his shift. Maybe he was adjusting to the all-night schedule. It helped that, after his first night, Kimble seldom sent him out to the city suburbs on errands. Mostly, he ran errands between saloons, restaurants, and whorehouses. It was a world full of drunkenness, addiction, and vice.

Once they got to the bottom of Glad's disappearance, he'd do everything he could to help Millie Trumbull end the use of child messengers for good.

Upon returning to Speedy, Sage had asked Kimble, "How come you never send me on errands to Vera Clark's whorehouses?"

After a phlegmy chuckle, Kimble explained, "I do that, we might lose her business. She wants only young messengers—the younger, the better. Sez she gets a kick out of being the first to introduce them to certain 'manly pleasures.'"

Sage had to ask, "You think that's okay? Some of these kids are less than ten years old."

Kimble shrugged and said, "Gonna happen to them sooner or later. Might as well be Vera doing it. Never had no complaints from the ones she's educated."

Sitting in a café and shoveling in breakfast, Sage puzzled over how to get Terry out of Speedy's clutches, find Glad and ruin both Vera Clark's and Speedy's businesses for good. His biggest concern, though, was how to get Terry into a safe situation as soon as possible.

It was as he was heading back to Mozart's and bed, that the various bits and pieces snapped together in his head. He realized why Matthew had given up the messenger job he loved and why the schoolboy messengers had vanished from the farmers' market. Speedy hadn't limited itself to attacking other messenger companies; it had gone after the independent messengers as well. He gave himself a mental kick in the head that it had taken him so long to make that connection.

Sage changed direction and caught a trolley up to the West Side High School at 14th and Morrison. He had to talk to Matthew.

The school was an ornate stone pile of gothic towers, pointed arches and useless spires prickling its roof. The reception he received was equally prickly. "Well, I'm not sure it is proper for me to call him out of his classroom on just your say so," said the primly officious school secretary.

"It's important that I speak with him immediately. I am carrying a message for him. It's a private family matter," Sage insisted.

The woman arched an eyebrow, clearly exasperated that Sage refused to be more specific. Sighing heavily, she beckoned to a nearby student. Scribbling something on a piece of paper she handed it to the boy saying, "Matthew Mason is in Mrs. Grady's history class. Please deliver this note to him."

Five minutes later Matthew rushed into the office, spied Sage in his Speedy Messenger cap and came to a dead stop as fear turned him rigid.

Sage didn't want the secretary listening so he stepped into the hallway. Beckoning Matthew to follow, he said nothing until both were outside on the school's front steps.

"Everybody is fine," were Sage's first words. Matthew's reaction confirmed that Sage had discovered the reason for the young man's odd behavior during the past weeks. Relief seemed to buckle Matthew's legs because he grabbed the side of the stone arch to stay upright.

Sage gestured down the steps, "Come on, we're going back to that café down the street and talk this through. I need your help with something."

Once they'd sat and had given their orders, Sage started talking. "I am going to tell you what has been going on. If I get something wrong, you tell me, okay?"

At Matthew's cautious nod, Sage continued. "A while back, some men came to you and told you they wanted you to work for one of the messenger companies. You refused."

Matthew nodded and Sage said, "You weren't the only one. They asked that of all of your messenger friends, all the boys who hang out at the farmers' market after school."

Matthew's eyes widened and Sage continued, "Most of them said 'no', just like you. But for some reason, it was you that they focused on the most. Why was that, Matthew?"

Surprisingly, Matthew responded, "My bicycle and the fact I had a route of regular customers. They wanted that route."

"They threatened you and your family."

Sage's statement brought tears to the young man's eyes. "Not just Aunt Ida and Uncle Knute but you and Mrs. Clemens. They said they'd burn down Mozart's with everybody in it."

"They've beat you, haven't they? You never fell off your bicycle like you told your Aunt Ida."

Another nod, so Sage asked, "Why didn't you tell us what was going on? We've handled worse situations than this before."

"I couldn't. He said if I did, he'd kill me and burn down Mozart's. He knows all about us. He even knew Mrs. Fong was sick."

"When and where have you seen him?"

"He hangs around outside school. I try to sneak past him but he's caught me and pushed me around. He only punched me once."

"Who is he?"

"He's never said his name. But he's a big guy."

"Which messenger company does he work for?" Sage asked, though certain of the answer. He wasn't disappointed.

"Speedy Messenger Service, up in the North End. He waits around the school, watching for when I leave to go home. And you are right. He's scared off all the other messengers down at the public market."

"When's the last time you saw him?"

"Day before yesterday."

Sage relaxed back in his chair. "He gave you that black eye?"

At Matthew's nod, Sage continued, Okay Matthew, if you are willing, I am going to give you the opportunity to get even with that big guy and get your life and, your friends' lives, back to normal."

For the first time, light shone in Matthew's eyes. "You'll let me help?"

Sage chuckled. "You might not be so eager when I tell you what I need you to do. It will mean missing some classes and it could be dangerous."

Matthew's eagerness didn't abate. "Mr. Adair, I am willing to do anything that will bring this to an end for me and the other messengers. Some of the fellas are saying they need the messenger money, for food and stuff. We're all scared."

And so Sage told Matthew about Glad, Terry and Speedy.

SIXTEEN

Sage had two more stops to make before he could lay his head down. Fortunately, Philander Gray was in his law office. He listened to Sage's story with mounting outrage.

"Do you think you can round up enough credible witnesses?" was his only question.

Once assured witnesses wouldn't be a problem, Gray said thoughtfully, "Problem is, we don't know who is underwriting the Speedy operation. It could be someone with close ties to the police or the prosecutor's office. We don't want to alert those criminals that we're on to them. If we do, they might kill someone else to cover their tracks. I don't think I could live with that."

"You're right. Before we set the trap, we need to know everyone involved. So far, I only have Prang and Kimble. They're just underlings. And then, there's the 'big guy' who threatened and attacked Matthew. I am sure he's not the head guy either."

"You nail down all the miscreants and we'll snap that trap shut on every last one of them. Until then, I'll do some research so that, when we know it's safe, I can lay all the legal arguments in the prosecutor's lap."

Millie Trumbull was also in her office and greeted him with a warm smile. "Why Mr. Adair, it looks like you're still working undercover as Mr. Miner."

"I am and I've learned some things you ought to know."

She was grim-faced as he told of Speedy's operation and Doug Spencer's death. She turned furious when he explained Vera Clark's role in "educating" the youngest messengers. "I want to rip that woman's throat out with my teeth!" she declared.

She stood and began pacing her small office. "Do you know that surveys of detention home inmates show that the number of former child messengers far exceeds that of children working in any other profession? Former newsboys run a close second."

As she made her final point, her eyes turned from fire to cold steel. "And, when arrested, a high proportion of those young boys are ravished by venereal diseases. We are exposing our children to parts of life they are neither ready to see nor experience." Now her eyes glittered with unshed tears as she asked, "When are we, as a nation, going to take responsibility for these defenseless children?"

"You're right, in every single respect," Sage assured her. "But hold off on the throat-ripping. To stop Speedy, we have to be patient and plan carefully. Otherwise, some of the scoundrels will escape. What proof does your board need to close that operation down? Or, at least wound it so badly, that it has to close down?"

"The Child Labor Commission inspects. We surprise inspect. That's where our proof comes from. Someone telling us of a situation is what usually triggers an inspection. So, that avenue is not too high a hurdle.

"What we need is the kind of proof that will convince members of the Common Council to change our city code. We must forbid children less than sixteen years of age from entering saloons and vice dens. And we have to outlaw direct telephone lines between whorehouses, saloons and messenger companies."

She stopped pacing and took her seat again. "If you are right and, the Speedy people have gone from committing civil violations into criminal acts, that'll be our best chance of stopping them. For certain, our Commission's fines won't be enough."

Both of them stiffened and fell silent at the sound of the outer office door opening. Footsteps crossed the floor and a slight, narrow-faced, bat-eared man of about thirty stepped into Millie's office. She whooped upon seeing him and jumped up to wrap the fellow in a big hug.

Sage rose to take his leave, figuring he was intruding on a reunion.

"No, no! This is perfect! Sit down, Mr. . . . ah . . . Miner," she said. Turning to the man Millie said, "Henry, this is Mr. John Miner. He is doing some undercover work for us."

Turning back to Sage she explained, "This is Mr. Henry Russell. He works for the National Child Labor Committee though usually back east and in the South." The two men shook hands and sat down.

Millie had a calculating look on her face. "How long are you here for?" she asked Russell.

"Just overnight. I'm on my way down to California. The Committee wants me to record the newsies in Sacramento, San Francisco, and Los Angeles."

Sage and Millie exchanged glances—his puzzled, her's merry and teasing as she said, "Henry is the National Child Labor Committee's photographer. He wriggles into factories and takes candid photographs of children working. The Committee uses his photos to show the need for child labor laws. We've learned that a photograph of a seven-year-old girl working on a textile loom packs a bigger wallop than a ten thousand word report from notables saying the same thing."

"That's got to be dangerous for you," Sage commented to Henry.

The other man laughed. "Well, I must admit that I've had to run for my life a time or two. Still, I've taken some great pictures."

Millie leaned forward over her desk, her face earnest. "Henry, could you stay a few days here in Portland? Maybe take some photographs for us? It would be a great help and right in line with what the Committee wants."

It was noon before Sage crawled into bed. He was bone-weary tired but also hopeful. They had a plan. And, there was a whole crew of people willing to lend hearts, minds, and skills to its success. Still, his last mental image before sleep took hold remained that of Glad Tobias's impish grin.

Sage slept straight through Saturday into late Sunday morning. Sunday was the only day Knute didn't work so it was the rotund Swede who answered Sage's knock with a huge smile.

"Mr. Adair, Matthew said you vant to talk vit me and the fru," he said in his singsong Swedish accent. "Please come in and have a seat."

Sage's remodel of Mozart's had created a spacious apartment that used the entire second floor.

Within it, Ida and Knute had created a bright, homey place with cushioned furniture, polished tables and gingham curtains on the windows. Yellow was their favored color.

Matthew entered from the kitchen to sit on the sofa, followed by Ida.

"I'm sorry to disturb your Sunday," Sage began, only to have Ida wave a dismissive hand at his apology. "Matthew told us what has been happening to him. We are so grateful to you. We were at our wit's end."

Ida's normally cheerful, apple-cheeked face reflected that remembered anxiety and Matthew reached out and took her hand. "I am so sorry, Aunt Ida. I just didn't know what to do." His aunt wrapped an arm around his shoulders and gave him a hearty squeeze.

Knute sat on the boy's other side and patted his knee. "That's okay, son. It vas a difficult situation for you."

Eyes stinging, Sage gazed at the three of them sitting side-by-side and so full of love for each other. This child was being given a chance, a head start in life. Ida, besides being a great cook, was one of the most cheerful and kindest people he had ever met. Knute, equally round and apple-cheeked, had stepped in to lovingly father his wife's nephew during those terrible days when Matthew was reeling from his brother's murder and his own jailing.

"I want you both to know that I will understand if you don't want to give your permission for Matthew to help me stop what the Speedy Messenger Service is doing. I will do my best to see that he's not in danger but I can't guarantee that there isn't some risk,—" Sage began.

"Vhat is it that you need our Matthew to do?" interrupted Knute.

"I need him to befriend a boy and provide a safe place for that boy to stay. I want to install Matthew in a safe boarding house and have the boy, Terry, stay there, too, if he's willing. It would mean that Matthew can go to school in the morning but might need to miss a class or two in the afternoon."

"Vat is the danger to our Matthew?"

"I don't think there will be any, but we are dealing with criminals. I plan to tell Terry that Matthew needs help with his rent to stay in school but that he's had trouble with Speedy Messenger and doesn't want them to know where he lives. If I'm right, Terry will protect Matthew. If he doesn't, we'll move Matthew out of there immediately.

"And there are two extra layers of safety. A friend of mine, Stuart Franklin, runs the boarding house. He's helped me before. I stopped and talked to him. He'll move one of his permanent boarders out temporarily to another rooming house and Matthew can take over his room. Stuart will be on hand every minute that Matthew is there. And, I will ask Mr. Fong to have one of his cousins watch over the house just to make sure there's no problem.

"How many days will Matthew be gone?" asked Ida.

"I thought we'd give it no more than a week. If Terry won't let us help him by that time, we'll have to try another angle."

Ida and Knute exchanged a look after which Ida gave a slight nod. Knute leaned forward to say, "Okay then. Ve trust you, Mr. Adair. But please take care of our Matthew. Ve love him, very much." Knute gave the boy's shoulders a strong squeeze, saying, "Matthew, you must do exactly vhat Mr. Adair tells you to do. And, keep up vith your studies."

Matthew nodded eagerly, his eyes shining. "I promise." Looking at Sage he asked. "When do we start?"

"Well, it being Sunday, Terry's not working. So, tomorrow after school I'll introduce you to him before he goes to work. Then, if he's agreeable, I'll bring him to your place first thing Tuesday morning before school."

Matthew's enthusiasm was worrying. The anxious faces of Ida and Knute said they also remembered times when Matthew hadn't done "exactly what Mr. Adair told him to do."

"Okay then, let's head over to Stuart Franklin's with some of your things," was all Sage said.

On the way to Franklin's boarding house, located on the western edge of the North End, Sage told Matthew about Franklin. "He used to row out and intercept ships leaving the mouth of the Columbia River. He'd call out for shanghaied men to jump ship. When they did, he'd pluck them out of the water and row them back to land. Unfortunately, the shanghaiers beat him so badly that he can't do that anymore. So now he runs a safe boarding house for sailors."

What Sage didn't tell Matthew was that it was Sage who bought the house and had Franklin run it and keep all the profits. He figured it was the least he could do for a man who'd been nearly beaten to death for trying to save men from ship-board slavery that frequently ended in death.

Franklin's large boarding house had a wide veranda, a small vegetable garden and flower beds that burst into bloom every spring. Every time he visited, Sage saw that the retired rescuer of sailors had made yet another improvement, despite suffering from chronic pain.

Franklin opened the door with a wide smile and said, "Greetings! You must be Matthew. Come in, come in."

Pocket doors opened into rooms on either side of the spacious entryway. One room was the parlor for sitting, reading, visiting and game-playing. The other was the dining room. Sage had eaten there a few times and the food was good, thanks to the old ship's cook Franklin had hired.

"I'm putting you upstairs in the front," he said to Matthew as the three of them mounted the stairs to the second floor. "It's one big room and right beside my own."

It was a corner room with two single beds, one on each side and a table and two chairs between them. Light streamed in through windows on two sides. Two wardrobes with hanging sections and drawers stood to either side of the door.

"This looks right nice, Mr. Franklin," said Matthew, as he put his duffle on the farthest bed and his school books on the table.

SEVENTEEN

Lucinda was all smiles as she sat squeezed into a small, non-descript coach with Sage, Matthew, and Henry Russell. Despite the discomfort, she'd jumped at the chance to change into what she called her "kitchen dress" of faded calico and spend late Monday afternoon cooped up with the three of them. Fong sat outside atop the driver's seat.

"There he is!" Sage said. "Come on!"

He and Matthew jumped out of the coach, but not before he gave Lucinda a quick kiss on the lips and tipped his hat to Henry Russell who'd snapped quite a few pictures of underage messengers entering and exiting Speedy Messenger from his window seat. "Good luck," he said to them both.

Once they reached the boardwalk, the coach rolled off and Sage and Matthew hurried to intercept Terry half a block from Speedy Messenger.

"Yo! Terry!" Sage called to halt the boy. Terry stopped and turned toward them. His face was pale and exhausted.

"Hey there, Mr. Miner," Terry said with a smile that didn't reach his tired eyes.

"Terry," Sage said, "I want you to meet my friend, Matthew Mason. I think you could help each other out. Matthew, this is Terry Tobias."

Terry looked puzzled but he stuck out his hand. "Pleased to meet you, Matthew," he said.

"Matthew here is from out of town and going to high school. His folks send him money but not quite enough. He rents a room with a spare bed. His place is nice and quiet and comes with breakfast and dinner. I thought you might be interested in staying there. He leaves for school early in the morning and doesn't come back until after noon. You'd be able to sleep undisturbed," Sage said, as Matthew nodded eagerly.

Terry shook his head. "I appreciate you thinking of me, but I can't afford a place like that. I've got to save money for my family."

"How much are you paying where you're staying now?"

"$2.50 a week, but that don't include any food."

Matthew jumped in. "That'd be perfect. I'm only short $3.00 a week. What with the food and all, you can save even more money."

"What time do they serve dinner?" Terry asked, his interest finally caught.

Sage jumped in because that was a question Matthew couldn't answer. "That's the beauty of this place. It has mostly sailors boarding there. They come and go at all hours, so the manager keeps a pot of soup on the stove all day in case they miss mealtime." Sage shut up, fearing he'd enthused a bit too much.

Terry looked skeptical and asked hesitantly, "It wouldn't bother you rooming with another person? Or, having me coming in to sleep so early in the morning?"

Matthew grinned. "That's the beauty of it. It won't hardly be like having another person there 'cause you work nights. Mostly I'll be gone when you're sleeping and you'll be gone when I'm sleeping. Besides, Mr. Miner's right. If I don't get someone to help with my rent, I'll have to move and I surely don't want to do that. It's a great place."

Pity tugged at Sage as he looked at Terry in the dusky light. No kid should have this boy's worry and woes. Hope flickered across the boy's face but his tone remained cautious as he said, "Well, okay. I guess I can give it a try. I'd have to get my stuff and come over in the morning. Where is it?"

Sage jumped in. "How about I meet you after work and take you there?" he asked.

Terry agreed and soon the two of them were on their way to Speedy Messenger while Matthew headed back to Franklin's to settle in before his new roommate arrived.

"Where the hell were you on Saturday, Miner?" Kimble demanded the minute Sage entered the office. "This is a six-day-a-week job, not some five-day, union job."

"Sorry, boss. I laid my head down and just didn't wake up until Sunday," Sage said apologetically. "I guess maybe I'm still adjusting to the night hours."

"Well, Number 37, you better be adjusted now 'cause I'll boot your butt down the street if you miss another night," Kimble growled. He looked like he wanted to continue but a call box jingled and he had to answer it. Soon messengers were scurrying out, Sage among them.

When Sage and Terry met again, their shift was over and dawn glowed bright along the cloudbank's eastern edge. "Are you certain sure my moving in with your friend is on the up and up? And that he's only going to charge me $3 a week?" Terry must have spent the night questioning such unexpected good fortune.

"Positively sure. There is only one small condition," Sage said and watched the hope die in the youngster's face.

"No, no. Nothing bad. It's just that Speedy Messenger tried to recruit Matthew to work for them. When he refused, they threatened him. So, it's very important that they not know where you and he are living."

Terry huffed out a gust of air. "Don't worry about that. I sure don't want them to know where I or my friends live."

They reached the dilapidated clapboard where Terry had been staying. A toothless old crone met them at the door and demanded money before she'd let Terry enter. When he told her all he wanted was the bundle of clothes he'd left with her for safekeeping, she charged him five cents for storage. Once that was paid, they set off for Franklin's.

The boarders were sitting down to breakfast when they arrived. It was a fine meal of fresh bread, eggs, potatoes, sausage, and plenty of coffee to wash it down. Terry took a seat beside Matthew, a slightly dazed look on his face as he surveyed the bounty and realized some of it was for him.

Sage joined the group and ate heartily, his gusto coming from the fact that he'd found a safe place for Terry. Next, he had to get the boy away from Speedy and find Glad. Despite the way it looked, he was certain those two aims were "twined like the strands of a braided rope," to use a phrased coined by a cowboy friend. If they were, it meant that once they found Glad, Terry would be free to leave Speedy.

In the meantime, he hoped Matthew would learn more from Terry. And, perhaps Lucinda and Henry Russell had uncovered some helpful information. Spirits high and stomach full, he set off for Lucinda's. He was looking forward to seeing her and, not just because he was interested in what she might have to tell him.

Elvira answered the door still in her robe with a scarf wrapped around her head. His John Miner outfit didn't surprise her. She'd seen him wearing a variety of disguises, John Miner's being only one of them.

Her answer to his first query stunned him. "Why no, Mr. Adair, she didn't come home all night. I thought she was with you."

"What?" Alarm stiffened every cell in Sage's body. "You haven't heard from her or anything?"

Elvira stepped forward and grabbed his arm. "No, I've heard nothing since she left with you yesterday afternoon. Where is she?" Alarm had now seized hold of her as well, creasing her dark-honey face and tightening her grip.

Sage patted her hand, turned on his heel and threw the words, "I don't know. Don't worry, I'll find her," over his shoulder as he raced back down the stairs.

Heading to Mozart's, Sage kept going over what he knew. Fong, Lucinda, and Henry Russell had left to stake out Vera Clark's house. The plan was to take pictures of the young messengers entering the house and see if the mystery man Sage had followed to the Imperial hotel returned. Lucinda's task was to signal Russell to photograph any monied man she recognized entering Clark's.

Could all three of them have been kidnapped? "No! No way that could happen with Fong there," he told himself in fierce tones that caught a passerby's attention. He clamped his lips together the rest of the way and tried to calm himself by breathing deeply, like Fong had instructed.

He reached the trap door in the alley, flung it open and moments later was running up the hidden stairs to Mozart's third floor. When he burst into his room, he found his mother already there, standing beside someone stretched out on his bed.

"Who? Lucinda?" he demanded.

"It's that man named, Henry," his mother replied. "He got hit in the head and is unconscious. Fong brought him here last night."

"Why didn't you come to get me? Where's Lucinda?" Sage demanded.

"Fong's out hunting for her," Mae said, putting a placating hand on Sage's forearm only to have him angrily shake it off.

"You should have come got me," he repeated.

"Fong and his cousins are out looking. You couldn't have done anything more."

As if her words summoned him, Fong appeared in the doorway. Sage whirled toward him and said, "What the hell happened? Did you find Lucinda?"

Fong paused, seeming to draw on inner strength because he calmly gestured to the table in the alcove and said, "Best you sit down, Sage. Then I tell you."

Sage took a seat. Mae left the room while Fong checked on Henry. He took the chair across from Sage, saying, "We wait for Lady Mother. She has not heard story either. I drop Mr. Russell at kitchen door and leave quick to find Miss Lucinda."

Sage took a deep breath, again fighting for calm. Wild emotion was the last thing they needed in such a dire situation.

Mae entered with coffee and biscuits. Setting the tray down, she took the third chair. The three of them were silent as she filled cups and passed the plate. Sage accepted the coffee but shook his head at the food. After taking a swallow and a bite, Fong began to speak.

"We wait outside Clark houses. Mr. Russell, he across street taking pictures. I also stand across street to protect him. Miss Lucinda stay in carriage to watch for boss man. Plan is Russell take his picture and then we jump in coach and follow him. Meantime, Russell, he take pictures of boy messengers going into houses."

Fong swallowed a sip of coffee and a bite of biscuit. "Next thing happen, two men run, grab Mr. Russell camera and start hitting him with clubs. I go to help. We fight. Then Miss Lucinda scream."

Shame filled the Chinese man's face, "I could not save her. Big man with gun push her into cab. He yell he kill her if I follow. I watch cab drive away."

"Meantime, two men run away also. Mr. Russell on ground knocked out, camera broken. I put him in coach, bring him here."

"My God, what are we going to do?" Sage asked of no one in particular. He rubbed his face with both hands as if he could scrub away the awful news.

"One bit of helpful information," Fong said.

Sage looked up sharply. "What?"

"Cab driver have big knife scar on side of face. Cousins looking for him now."

"Tell me about the man with the gun," Sage said.

"He is very tall. More tall than you. Big shoulders, like ox," Fong answered promptly.

That description rang a bell. It sounded like the fellow who'd grabbed Glad and turned him upside down. And, the cab. That night the big man had thrown Glad into a cab. It could be that the scar-faced cabbie was part of the gang. He'd have to be. No honest cabbie would help kidnap boys and women off the street, especially at gunpoint.

"Okay, then," Sage said. "Did any of Russell's attackers look familiar?"

Fong nodded. "Two who attack Mr. Russell same ones who attack at Miss Lucinda's house."

"Where's my camera?" came a croak from the bed. Russell was struggling to sit up.

Mae rushed to his side, picking up a partially crushed Brownie camera to show him. "I'm afraid your camera's ruined," she said, holding it out.

Russell took the box in his hands and turned it around. "Whew! I don't think they damaged the film cassette. Just the aluminum casing is dented. That means I've still got the unexposed pictures," he declared, as he flipped back the blanket and swung his feet to the floor. "Got to get this film developed." He swayed on the edge of the bed and turned a light shade of green.

"Oh, no you don't," Mae said, taking the camera out of his hands and gently pushing him onto his back. "You need to rest a bit. You've gone green around the gills."

Sage crossed to the bed and said, "Mrs. Clemens is right. You can't get up just yet. Besides, your pictures of the kids can wait."

"Kids, hell," responded Russell. "When I saw those two galoots run at me, all ugly-faced, I snapped their damn photograph."

EIGHTEEN

"SAGE, YOU NEED TO SLEEP," Mae said, as she stood behind him as he shaved.

"I tried. But every time I close my eyes I see Lucinda's face."

"What do you think you can do that Fong isn't already doing?"

He rinsed his face, patted it dry with a towel and turned to ask, "Where is he? I need to speak to him."

"He's downstairs. He's as bad as you are. I don't think he's slept a wink since yesterday morning. Hanke's down there, too."

"Where's Henry?"

"He's shut up in Ida and Knute's bathroom developing his pictures. He limped in there right after you delivered that suitcase from his hotel."

'Cameras have come a long way since glass plates," Sage remarked. "I hope he got a good picture of those two thugs."

The three silent and glum men sitting in the kitchen were oblivious to the noon meal commotion.

"Mr. Fong, I forgot to ask you whether you and Lucinda saw that strange man around Vera Clark's house," Sage said.

Fong frowned in concentration, clearly trying to recall something. "Maybe Miss Lucinda saw him. Just as men attack and I run to help Mr. Russell, I hear her say very loud, "Good Lord, I didn't expect to see him.""

Sage edged forward on his chair. "Who?" he demanded.

Fong shook his head regretfully. "I not see. Too busy fighting."

Sage turned to Hanke. "Sorry, Sergeant. I should have said, 'hello.'"

Hanke waved the apology away. "Don't worry about it. And, sad as it is, I have to thank you. Our little carrot-top fellow in the mortuary is Doug Spencer. His pa identified his body this morning. He might be an old sot, but I believe he loved his son. Terrible business."

"Was he able to explain anything, like the marks around the boy's wrists and ankles?"

"No, though if the perpetrator had been there, I believe the father would have killed him on the spot. All Mr. Spencer knew was that Doug was working for Speedy Messenger and that he and another boy wanted to start a messengers' union."

"The other boy was Terry Tobias, Glad's older brother," Sage told him.

"I can't believe they'd kill a kid over that. The newsboys have had a union for a few years and it hasn't caused any problems. Mostly, it's just a safe place for them to gather and socialize."

"That's the problem with power. It leads to arrogance and the mistaken belief that only the powerful know how the world should work," Sage said, and added bitterly, "Of course, that means they always make sure the world works to their, and their offsprings', benefit."

Mae entered the kitchen followed by Henry who looked vigorous and excited despite a whopping black eye. He was waving a piece of paper as he declared, "Got 'em!"

He came to a dead stop and tamped down his enthusiasm when he caught sight of Hanke in his brass-buttoned uniform. Sage was quick to reassure. "Henry, this is Sergeant Hanke. He's a friend. He's the one you need to show the picture to."

Hanke stood and shook Henry's hand as the photographer said, "Henry Russell, Sergeant Hanke. I'm glad to know you're a friend. Unfortunately, my back and shoulders have felt a policeman's billy club more than once. I've learned to be cautious."

"Sorry to hear that, Mr. Russell," Hanke said. "You have a picture to show me?"

"I do," Henry's enthusiasm had returned. "These are the fellows who attacked me," he said, handing the Sergeant a picture.

Hanke stared and then a slow grin spread across his face. "I'm pretty sure we've arrested these two before. I'll need to ask the arresting officer but I know who he is. He just might know where to find them."

Sage jumped in, hopeful for the first time that morning. "You'll look for them and arrest them? Lucinda was grabbed at the same time as those two attacked Russell here. I'll bet anything their attack was a diversion so the big man could snatch her." He pointed at Russell's picture in Hanke's hand. "Those two know who's behind all this messenger uproar, I'm sure of it."

Hanke stood and donned his tall beehive helmet. "I'll do my best. I'll send word when we have them in custody." He turned to Russell. "Any chance I could get more copies of this picture? I can send it down the rail lines just in case they've skipped town." At Russell's nod, Hanke said, "Send them to me at the station. He turned to Sage, saying, "I presume you'll want to be there for the questioning once we catch them?"

"You'd allow that?"

Sage's question drew a rueful smile from the big Sergeant who said, "I suspect it would be hard to keep you away. Besides, I know how much she means to you." With that, he was out the kitchen door and heading down the alley.

Fong cleared his throat. "We maybe soon find cab driver. Cousins have seen him. They know places he goes. They looking for him."

"If they find him, I want to know. I don't care whether I am working or not."

Fong nodded. "We find cabbie, you want me to deliver him to Sergeant Hanke?"

"Hanke can deal with Henry's attackers. You and I will take care of the cab driver."

"We use crimp cell again?" asked Fong.

"You're not going to kill him, are you?" Henry piped up for the first time since handing over his picture. The distress on his face said he feared he was hearing a murder being planned.

Fong and Sage turned mystified faces toward the photographer and then Sage laughed. "Lord, no. We might make him think that, but don't worry, what we plan usually works without touching a hair on his head."

It was pitch black and smelled dusty. At least the thug hadn't drugged, knocked out or otherwise interfered with her. It had all happened suddenly. One minute she was watching the photographer, then there'd been the fight and then she'd been forced into a cab. They'd ridden around for at least an hour with the big lump beside her saying nothing and ignoring all her questions. Canvas rain flaps hid the street and they'd made so many turns that she'd lost track of their direction. When the cab finally stopped and the door had opened, she expected to see a rural scene. Shockingly, the cab had stopped across the street from where they'd grabbed her. A frantic peer into the dark surroundings, as the big man yanked her out of the cab, yielded the disappointing fact that Fong and the small coach were nowhere in sight.

A few jabs with the gun barrel got her across the boardwalk and into the middle house of Vera Clark's brothel. Before the man could knock, the door was snatched open. A dirty, scraggly-haired old slattern shooed them inside. "Hurry up. We don't want anyone to see. The customers are all upstairs but who knows when someone will come down," she said.

The big man grabbed Lucinda's elbow and shoved her down a narrow hallway. Lucinda opened her mouth to yell but snapped it shut when the gun barrel jabbed painfully into her ribs. Seconds later, the three of them were swiftly descending cellar stairs. At the bottom, stood a door with a brass padlock holding it shut. The woman slipped past them and unlocked the padlock. At the man's nod, she lifted the padlock from the hasp and pushed the door open. It was pitch black on the other side.

Before Lucinda could say anything, a firm hand on her back shoved her forward with such force she fell to her knees onto a dirt floor. Even as she struggled to rise, the door slammed shut. Seconds later, she heard the padlock rattle in the hasp and snick shut. Footsteps mounted the stairs and the upstairs door slammed.

Lucinda carefully rose to her feet. She reached out but it was so dark she couldn't even see her hands. She touched nothing. Slowly she turned in a circle and still there was nothing. There was a smell though. Besides dust, there was the unmistakable stink of a slop pail. That meant she wasn't the first person imprisoned here.

Fear made her sway on her feet. She pushed it down. Sage and Fong are coming for me, she told herself. I just have to figure out how to help them find me.

Slowly she slid a boot forward, her hands outstretched. Eight steps forward and her fingers encountered a rough plank wall. She stepped to her right, trailing her fingers along the wall. A few steps more, she felt a door frame. Frantically, she felt for the door and eventually encountered a knob. She turned it and pulled. Nothing happened. She kept feeling and found the hasp and padlock that held it shut. "Damn it," she said aloud.

This second door might open into a larger basement space or to the outside. No light leaked from under the door so the first option was more likely. Given they were in the heart of the North End, the underground could be on the other side.

She stood thinking. First things first. She had to get that padlock off the door. Once inside the underground, she could stumble around until she found a Chinese home, gambling den or opium parlor. She'd find help there. All she had to do was say Fong's name.

She started groping through the pitch dark again and soon reached a corner. She turned and kept going, vowing to systematically search every inch of the cellar. There must be something helpful down here. Just as she had that thought, her boot smacked a wooden crate. Its lid was off and she plunged her hands inside. She encountered fabric. Burrowing deeply, she felt only more fabric until something sharp pricked her finger.

She jerked her hand out of the crate, sucked on the finger, and then gingerly began feeling for whatever had pricked her. Something sharp lurked in these clothes. Something that could come in handy. Encountering the rigid felt of a lady's hat she carefully fingered its surface and, at last, encountered the cool metal of a forgotten hat pin.

She drew it from the hat and her exploring fingers told her that it was long and sharp. With a grim smile only a ghost could see, she carefully pinned it inside her bodice. Her spirits rose. She had a weapon.

Further rummaging revealed the crate held nothing that she could use against the padlock. She continued moving along the wall once again. And, again, her foot encountered something interesting, another crate. This time, the crate's contents were the opposite of soft fabric. It held tin cans. Picking one up, she shook it. Something sloshed inside. "If I find a can opener, I won't starve," she said aloud.

There was nothing in the second crate she could beat against the padlock. She continued along the wall until a faint rustle froze her steps. "Who's there?" she demanded. Only silence greeted her question. Nothing moved in the deep silence.

She stepped out again despite sensing that something alive was inside this cellar with her. Probably just a mouse or rat, she told herself only to shudder as her imagination conjured up a beady-eyed, sharp-toothed rat eyeing her ankles. She was glad she wore walking boots. Taking a deep breath, she stepped off again. Five paces later, she stumbled into the room's second corner. She turned and moved along this third wall.

It held the door to the upstairs but she didn't bother messing with it. An escape into the upstairs would be no escape at all.

For a moment, she sagged against the wall, weary with defeat until she thought of Mae Clemens and heard her voice saying, "Buck up girl, there are worse spots to be in." Lucinda's resolve stiffened and propelled her forward. Reaching the third corner, her foot hit something hard that rolled away across the dirt floor. Dropping down onto her knees, she felt for the object until she found it. Quickly her fingers roamed its contours. It was metal, about two feet long, round and had openings on both ends—a metal pipe. Excitement sent her to her feet and bumbling across the room to the underground door.

Reaching it, she found the padlock with her fingers and gave it a good whack with the pipe. The pipe clanged but padlock stayed secured. She attacked the hasp and it didn't even bend, though a splinter of sharp metal sticking up meant the pipe had done some damage.

She hit the hasp another good whack in the hope she could eventually loosen the screws that held it to the door frame. As she fingered the hasp to gauge her progress she heard the door at the top of the stairs open. She moved to the crate holding the clothes, tossed in the pipe and hurriedly buried it. Then she went back to stand in front of the door to the stairs.

Nothing happened. She held her breath and in the ensuing silence, she heard heavy breathing outside the stairway door. She recognized its rasp. She'd spent hours listening to it come from the big man while they wheeled aimlessly around the city. After what seemed like forever, the breathing sound faded and boots thudded up the wooden steps.

Lucinda sighed. She'd have to be more careful. Blindly stumbling over to the crate, she fished around and finally found the pipe. She also found what seemed to be a heavy brocade jacket. She carefully wrapped it around the pipe and crossed back to the door to the underground. This time when she hit the hasp, it yielded only a dull clunk.

"Won't do you no good breaking the padlock. That door's been nailed shut. I seen him do it."

She jumped and dropped the pipe. The small voice had come from the one corner in the cellar she hadn't explored.

NINETEEN

"Good Lord, you almost gave me a heart attack," Lucinda exclaimed, a palm pressed against her chest. She swallowed and said, "Glad Tobias, is that you?"

"Yes, it's me. How do you know my name?" The voice was small and cautious coming out of the black.

"Oh sweetie, you have no idea how happy I am to find you. There are so many people looking for you."

"They are?" Wonder and hope strengthened his voice.

"Glad, how are you?" she asked into the dark.

When he spoke again, he'd moved closer. "They left me with jars of peaches and other things. And they gave me a pail of water. "Fraid there isn't any can opener like you hoped," he added with a chuckle.

"How come you didn't speak up sooner?" she asked.

"Since you're a woman, I figured you must be one of them women that I saw upstairs when they was bringing me down here. Thought maybe they was locking you up as a punishment. They done that once and she kept hollering I was someone she didn't like much. It was like she was drunk or something."

"I most assuredly am not one of Vera Clark's women," she said hotly before calming down and asking, "How long have you been down here?"

"Don't know. Seems like forever. They grabbed me off the street and I've been here ever since."

"Do you remember being in the Slap Jack saloon and meeting a man named, 'John Miner'? I think he bought some of your papers."

"Why sure enough I remember him. He was a nice man. That's where they took me, right outside Slap Jack's."

"Well, John Miner saw them throw you into that cab. He and a lot of his friends, including me, have been looking for you ever since."

A sniffle sounded in the dark. Reaching out she touched a bony shoulder and gently drew the boy close, wrapping both arms around him as he let go a sob. Her heart felt like it was breaking. What kind of monsters would keep a boy in a pitch-dark cellar for over two weeks?

Still sniffling, Glad said, "I been terrible worried about my family. They need me. We was barely making a go of it, no matter how hard we all tried. They need what I make selling newspapers." More sobs escaped him and she held him closer.

Once he'd calmed she said quietly, "I have some good news for you. John Miner and other people have been looking after your family. Your mother has seen a doctor and is in the hospital getting well. Carrie Lynne and little Emma Jane are being cared for in a children's home until your mother is well enough to take care of them. And, your brother, Terry, has a safe place to stay with plenty of food."

Glad dropped the arms he'd wrapped around her waist and stepped away but kept hold of her hand. "Really? You're not just telling me that? The bad man can't hurt them?"

"Oh, honey, what did he tell you?"

"He said that he would hurt them if I tried to get out of here or made any noise. He knows that they live down in Sullivan's Gulch and everything."

"Well, all four of them are safe. And, none of them live in Sullivan's Gulch. Not anymore. Those days are over. When your Ma is better, all of you will live together in a much better place." Of course, Lucinda only assumed that was true since they hadn't discussed what would happen to the Tobias family after the Speedy Messenger mystery was solved. She was counting on the fact that Sage had money, and always did the right thing by the people he met. She smiled and let her thoughts linger on the handsome, kind and exasperating man she'd come to love.

Glad interrupted her romantic digression. "Even Terry is safe? Isn't he still working for them?"

"You mean for Speedy Messenger?"

"They're the ones alright. They took me because they didn't like Terry and Dougie trying to start a union. He said it was messing with their plans. They took my copper wristband that Ma gave me for my last birthday. They said it was to prove to Terry that they had me."

"Did you see Dougie?" she asked gently.

His tone was subdued as he said, "I think it was Dougie who died. I heard them coming down the stairs and then there was a loud noise and shouting and thumps like someone rolling down the stairs. A little while later they brought a body in. I couldn't see him but I felt him."

Lucinda couldn't see the boy but the hand she was holding trembled. Glad continued, "I felt all over him. He was short and small, just like a kid. At first, I thought they'd killed Terry but the boy I felt had longer hair. And, there was a kerchief around his neck. Dougie always wore a kerchief and Terry never did. Anyways, his chest didn't move and no breath came out his mouth."

"Did they keep his body in here very long?" She forced herself to stay calm and matter of fact despite feeling burning rage. The monsters. How could they have inflicted such horror on this child?

Glad's voice was soft, almost musing as he answered, "It seemed like forever, but maybe not too long. They come in to switch out the water and slop pails. Next time they did that, they took away his body."

After a pause, Glad said, "I don't think they meant to kill him."

"What makes you say that?" she asked.

"It sounded like he tripped going down the stairs. Besides, I think they wanted him alive. They talked about selling us to shanghaiers. Leastways, that's what I heard through the door. They fought out there when Dougie fell down the stairs. The boss woman was swearing and a-screeching. She's the one who talked about selling us onto the ships."

Vera Clark, Lucinda thought. She'd sell her own mother for the dope and booze.

Glad's voice was thin as he asked, "Miss, what are we going to do? I don't want to go on no sailing ship."

Lucinda pulled him close again and said to the top of his head. "Don't worry, we'll figure something out."

Sage lingered in Franklin's kitchen until Franklin had handed Terry a cloth sack holding a sandwich and apple as he went out the door.

Once the boy was gone and the front door closed, Franklin limped into the kitchen scowling. "He's eating okay but he certain sure isn't sleeping. I don't think I've seen a boy as tuckered out as he is," he said.

Sage went up to the boys' room where he found Matthew sitting at the table. Despite his books being open, he was gazing out the window and frowning.

"You doing okay?" Sage asked him.

Matthew heaved a sigh. "I'm fine. The big man didn't show up outside school this afternoon. That makes three days in a row. I think he's forgotten me. But, Terry is powerful worried. When I came in after school, he was sitting on his bed, turning a copper wristband round and round 'til he liked to wear it out. I asked him about it. He said it was his brother's. But he wouldn't say anything else. I was afraid to push it. Sorry I couldn't get him to say more."

Sage's mind had stuck on the word 'wristband'. A memory broke the surface but sank before he could catch it. He said, "It will take time. Just try to take his mind off his worries as best you can and if you get the opportunity—"

Sage didn't finish because that elusive memory surfaced again. "By Jove, Matthew. I just realized something. Glad was wearing a copper wristband just before they threw him in that cab. I bet they gave it to Terry to prove they have his brother. It explains why he's been cooperating with them. I suspected it, but now, thanks to you, we know it for sure."

Matthew looked gratified. Sage patted him on the shoulder. "I'm off to Speedy Messenger," he said over his shoulder as he headed for the door.

"Well, well, what do we have here? Miss High and Mighty herself." Vera Clark's voice was thick with drugs, drink, or both.

If she'd been by herself, Lucinda would have tried to overpower her but the same huge man blocked the exit, holding a kerosene lantern high. Lucinda took advantage of the light to survey her surroundings.

It was a dirt-floored storage room with brick walls on four sides and wood frames around the two rough-planked doors. A pail stood in the corner farthest from the stairs. Further along the wall, stood another. Water and slop pails, she realized. Other than that, the room was pretty much as she imagined it. Two hand-hewn spikes secured the padlocked door she'd surmised led into the underground.

She looked down into the elfin face that had captivated Sage. The boy was staring at her, his expression one of hope and fear beneath tear-streaked filth. She wanted to pick him up, assure him that everything would be alright. Instead, she tore her gaze away and said, "Vera, I'm sad to see that you're mixed up in this." Lucinda made her tone regretful. No sense antagonizing the woman.

"Oh, please. I am so sick of your butter-won't-melt-in-your-mealy-mouth airs. You're no better than I am."

Lucinda shrugged but kept her lips clamped shut.

"Oh, oh. The silent treatment. As if that's really going to work. Maybe if you begged a bit? But you won't do that, will you? Well, we'll soon see how long that lady act lasts." Clark would have sounded more threatening had her words not been slurred. She turned to the man. "Go ahead and switch out the pails."

He put the lantern down on the dirt floor and, for a moment, Lucinda felt a rush of hope. If he carried the two pails upstairs, Clark would be alone.

The big man crossed, picked up the two pails, and headed for the stairway.

Lucinda readied herself, confident she was stronger and certainly soberer than the other woman. Momentarily, she regretted that she'd never asked Fong for lessons in that fighting technique he'd taught Sage. When she got out of this, she would. Reality tamped down her optimism. Even if she overpowered Vera Clark, they'd still have to get out of the cellar, up the stairs and out the front door before the man came back. How likely was that?

Her plan hit the wall when the big man only put the pails on the steps and picked up two replacements he'd already carried down the stairs. Vera Clark wasn't being left on her own. If Lucinda's thoughts at that moment had been audible, even Vera Clark might have been shocked at just how unladylike they were.

Vera Clark's smirk suggested she'd been following Lucinda's thoughts. Rather than commenting, however, Clark said, "I like picturing you squatting over that pail. Bet you haven't done that in a while. It'll be lots of fun in the dark, just ask the boy."

Clark moved toward the door only to pause and turn back. "But, don't worry, you'll only be needing it for a short while. Willard tells me you saw the boss man. Too bad. It means that, in a day or two, you and the runt will be on a sailing ship. Him they might keep. But you, Lucy Collins, you, I think, will be taking the long swim once all the sailors are done having their fun."

"Vera, he's just a little boy," Lucinda said softly, pleadingly.

"We were just little girls, younger than him. We survived, didn't we?"

Clark quickly stepped out and slammed the door shut. Her cackling continued even after she had padlocked the door and was climbing the stairs.

"What are we going to do?" Glad asked in a trembling voice.

She squeezed him around the shoulders and paused to think before she answered. She was remembering what the lantern light had revealed.

"How long do you think we have before they come back to swap out the pails?" she asked.

"It's different all the time. Usually hours and hours but sometimes it seems like a whole day," he answered.

"Okay, then," she said. "I think I know exactly what we need to do."

TWENTY

"Mr. Fong! Why are you here?" Without waiting for an answer, Sage dodged into a nearby doorway, Fong at his heels. He'd worried all night long, his thoughts fixed on Lucinda, imagining her fearful and hurt. When not worrying, he pictured her in better times, the light in her honey-colored hair, her laughing eyes, and the secret sorrow that sometimes turned her silent and withdrawn. He'd even run through various guilty memories, the days he'd left her alone with no word and worse, the attraction he'd recently felt toward that school teacher, Valentine Pritchard. What had he been thinking? Maybe that was it. He hadn't been thinking at all. There was no braver, stronger, or more loyal woman than Lucinda Collins, she'd proven that more than once.

"Cousin's find him. They watching him now," Fong said quietly as if sensing Sage's despair and wanting to console him with hopeful news.

"The cabbie? They've found the cab driver?" Sage's pulse quickened.

Fong nodded and asked, "You done with delivery?" That was a good guess. As they'd arranged, Sage took the same street back to Speedy Messenger after every errand. That's how Fong had known where to intercept him.

"Do you have him locked up somewhere? Can we question him?"

"He still loose but no matter where he go, cousins follow. They not lose him."

Fong's confidence was justified. In truth, Fong's 'cousins' were unrelated to him by blood but rather they were members of the same fraternal organization they called a Tong. Because the Chinese were slight in stature most whites grossly underestimated their determination, bravery, and skill. Yet, these were men who had survived perilous journeys to the land they called Gold Mountain after leaving behind family, language, and everything they held dear. Upon arrival, they were exploited, having no choice but to take the hardest, most dangerous jobs, building railroads, digging mines—doing what few white men were willing to do. Sage had come to respect them and he held, in awe, his friend who now stood beside him.

That awe was seemingly something he shared with the cousins who also venerated Fong Kam Tong. A former soldier in San Francisco's tong wars—Fong'd been a dreaded bo hoy doy—a hatchet man. But he'd left that all behind, gathered up his wife, Kum Ho, and moved to Portland where he served as a mediator between the Tongs. His skill with the hatchet, with the snake and crane martial art, and his wisdom had made him one of the Chinese community's most important leaders. Yet, he moved humbly among the whites, concealing his amazing abilities and looking like every other small and vulnerable Chinese immigrant.

"Let's go get him!" Sage said. He was done working for Speedy. There was no point in continuing the ruse. He was rarely in the office and, even when he was, Terry usually wasn't there. Now that the boy was living at Franklin's it would be easy to see him. Besides, the most important question had been answered. They now knew who had taken Glad. What they needed to know, and didn't, was who wanted to take over the messenger services in the city. It sure wasn't the two thug brains running Speedy Messenger.

He needed the freedom to find the boss man. Snatching the Speedy cap off his head, he tossed it into a nearby barrel. "Let's go!" he said again.

Fong led them through the streets to a wood-frame house behind the rail yards. They stood in the weeds as Fong pointed toward a window on the second story. "That is his room," he said. "In corner of house," he added.

"I wonder if the landlady keeps the front door locked," Sage said as he tried to remember his lock picking lesson.

"Nope, door not locked. Boarders come and go but we not see them unlock door."

Sage grinned at Fong. "I don't relish the idea of us hauling him out of that house and to someplace where we can question him."

"We not need to move him. I use pig sticker to persuade him to talk right where he is." Fong patted the knife sheath sewn into his waistband.

A minute later they were creeping across the porch. Fong glided soundlessly as if he were moving an inch above the rough boards. Sage struggled to step silently, his boots feeling both heavy and clumsy.

Reaching the door, Sage carefully twisted the doorknob and pushed. It was dark and soundless inside. Even the evilest of doers tended to be asleep at three in the morning. His nose twitched, rebelling against the stale smells of grease, tobacco, dirt, sweat, and mold—poverty's scent was universal.

Fong followed him into the dark hallway and silently closed the door. They both froze, listening for movement but all remained silent save for the faint sound of distant snoring. They crept up the stairway and down the hallway with Sage hoping that no one would need to use the backyard outhouse. The doorknob to the cabbie's room didn't move. The landlady might trust unlocked doors but not so her cabbie tenant.

He and Fong exchanged grimaces of frustration until Sage felt in his pockets for his wallet and found the paper-thin piece of whalebone Franklin had given him. Carefully, he slid the flexible piece of white between the frame and lock. He grinned at Fong when the latch snicked. He eased the door open and peered inside.

It was a small room. Someone lay beneath blankets on a single bed standing against a side wall that contained a second window. The stillness inside contrasted with the snores coming from another room down the hall. He opened the door wider and slipped inside. Fong followed and again closed the door behind them. Enough light came from the curtainless windows that Sage could see that the only other furnishings were a small bureau and a single ladder back chair, both of which stood against the wall opposite the bed.

Sage turned to gesture Fong toward the end of the bed. As he did so, the mound on the bed erupted. Taken by surprise, Sage simply watched as the figure flung the bedside window wide and climbed out. Fong, however, was already in action, pushing Sage aside, jumping onto the bed, and to the window. He started to jump through it but paused as a crash sounded.

No longer immobile, Sage leapt to the window and saw bottles, boards and who knew what else piled below. On top of the mess lay the wooden ladder that the cabbie had knocked down once he'd reached the ground. It was too dangerous to jump.

"We better leave. He make big noise," Fong observed.

Sure enough, there were sounds of stirring elsewhere in the house and a woman cried out a query. Muffling his voice with his hand, Sage called, "Sorry, dropped something."

They stood motionless in the cabbie's room, waiting for the house to settle down. Sage shook his head in disgust and mouthed the word, "sorry," in Fong's direction. Fong shrugged in return. "That happen sometimes," he said.

But never to Fong, Sage thought ruefully. One thing for sure, another Fong lesson is in the works once this is over. What the heck was I thinking—standing there like a stump instead of grabbing him? He answered his own question: Nothing, I was thinking nothing.

"They're coming!" Glad whispered.

Lucinda quickly lifted the wooden crate and set it in front of the second door, the one she hoped opened into the underground. She sat on the crate and spread her skirt wide. Earlier, she'd tossed all the clothes to one side and flipped the crate to make the seat. Once seated she felt Glad's small hands on her knees and then he crawled onto her lap. She hugged him close.

The door crashed open and Vera Clark stepped into the room, her big sidekick again holding the lantern high like some perverse Statute of Liberty.

"Oh, how sweet, holding the little kid on your lap while he sleeps. Too bad we don't have a camera, right Willard?" she said to the big man at her side.

"Shh, you'll wake him," Lucinda said quietly, nodding down at the boy who lay with his eyes closed.

Clark shrugged and turned to Willard, "Drop the food bag on the floor, they'll find it if they get hungry enough." Turning back to Lucinda she said, "We've experienced a bit of a delay. It seems your friends are looking for you. One of our men had to jump out his window and go into hiding. That means you and the kid will be leaving us a bit sooner than planned. I'm closing up shop and moving on."

Lucinda tried not to show relief at knowing Sage and Fong were getting close, only asking, "Are you're going to keep us shut up down here? I can understand doing that to an adult, but to a child like him?" When Clark didn't respond, Lucinda added, "You make me sick."

"If you're going to throw up, don't miss the pot," Clark said with a ghastly smile.

She turned to Willard. "Come on. It appears Miss Fancy Pants Collins doesn't care for our company."

With that, they shut and padlocked the door and the light beneath it rapidly dimmed as they climbed the stairs.

For a moment, Lucinda sat liking the feel of the boy on her lap, all warm, bony and small. But, at the sound of the upstairs door closing, Glad rolled off her and scampered to the stairway door. A moment later he whispered, "They're gone." Then he was back beside her, helping to lift the heavy crate to one side. They daren't leave suspicious tracks by dragging it across the floor.

Lucinda dropped to her hands and knees and groped for the length of pipe she'd been using as a digging tool. Glad was beside her, his fingers searching for the glass jar he was using to toss the dirt she loosened onto the pile they'd hidden beneath the clothes.

Soon they were back at work, her loosening the dirt before the door, him scooping it out with his jar.

She didn't know if her idea would work but at least it kept them busy and Glad's spirits seemed to rise with every scoop he tossed. The possibility that the door opened into the underground had given her the idea. What she hoped was that, at some point in the distant past, someone had dug a tunnel from the Clark house's cellar into the underground beneath the neighboring brick building. Or else that the door simply opened onto a stairway that led outside. Either way, possible escape lay behind it.

If they dug a big enough hole beneath the door, then Glad could slither under it and go for help. They'd never be able to make the hole large enough for her to escape but she hadn't told him that.

She gave a little squeak of excitement when the pipe slid under the door for the first time. Frantically, she stabbed at the dirt, fury, and hope giving her strength. The gap beneath the door deepened until she was able to thrust the groping fingers of one hand beneath it. She felt more dry dirt. She sat back on her heels.

"It feels dry on the other side. I think that means the door leads into the underground," she told the invisible boy breathing at her side. "You ever been in the underground, Glad?"

"Nah just heard tales of it. Terry told me to never ever go down into it."

"Well, I've never been in it, either. But Mr. Miner has described it to me." Lucinda said. "It's just the open basements of every building on every block. There are tunnels under the street that let you walk from one block to the next. It is very dark, like here. But, Mr. Miner says, you can hear the people above you walking and talking, so it's not all that scary."

"With you beside me, I won't be scared," came his solemn vow.

She bit her lip but only said, "Come on, we've got to hurry. We don't know when that awful woman will come back."

Hope invigorated their efforts and soon, the gap beneath the door felt wide and deep enough to Lucinda's probing fingers. But now the tricky part came, they had to dig far enough out, on both sides of the door so Glad's body could slip into the hole, beneath the door and wiggle out on the other side. Lucinda lay on her belly gouging out the other side, dust coating her lips and filling her nose. She kept her eyes squeezed shut. She could only imagine what she must look like, a grubby mess of sweat-streaked dirt. She smiled grimly. At least she wasn't wearing one of her better dresses.

She allowed herself a second smile at the thought of how Elvira's face would look when Lucinda handed her the dress to wash. She could even hear the woman's voice, "Lawd have mercy, Miss Lucinda. We might as well throw this dress on the burn pile. It will never come clean."

Lucinda's eyes stung with a mix of unshed tears and dirt at the thought of her friend's face. Elmira was brave, loyal and loving. As Mae Clemens once said, "Miss Elvira isn't afraid to tell anyone and everyone exactly how the cow ate the cabbage but that heart of hers is pure gold."

And, of course, that thought trail led to Mae Clemens. Most respectable women like her would have nothing to do with a parlor house madam. But Sage's mother had immediately taken to her, making clear that she thought Lucinda a suitable companion for her son. Sometimes she acted like the mother Lucinda had never had. A few times Lucinda had wondered whether Mae didn't want her son to . . . No, she wouldn't think of that. Those kinds of thoughts always sent her to a sad, lonely and despairing place.

Despite her whirling thoughts, Lucinda's hands and arms kept working as did Glad's. When she felt she'd loosened enough dirt, he took her place to scoop it out. Finally, she believed they'd cleared enough space for Glad to slip out the other side. Now came the tricky part. They had to make enough space on their side of the door for him to slip under it. She feared that her skirt and the crate wouldn't be able to hide a hole that big.

"Let's eat and drink something before we finish the job," she said to him. They lifted the crate before the door. Glad retrieved the bag Willard had dropped on the floor. It offered bread, cheese and a jar of water. It tasted good although the bread was stale and dry with sawdust, the cheese hard, and the water tainted with dill pickle juice. Lucinda would have felt grateful except she knew Clark's only motivation was to keep them healthy enough to sell.

They chewed in silence before Lucinda finally said, "This is the dangerous part. You need to stand by the door to the upstairs and listen for any sound of them returning. I'll dig like crazy."

She reached out in the dark and felt for his hand. "Glad, you are going to have to go into the underground without me."

"No, no. I won't leave you." Fear and tears thickened his voice.

"Sweetie, I can't fit under that door. It's going to be hard for you to get to the other side and you are much smaller."

"We can dig some more!" Panic edged his words.

"Glad, you know we don't have time to make that hole big enough before Clark and that Willard fella come back. You have to go for help. You have to rescue me."

"I don't know where to go."

"You're going to take the pipe we've been digging with. Hold it in front of you like a blind man so you don't run into things. Listen to the sounds of people overhead. Look for light. Mr. Miner says many Chinese live and work in the underground. You'll see their light through cracks in plank walls and around doors. Knock on one of those doors. If you see men walking with lanterns hide and don't make a sound. They might be shanghaiers. Only go to Chinese men."

"Chinese? Why would they help us?"

"They will help because Mr. Miner is friends with them and because I will tell you three words. I want you to repeat them over and over so that when you do find a Chinese person, you will say those words. That's all you have to do."

"Are they magic words?" Glad sounded puzzled and hopeful at the same time.

Lucinda laughed. Fong would be tickled at the idea his name was magic. "Yes, Glad, 'magic words'. Here they are: 'Fong. Kam. Tong.' I want you to say them over and over to yourself."

They lifted the crate away from the door and she began digging. Glad went over to the door and she could hear him softly repeating Mr. Fong's name. At last, she decided she'd made the hole large enough. "Glad, honey. Come over here and lay on your back. Let's see if you can scoot under the door, I'll push from this side."

He crossed the floor, laid down and began to wiggle into the hole. With her fingers on his chest, he started inching his way under the door, head first. "Ouch, I scraped my nose," he said.

"Turn your face sideways," she instructed. She grasped his two thin thighs and said, "Tell me when your head is on the other side and I'll push you through. Keep your shoulders and arms down."

Seconds later, his muffled voice sounded from the other side of the door. "Push!"

She pushed until his coat buttons snagged. Carefully she unbuttoned them and spread his coat open. Her fingers told her that his clearance was less than a quarter of an inch. She pushed again. This time his torso slid under so that only his thighs and feet were on her side. They'd done it! Such intense joy filled her that she was surprised it didn't light up the room. She felt his heels dig in and he gave a mighty 'oomph' as they both pushed.

He was out. She leaned down and shoved the pipe through. "Here's the pipe. Get away, hurry, hurry. Find and go through at least three tunnels before you look for help. Try to go straight out from the door. That's east. Go straight and find two tunnels heading east. Once you're through them, you'll need to turn right and go straight again, through at least three tunnels. One will be very long. That's Burnside street. Two more tunnels after that, you should find some Chinese people."

"Okay," came the small voice. "I'm sorry I'm leaving you." His flailing hand reached under the door to find her's. They held on momentarily until his was withdrawn. She heard the sound of footsteps stumbling away, a distant thud and a quiet curse and then no sound at all.

She sat back on her heels. Then she went to work using the jar to rapidly fill the hole. Once she'd filled in enough that the crate could cover it, she started on the pile of clothes. Wadding some dresses into a roll she covered them with more clothes, trying to make it look like a small boy slept beneath them. The longer it took them to realize Glad had escaped, the safer they were. Having done the best she could, she rested, letting her imagination trail the small boy as he stumbled through the darkness, his eyes and ears searching. Lucinda wrapped her arms around her abdomen and bent over, fighting the fear and finally letting loose the tears she'd been holding at bay. Had she sent that child into even greater danger?

TWENTY ONE

"We're not finding her anywhere!" Sage's hands shook as he raised the coffee cup to his lips. "And now we've lost the cabbie." He'd told Mae about the cabbie jumping out the window and eluding his Chinese watchers. He'd also confessed to freezing and impeding Fong's efforts at capture.

"Don't worry, we'll find her. Our Lucinda's resourceful. Wouldn't surprise me if she escapes all on her own." Mae's tone carried only optimism.

"It's been over a day. I am sure that Clark woman's involved but Fong's cousins say everything is normal at her houses. Besides, Fong said they drove Lucinda away in the cab. They didn't rush her across the street and into the house."

Mae could think of nothing more encouraging to say because her fear regarding Lucinda's safety was also growing despite the brave show she was putting on for her distraught son. Maybe they had lost Lucinda for good. Hush those thoughts, she silently chastised herself. Fear wouldn't help, only doing. So she continued, "Lucinda is strong and she's survived worse things, far worse things than you or I can imagine. Don't you dare give up. She never did, even when most folks would have."

Her words triggered a sharp glance from her son. Lucinda had always been very private about the years before he'd met her. Guess maybe she hadn't been so private when talking to his mother. For some reason, that realization sent a frisson of jealousy through him.

Mae saw the expression on his face and interpreted it correctly, "There are some things that are easier to tell another woman," she said softly.

Sage said nothing though his imagination stirred with the image of Lucinda as a child and the possible horrors others had inflicted on her.

"Fong's cousins are watching the ships and the trains?" Mae asked, her question a welcome intrusion into his thoughts.

Sage stirred. "Yup, he has men posted on the wharf and at the station looking for any woman being manhandled aboard."

Mae wanted to stay and comfort him but she couldn't. "Millie Trumbull came by. She said Carrie Lynne and little Emma Jane are both healthy, no TB."

"Well, that's good news. I think Terry Tobias is also okay given how hard he works. I haven't seen him cough, act sickly, or show a fever," Sage said.

"Good. I want to take the children to see their mother today. I'd like to take Terry too, but that would mean telling him that you're involved."

Sage raised a weary hand to wave away that particular worry. "Doesn't matter now. I'm not working at Speedy anymore. It's high time Terry learns that there's a lot of people looking for his brother. Maybe it'll raise his spirits. He might even be able to sleep once he knows."

Terry and Matthew were both in their room at Franklin's boarding house. Matthew was quietly reading on his bed while Terry had been trying to sleep but he'd mostly been tossing and turning. Both sat up at the sound of people climbing the stairway.

At a soft tapping on the door, Matthew jumped to open it. Mae Clemens stood in the doorway holding Carrie Lynne's hand. Behind her stood Millie Trumbull, holding baby Emma Jane.

Terry leapt from his bed. Joy and fear raced across his face as he looked from his siblings to the two women. Mae felt a surge of pity and rushed to reassure him. "Don't worry, Terry. We're not here to take you back to the Children's Aid Society. Mrs. Trumbull and I are here to take you children to see your mother in the hospital."

As the five of them rode the Oregon Water and Power train to the sanatorium, Mae explained how Mr. Miner had met Glad and witnessed his kidnapping. "That's why Mr. Miner has been working at Speedy

Messenger. We figured that you might know something about the kidnapping but were too afraid to talk about it."

Terry's face paled but he made no denial, saying instead, "They took Dougie and Glad. Told me to stop stirring things up and be a 'good boy.' They gave me this." He pulled a copper wristband from his pocket. "This is Glad's. Mother gave it to him for his last birthday."

Mae nodded. "Yes, it took some time but we figured that out. We've been searching for your brother these last few weeks. Yesterday, the same people took one of our friends. Her name is, Lucinda Collins. She was helping us look for Glad. Now, we're searching for both of them."

Terry's eyes filled with tears. "Mr. Miner's been trying to find Glad? And, is he looking for Dougie too?"

Mae and Millie exchanged looks, with Millie giving a slight shake of her head. It would do Terry no good to learn that his friend was dead. So, Mae only said, "Mr. Miner and a whole lot of others, including the police, are out looking for them. We're certain that Vera Clark woman and Speedy Messenger are both involved."

A thoughtful look settled on the young boy's face. "Something kinda peculiar is going on at her house."

"What do you mean?"

"Well, last night she yelled a lot. Didn't even try to—" here he flushed and couldn't finish.

Mae nodded. "Mr. Miner told me how she likes to embarrass young boys, so you don't have to explain. But, what did you see?"

"There were travel trunks in the hallway and her maid was running up and down the stairs loading things into them. I think Mrs. Clark's fixing to leave."

Millie and Mae exchanged looks. "That cabbie raised the alarm, I'll bet," Mae said.

"Cabbie?" Terry echoed.

"Yes, there's a cabbie that seems to be involved. He has a bad burn scar on the side of his face," Mae said.

"I've seen that fellow a bunch of times. He's always with Willard," Terry said.

"Who is Willard?" Mae asked sharply.

"He's this huge man who comes by Speedy Messenger to pick up the earnings. That cabbie you were talking about is the one who always brings him."

"Where does he take the money?" Mae prodded.

Terry shrugged. "I don't know. I guess to the owner of the messenger company."

"Who is the owner?" Mae was leaning forward, her urgency telegraphing to little Emma who began fussing. Millie tried to jiggle her quiet but it didn't work. Carrie Lynne reached out and took the baby into her arms. Emma's eyes widened and she touched her sister's braid before sticking a thumb in her mouth and going quiet.

Mae tried to relax. "Do you know who the owner is?" she asked again.

Terry shook his head. "He never comes down to the office. Sometimes, Willard comes and runs things while Pringle and Kimble leave for a meeting with him."

Mae and Millie exchanged disappointed looks that Terry caught because he added, "I know the owner is a lawyer, 'cause I heard Willard say one time that the meeting was canceled because a judge ordered the boss to show up in court with his client. Leastways, that's how come I figure he's a lawyer."

Millie's lips twisted but all she said was, "It figures."

Mae pondered the situation before saying aloud, "Wonder where we could find that Willard fellow."

Terry straightened on the wood slat bench. "He's easy to find. I seen him a bunch of times at Mrs. Clark's."

Mae was putting the pieces of information together when Terry spoke up. "That Willard is mean. Once they caught a Speedy messenger stealing from a customer. Willard hurt him so bad that he went to the hospital. And, he's got a gun. I saw him cleaning it right there in Vera Clark's parlor."

The group fell silent while the electric train, purportedly the first of its kind in the country, rolled serenely on. Soon they were passing Milwaukie's brickworks and orchard fields. Mae, however, felt anything but serene. She twitched in her seat, fighting an overwhelming urge to jump off the train as soon as possible and catch the next one heading back to the city. Mr. Fong and Sage needed to know Terry's information.

At last the train braked to a stop at Park and River Road and they disembarked. Millie cast a sympathetic look at Mae. "Nothing you can do now. The return train doesn't arrive for another hour. We'll make sure we catch it."

Mae took a deep breath and nodded. She forced herself to focus on the children who were looking from her to Millie as if sensing an urgency they didn't understand. "Come, children, let's go see your mama," Mae said, with all the lightheartedness she could muster. She took hold of Carrie Lynne's hand, while Millie hefted Emma Jane onto her ample hip.

The TB Sanatorium sat in a park-like setting. They trooped up the long grassy drive that wound beneath towering fir trees toward a row of small cottages sitting atop a bluff high above the river. The tiny white-washed structures had screened-in porches fronted by neatly tended gardens. The sunlit air was crisp and carried a sweetness untainted by the city's woodstoves and horse manure.

As they walked, Millie Trumbull spoke pridefully about the facility. "Our cottages have hot and cold running water and even soaking tubs. We have a health center with an x-ray machine to track the disease. Our patients spend every minute breathing this clean, fresh air. We give them healthful food in spotless surroundings. Most important, we make sure they have complete rest." She looked directly at Terry and said, "We are taking very good care of your mother but she is still very sick. Fortunately, her TB is in only one lung. That makes it easier for her to get better."

The children listened quietly as they gazed owl-eyed around them at the sanatorium's extensive grounds. When they were close to the tiny cottages, Millie Trumbull made them all stop. She looked soberly at the two oldest and said, "You will be visiting your mama on the screened porch of her cottage. She's waiting for you. It is important that you don't hug, kiss or touch her because TB is very contagious. We don't want you three to catch it. And, she doesn't want that either. We can't have her worrying."

Millie led them up the steps of the nearest cottage and opened the screen door onto the veranda. Three women lay in beds, blankets pulled to their chins. Mary Tobias occupied the bed farthest from the door. Upon seeing her children, she broke into a wide smile and struggled to sit up until a white-aproned nurse quickly stepped forward and gently pushed her back down against the pillows.

"Now Mary, you must stay lying down." The nurse turned toward the children who were eagerly looking toward their mother. "Come closer, children. Your mother can only whisper because we want her to save her lungs. Please remember that you cannot touch her just yet. But I know she wants to hear about you children. She's been very worried and that's not good."

The nurse turned to Millie Trumbull. "How good to see you, Secretary Trumbull," she said respectfully but also with some warmth. "Dr. Lane was here this morning and says we are at full capacity, forty patients." There was pride in the woman's voice.

The children, meanwhile, edged closer to the bed with Carrie Lynne holding Emma Jane on one side and Terry on the other. Mary looked at her children and smiled wide, even as tears coursed down her cheeks. She began whispering to them and they nodded and chirped in return.

Millie, Mae and the nurse retreated to the cottage's doorway where the nurse ushered them inside. The room was simply furnished. Three single beds stood against three walls, each bed having a chair and a small dresser beside it. Every wall sported a screened window. Heavy blankets piled atop each bed would keep the patients warm as the night chill flowed through the open windows. A bathing room, with toilet and tub, filled the corner of the fourth wall. Millie stepped into the tiny room to turn on the tap. She nodded with approval when hot water hit her hand.

"How is Mary Tobias doing?" Mae asked.

"She's very weak and restricted to her bed. She's only allowed up to go to the toilet and to her bed on the veranda. We have to help her do both because she's so weak. But she's determined to get better and doing exactly as she's told. Since only one lung is involved, Dr. Lane is optimistic about her outcome. Even so, we're looking at nearly six months before she can leave. I know she's been worried about her children. It will do her a world of good now that she sees they're okay."

A puzzled look crossed the woman's face, "But, I thought Mary said she had four children. Isn't there another boy?"

Millie straightened and said, "There is another boy but some bad men took him. His name is Gladney but his family calls him, 'Glad.' I expect her son, Terry, is telling her right now that we have a lot of people looking for him. Please do your best to reassure her that we will find him," Millie said in a firm tone that Mae had not heard from her before.

Soon the five of them were heading back down the grassy drive to the train stop. The children and their mother had benefited from the visit. But their brief visit had tired Mary and, even before they'd left the porch, she had drifted off to sleep. The two children chattered as they headed away down the lane, their worries lighter now that they'd seen their mother receiving good care. Mary, in turn, was also reassured at seeing all three children well taken care of. With tears in her eyes, she'd thanked Mae and Millie for their efforts to find Glad.

Back aboard the train, urgency seized hold of Mae. If her hand had been on the train's throttle she'd have pushed it to full and blasted through every station without stopping. But she wasn't at the controls so she gritted her teeth and smiled while begrudging every station stop, every boarding passenger, and every curve slowing their return to Portland.

TWENTY TWO

His neck had a crook in it from sprawling on the splintered board-walk with his head lolling against the brick wall. He looked at the bottle beside him and again wished it held something other than weak, cold coffee. And, not for the first time, he wondered whether he was wasting precious time. But what else could he do? He'd looked everywhere. This was the place that drew him—why he didn't know. It teased like a faint light behind fluttering leaves.

He'd been playing the wastrel drunk and keeping an eye on Vera Clark's three houses for over five hours. He had memorized every single shop, house, and light post as far as he could see in both directions. The sign of every café, barbershop, job agency, gambling joint, crib, grill, and saloon was engraved on his memory. He'd counted every raggedy awning, furled and unfurled, more than once.

It had been a mistake to start so early in the day. The brothel business didn't really get going till sundown. Strangely, she'd had not a single customer. Despite being near Erickson's saloon, not a soul had knocked on the doors of Clark's three houses.

Dusk was minutes away. Down the street, a lamplighter used his long stick to light the only gas fixture on the block. The intersection's electric light began glowing dimly, its gradual brightening a harbinger of the eventual extinction of the lamplighter's job. Lucinda had been missing for three days.

With a groan, Sage rose. The darkening sky meant that he and other unfortunates could now occupy the crib rooms for which they'd already paid their twenty-cent rent—though, in his case, he'd paid an extra ten cents for the privilege of having the first pick of rooms.

It was marginally warmer inside. After receiving his key from the bored desk clerk, Sage headed upstairs. As he climbed, plaster crumbles crunched beneath his boots and the breath-catching smell of stale urine, tobacco smoke, and musty filth filled his nose. His room door, only slightly stronger than cardboard, shook beneath his hand as he unlocked the padlock. He saw what he expected when he entered the 6 x 5 x 10-foot space. Chicken wire filled the gap between the top of the thin plywood walls and ceiling. A narrow cot, single chair, door hook, and oil lamp on the window sill were the only furnishings. But he didn't care since the window faced the right direction. Sage moved the chair in front of the window, raised the sash an inch for fresh air and left the lamp unlit.

"I 'bout gave myself heart pain getting here and still no Sage!" Mae was pacing her room, her impatience mounting. The sinking sun's gold had faded from the laced-edged curtains and the blackness outside was turning her windows into mirrors. "Grab hold of yourself, Mae Clemens. Anybody hearing you going on would think you demented," she scolded.

She stopped in the middle of the room, unsure of what to do next. She should be downstairs; the supper hour was in full swing. But she had to find Sage. Tell him what Terry had said about that Willard fellow and Vera Clark's trunks and the lawyer boss.

Fong had added to her frustration when he'd just come upstairs to say that the cousins couldn't find Sage. "They look everywhere in the North End, especially around Vera Clark's and they not find him anywhere."

"Well, I'm gol darned if I'll hang around here waiting." But, where should she look? Fong was certain Sage had planned to return to the North End. What was there that might keep him away from Mozart's?

She strode to the window, yanked aside the curtain and stared up and down the street. "That's it. I'm done sitting on my fanny!" She'd told Fong everything she'd learned from Terry. If Sage returned before she found him, then Fong could tell him.

There was neither moon nor stars. Unless passing under the street lamp or across lighted windows, pedestrians were merely shambling black shapes. In the next block, Vera Clark's red curtains began glowing as lamps were lit. Still, none of Erickson's booming business shifted toward Clark's. Their continued absence was making him uneasy. He fidgeted on the chair seat which hardened with each passing hour. Still, sitting inside was better than the rotten boardwalk and brick wall.

The neighborhood had turned lively. Drunks staggered and hollered their way down the street. Ladies of the night strode up and down the block, lounged in doorways and against the lamp post. Their face paint, ribald banter, and exaggerated hip-swings issued invitations to those who looked their way. Here and there the firm, purposeful steps of sober men contrasted sharply with the street side debauchery as did the swift boy messengers dodging drunk's grasping hands and ignoring the streetwalkers' teasing calls. He'd watched a young girl hurry past, a stack of newspapers clutched to her chest. All and all, it was a typical night in the North End with not a single thing hinting at where Lucinda might be.

His eye caught on the figure of an old lady. It was the second time she'd passed beneath his window. Her drooping skirt, lopsided hat and painful limp typified many destitute old women. Then he bent forward, squinting as the woman trudged through the gas lamp's wavering pool of light. When she reached the next block's end and turned to trudge back again, he was sure.

Slipping out the door and snapping the padlock shut, he went down the stairs, timing it so he stepped out the door and was at her side before she noticed him. In a whisper, he asked, "And just what is a lady of your quality doing down here?" Startled, she jumped and then slugged his shoulder.

"Ouch, that hurt!" he said aloud. The two streetwalkers by the lamp laughed, one of them calling out, "What kind of weird bugger are you? That'll teach you not to mess with old ladies!" Her companion added raucous guffaws.

He grabbed Mae's elbow and steered her away from the women. "Come on, let's get some coffee. They turned a corner and walked a block before entering one of the North End's minuscule cafés. She ordered coffee while he had a plate of sausage, kraut and mashed potatoes. While he chewed, she told him what Terry had said about the lawyer boss, Clark, and Willard.

"Whew," he said, sitting back in his chair. "That proves the connection. We thought Clark was trying to protect the pedophile's house. We were dead wrong. She's connected to Speedy Messenger."

"The Willard fellow sounds dangerous."

"I know he is. I'm sure he's the one who grabbed Glad. And, Fong said a big man pushed Lucinda into the cab. I'll bet that was Willard, too." Elbows on the table, Sage pressed his fingers against his skull until they turned white.

When he finally dropped his hands and straightened, his voice was firmer. "We have to find this Willard character and take him down. He has to know where Glad and Lucinda are."

"What about the two galoots that Henry Russell fellow photographed? Wouldn't they know?" Mae asked.

Sage shook his head. "As of noon, Hanke hadn't found either one of them. He said a rail clerk thought they'd boarded the southbound morning train. Hanke has telegraphed up and down the line. With luck, a not-so-welcoming committee will greet them at one of the stops. But, even if they're found, it'll take some time to get them back up here."

"Well, then, what about the cabbie?"

"He's disappeared too," Sage said, and felt that familiar flare of desperation. "It looks like we're down to Clark, Willard, the mysterious boss, and the two Speedy Messenger managers. I don't like it that Clark's packing up. It explains why she's had no customers all day."

"You think those Speedy fellows, Pratt and Kimble, know anything?"

"They sure the heck know who their boss man is and he's the one we want to catch. The others are just his lackey's. I think I'll go pay Kimble a visit. He's the one on duty tonight." Sage stood, tossed money on the table, clapped on his hat and headed for the door with Mae hurrying to follow."

"You've been outside Clark's house for six hours and haven't seen Willard. I got a feeling that we'd better not lollygag around much longer," Mae said, as she stepped onto the boardwalk. "I'm going to stay put outside Clark's brothel. Fong will be down soon."

Sage didn't argue. What he'd learned in the three years since they'd been reunited was that Mae Clemens's "feelings" were usually right. He handed her the key to the crib padlock and told her how to find it. After surprising her with a peck on the cheek, he headed toward Speedy Messenger.

Lucinda had spent what felt like hours in blackness. At least she thought it must have been hours. With no light and little noise, it was hard to measure time. For a long while she explored, keeping her hand stretched out and her steps tentative. She daren't injure herself—not when she might have to run. But she was achingly tired. The digging had been hard work and it seemed like forever since she'd slept.

Having explored every corner of the cellar, she'd returned to sitting on the crate. The next while was spent imagining Glad shuffling his way through the pitch dark, blindly holding the pipe before him as he hunted for the tunnels under the streets. She could imagine his eyes wide and staring, hoping for light glimmering from behind the cellar walls. Thinking about Glad took her through a gamut of feelings—hope, fear, and guilt.

Hope that he'd avoid capture by shanghaiers and no-good thugs and find some kindly Chinese. That Fong would be told and come to her rescue. But first, Glad had to get away and that's where her fear-filled thoughts lay. Even if he was beyond the reach of Vera Clark and her Willard thug, there were so many dangers in the underground for a ten-year-old boy—no matter how street-savvy he was.

As always, her circling thoughts eventually landed on guilt. She'd sent a child into the underground, without a light. What chance did he have?

She sighed heavily and tried to reassure herself she'd done the right thing. From what Vera said, Glad would have had no chance if he'd stayed in this cellar. Cabin boys on shanghai ships experienced a short, brutal life of starvation and abuse. Few ever made it back home.

She forced herself to stop thinking of the boy, stumbling through the dark. Instead, she thought of Sage. Knowing him, he'd be frantically searching for her. He'd pull out all the stops, haunt the streets above while wracking his brains to figure out where she was being held. Would he find her in time? Or was that carriage ride the last time they'd ever see one another?

She let herself escape into the remembered warmth of his thigh pressing against hers and the smell of him, a mix of musty John Miner clothes and the underlying clean scent of John Adair. Tears trickled down her cheeks, turning chill as they dropped onto her folded hands.

A sound she'd been listening for all along snapped her thoughts back into the cellar. Now it had come. Someone was descending from upstairs. The crack at the door's bottom began glowing brighter as the lantern advanced. Quickly she pawed at the pile of clothes to reassure herself that maybe it would fool that vile woman and her hulking sidekick. Glad needed all the time she could get him.

TWENTY THREE

SAGE'S HEART JUMPED IN HIS throat as every step brought a prayerfully whispered, "Lucinda." Panic was taking hold. If Vera Clark was packing up and the others had already left town it meant those behind this scheme wouldn't want to leave any loose ends. Lucinda and Glad were loose ends.

Ahead, dark figures huddled outside the Speedy Messenger door. That made no sense. It was a cold night. Why weren't they inside? A few strides closer and he recognized the messenger boys. Speedy's windows were dark with none of the feeble gaslights burning.

"What's the matter? Why's everyone outside?" Sage asked Christopher, the group's unofficial spokesman.

"They done locked us out. Kimble sent every one of us out on errands and when we got back he'd locked the door and done a runner. Turns out there weren't no real messages or errands. He just wanted us gone so he could lock up without our knowing. The bastards owe all of us money," he said, to angry, agreeing murmurs from five others.

Sage looked at their pinched, cold faces. "Where's Terry Tobias?" he asked.

"Kimble sent him out, too, but he ain't come back. It's kinda strange."

Sage swallowed hard. He didn't think his nerves could tolerate one more missing person. "What do you mean? Where was he sent? What's 'strange'?"

"Kimble sent him over to that Vera Clark's whorehouse. But I don't think he made it because she called up complaining. When I was heading out to fetch a bogus message, I heard Kimble on the telephone, trying to calm her down," Christopher said.

Sage thought back. Had he seen Terry outside Vera Clark's? Admittedly, he hadn't spent much time studying the children in the street. Terry could have been one of those flitting in and out of the pools of light. Somehow, he didn't think so.

"When did Kimble send you all out on the phony errands?"

"'Bout an hour ago." Christopher turned to the smallest boy who was sniveling and snapped, "Stop your gol darn blubbering. Kimble cheated every darn one of us out of our money!" The tense lines around Christopher's mouth said that, despite the stern words, he too was despairing.

"But Chris, we don't got no food ta home. We was counting on that money to eat tonight."

Sage looked into the small boy's thin face. Quickly he calculated the amount of money he had in his pockets. Wordlessly, he stepped forward and began handing out coins to their surprised gratitude. Once all his money was gone he said, "Boys, go on home. There's no point in staying out in this cold. Kimble won't be back."

They disappeared into the night, leaving him alone outside the office. Stepping forward he peered through the window and saw that no coin box sat on the table. Nothing of value remained—only the scarred and broken down furniture.

Fear bubbled up like acid in his throat. An alert had gone out. The rats were fleeing. Did that mean Lucinda and Glad were dead? Indecision froze him on the spot. What should he do next?

Cursing he began running toward Clark's. His pocket watch said 11:30. By this time, Fong should have joined up with Mae. They needed to talk. Make a plan. Figure things out.

This time, three weary people stood outside Hanke's apartment door. After his initial surprise, he gestured them inside. A thin layer of dust indicated that the sparsely furnished room seldom received attention from the busy sergeant. A sofa and a worn leather armchair sat next to a table holding an oil lamp. It appeared that the Sergeant read in his spare time because a shelf overflowed with books. An open newspaper on the floor and Hanke being fully clothed suggested he'd been reading when they'd knocked.

After directing them to seats, Hanke bustled about making coffee. Once they all held cups he said, "We've found the two who attacked your photographer. The Redding police caught them during the train sweep we'd requested." He raised a hand to still their sudden excitement, saying, "Unfortunately, street assault is not an uncommon crime as you well know. We want to go fetch them but Chief Hunt has to convince the board of police commissioners it is worth the expense of the train fare and the wages of two police escorts. Approval could take a few days and it's not guaranteed."

"But, they're involved in the kidnapping of Glad and Lucinda. Maybe in the death of that Spencer boy," Sage protested and leapt to his feet to pace.

"I know, I know," Hanke said. "I've told Chief Hunt our suspicions about their involvement in all that. He rightfully pointed out that we don't have an iota of proof. So, while he thinks we're on to something, he doubts the police commissioners will. They're tight-fisted with the money. Remember, we're policing a population that's doubled but with only half the men we had before. Thank the taxpayers for that—or rather the rich bastards who spend money every election cycle to prevent a tax increase. All to their own greedy benefit, I might add."

Sage whirled and said, "Hell, I'll pay for the damn cost. Tell Hunt that!" Frustration and fear put a sharp edge on his words.

Hanke raised an eyebrow but said, "Okay. I'll tell him that a mysterious benefactor wants to cover the cost. But, he'll think it strange and want to know more. What should I tell him?"

Silence filled the room until Mae said, "How about if I talk to Millie? See if she'll say the National Child Labor Commission is paying the cost. That would make sense. After all, it was their photographer who got clobbered."

"Great idea," Sage said with relief. "Can you ask her first thing tomorrow and let the Sergeant know?"

Glad's head was a swirling ache and his stomach was nauseous. He opened his eyes and panicked. It was pitch dark—was he blind? Where was he and why did his head hurt? Wherever he was, it smelled funny. He lay on his back. The sickness passed and the pain turned dull and centered in his forehead. He reached up to touch a painful lump.

Memory came roaring back. He wasn't blind, he was in the underground. He remembered the cellar, the awful woman, the big man, and the kind woman. "Lucinda," that was her name.

She'd helped him to escape from the cellar into the underground. He was supposed to do something. Something important. He lay in the dust, struggling to recall what it was.

Eyes brimming with tears, he rolled over onto his side, pulled his knees up and began rocking gently back and forth. Rocking always soothed him and cleared his mind ever since he was a baby. Gradually, his fear and despair lessened—enough that memory returned. He'd been walking in the dark like she told him, holding the pipe out to make sure he didn't run into something. But he had anyway. It must have been a board or a beam, the height of his forehead. When he started walking again he'd hold the pipe higher, maybe wave it up and down.

Pipe. Oh, no! Where was the pipe? Glad stopped rocking and sat up carefully after feeling overhead, making sure he wouldn't crack his noggin on something. Nothing was above him. He started patting the dust and, sure enough, his hand found the round metal length of pipe. He sighed with relief.

Now, what else? What was he supposed to do? Where was he supposed to go? A nonsense sing-song phrase slipped into his head. He squeezed his eyes shut, trying to get past the pain in his forehead to capture that phrase. And there it was, "Fong. Kam. Tong." After saying it aloud a few times, he was sure that was it. It sounded Chinese.

What did that mean? Why would he . . . then he remembered everything, as if someone had flipped a switch in his head. She'd told him, "Avoid any white men you might see in the underground. Find some Chinese men, say those three words."

Oh, Lord! He was supposed to be rescuing her. How long had he been knocked out? It could have been a day or two; leastways that's what he heard about being knocked out. Was she already dead? That Vera Clark would be real mad when she found out he'd escaped.

Glad clambered to his feet and stood undecided. What direction should he go? Carefully he raised the pipe before him, this time as high as his head. Nothing. He took another step and raised it again. "Thunk" it went and bounced in his hand. There was a beam, low down. This was what he'd hit with great force. Walked smack dab into it.

He thought back. He'd come to, lying on his back, his feet closest to the beam. That meant he had been moving toward the beam. So, that was the direction he'd walk. But how far?

She'd told him to get some blocks away before he looked for help. How many tunnels under the street had he already gone through since leaving Clark's block? Four. He remembered that. He'd counted each one aloud to help his memory. So, he was four blocks away from Clark's. The last tunnel had been way longer. That meant a wide street. Burnside was a wide street. He was supposed to travel across another block and through one more tunnel after Burnside. Then he'd be in the second block south of Burnside, right where she said he should find some Chinese people.

Okay then. He'd go forward through one more tunnel. That would land him five blocks from Clark's. Surely that was far enough.

Suddenly a faint light wavered in distance, getting brighter. Oh dear, that could be the big man looking for him or some other bad men—shanghaiers maybe. Where could he hide so they wouldn't see him?

Calm down, Glad. When the light gets closer, you'll be able to see what's around you. These basements got lots of junk in 'em. Once you can see, you can lay down behind some of it. Glad froze and watched as the light strengthened.

The rattling of the stairway padlock set her heart racing. "How long has he been gone?" she asked herself. "Long enough that he should have found help, yet, here I sit," she answered glumly.

She spread her skirts wide. She could only hope that when their light hit the pile of clothes, the hidden roll she'd fashioned would look like a small boy's body.

The door opened to reveal only Vera Clark and her henchman. Relief washed over her like a cool spring shower. They held no recaptured ten-year-old boy in their clutches. And, Clark's henchman was here, not off searching for Glad.

Clark must have seen Lucinda's relief because she snapped. "Don't know why you're so happy. It's not like I bring you good news. Like I told you yesterday, this is the day you get to smell the sea—at least until they make you drink it. Willard here will be returning in a few minutes to haul you both to the ship."

She said, "Yesterday," Lucinda thought with quiet satisfaction. That meant Glad had been gone for at least twelve hours. He'd gotten clean away from these two. A second thought dashed that momentary hope.

Surely, by now, he would have found some Chinese men? Said Fong's name? So, why hadn't they rescued her?

Clark's forehead wrinkled and she snatched the lantern from Willard's hand and raised it high. "Where's the boy?" she demanded,

"Shh, he's asleep," Lucinda gestured to the pile of clothes. "At least give him that moment of peace."

"Huh. Well, in two more hours he better be wakey, wakey, and ready to go. I've got a lot to do and the sooner the both of you are out of my hair, the better," Clark handed the lantern back to Willard and with a flip of her long skirt, she turned toward the door.

A slow sigh of relief escaped Lucinda. She'd thought it silent but something alerted Clark. She turned slowly to face Lucinda. "Wait a minute. Why hasn't that pile of clothes moved if the boy is under there?"

"He's dead tired, that's why," Lucinda said firmly.

Clark stared at her and keeping her hard eyes on Lucinda's, she said, "Willard, go give that pile a good poke. Make sure the kid's under there."

Lucinda didn't break their gaze even though her heart began thudding in her ears. This was it. God knows how this evil woman will react.

Willard shuffled across the floor and launched a kick into the pile. His foot hit nothing solid, nearly throwing him off balance. With a quick look at Clark, he put down the lantern and began throwing the clothes aside. "There ain't nobody here," he growled. He grabbed the lantern and raised it high, sending its light around the cellar. "That kid ain't nowhere in here."

"What?" Clark shrieked. "Where the hell is he?"

Willard's eyes narrowed and he moved toward Lucinda who clutched the crate as if it were a life raft in a roiling ocean. "Maybe she's done hid him under this crate," he said and gave Lucinda a one-handed shove that tumbled her into the dirt. He kicked the crate and it overturned, revealing emptiness and no child.

"Vera, come take a look at this," he said to Clark.

Lucinda looked at the hole she'd done her best to refill but, in the lantern light, there was no mistaking that the dirt had been seriously disturbed.

Clark looked at the dirt, at the secure padlock and then whirled to face Lucinda. "You stupid bitch!" she screamed, and slapped Lucinda across the face so hard that it sent her back onto her elbows. Clark didn't stop attacking. She sent a sharp-toed boot into Lucinda's hip and would have done it again except Willard pulled her away. "Ma'am, don't damage the goods. I'll find the boy. He can't have gotten far. It's pitch dark in there and he didn't have no light."

Clark took a few deep breaths as she struggled for composure. With a shaking hand, she smoothed back a strand of hair and shook the dust from her skirt. She turned to Willard and snarled, "Maybe we won't sell our Lucy. Maybe I'll just have you send her direct to hell."

TWENTY FOUR

Terry crouched behind an empty newsstand counter across from the hotel. Maybe the fellow he followed was a nobody—just one of Vera Clark's sleazy customers. But something told him he wasn't. Having nothing to do but wait, Terry pondered that question and finally decided that it was the man's business-like walk that made it seem like he wasn't a customer. Most North End brothel customers sauntered or staggered. This fellow had gone in and then come out of the middle house and down the steps like he was running from a fire and couldn't get away fast enough. And, he was posh. Too posh for a place like Vera Clark's. Posh like a lawyer. He knew that Mr. Miner and Mrs. Clemens missed seeing the fellow because Terry had watched them meet up and leave. So, Terry followed the stranger.

Now he was waiting outside the Imperial hotel. Terry smiled, mentally applauding his earlier boldness. Frustrated because he couldn't see the man's face well enough to describe it, he'd followed the man right through the hotel's front door. He'd got a good look at the fellow's face when the man stepped into the elevator and turned to face the door. Now, Terry would recognize him anywhere.

"Hey, you!" the desk clerk had called. "What do you think you are doing? If you have a message, you deliver it to the desk. You don't go up in the guest elevator!"

"Oh, sorry," Terry said turning away from the closing elevator door toward the desk. "I thought he was the fellow I was supposed to give this message to." Terry raised the envelope he'd been sent to deliver to Vera Clark.

"Who's it for?" asked the desk clerk, his tone a bit more helpful.

Terry said the first name that came into his head, "Vernon Clark."

The desk clerk quickly scanned his register and shook his head. "No. We don't have Mr. Clark registered here. You must have the wrong hotel."

Terry slapped the side of his head, apologized and quickly left. Once outside, he dithered, deciding to wait and see whether the posh man walked anywhere else. He'd give it an hour or so. If the stranger stayed put, then Terry planned to return to Franklin's boardinghouse because Matthew might know where to find Mr. Miner or Mrs. Clemens. He didn't know why but he was certain the man he followed knew what had happened to Glad. Finding his brother was all he cared about.

Glad crouched behind a pile of discarded furniture and watched as the two men with the lantern passed by. There was enough light that he could see that they were scruffy and he could hear them arguing.

"I told you we should have waited for Orville. He knows the underground. We'll be stumbling around here forever and never will find the meeting place."

"We done waited long enough for him. He's probably off getting his snoot full. The captain says he ain't gonna wait. Once the tide's up, he's lifting anchor whether the boy and woman are aboard or not."

Those words made the hair on Glad's head tingle and stand up. A squeak of alarm escaped his lips.

"What was that?" One of the men asked and they both stopped and looked around.

"Seemed to come from over there, by that pile of junk," said one of them. The lantern lifted higher and silence followed. Glad stopped breathing, hugged the dirt floor and hid his face in his elbow. If they came closer, there was no place for him to run. He was in a corner. The light brightened as they moved toward him. He trembled and then his jaw set in determination. He had to rescue Miss Lucinda, no matter what. If they saw him, he'd rush them. Knock their lantern away and run. His grip tightened on his trusty pipe.

"Ah, hell. I ain't seeing nothing. It was probably just a rat. They're all over down here. We better stop wasting time. We gotta find the right basement in the next few minutes," one said, and their footsteps moved away. Glad slowly raised his head and peeked through the spokes of a discarded wagon wheel. Sure enough, the two men were shuffling in the opposite direction of where he planned to go.

Carefully, he stepped from behind the furniture, taking advantage of the last remnant of their lantern light. Though they scared the heck out of him, his memory of the lantern-lit basement meant he quickly found the last tunnel he needed to go through before he could look for help.

It was very short. That meant he'd been right about his location because Ankeny Street was only one wagon wide. Once he traversed that tunnel and was beneath the next block, he stood still and listened. A murmur of voices and laughter came from close by. Carefully, with the pipe waving before him, he advanced toward the sounds, becoming filled with fearful elation. That could be salvation up ahead.

Faint lines of vertical light strengthened and, after moving closer, he saw even more light. Now there was no doubt. Ahead was a boarded off cellar with people inside.

Slowly he stepped forward until he could put his ear to a crack between the boards. She'd told him, "Only go to the Chinese people." He had to hear what language these people spoke. Seconds later he was certain it wasn't English. It was either Chinese or Japanese. Glad took a deep breath and stepped forward to put his hand on the boards. He began gently feeling for the door that must exist. As he did, his ear picked up a click-clack sound.

At last his searching hand encountered the cool hardness of a metal door pull. Taking a deep breath he knocked. The noise inside stilled until the only sound Glad heard was his own breathing. He knocked again, this time louder and heard someone shuffling in his direction.

A voice on the other side of the door asked a question in Chinese and Glad paused unsure what to say to make them open the door. Finally, he remembered. "Fong Kam Tong," he said, his voice sounding weak and frightened to his ears.

The person on the other side of the door asked a question, but again, Glad couldn't understand. So he repeated, "Fong. Kam. Tong." This time, saying it loudly.

The metallic rattle of a padlock lifting from its hasp followed and the door swung slowly inward. A raised lantern lit Glad's face. A surprised gasp sounded but at least the door didn't slam closed. A small Chinese man stuck his head out to survey the underground. After assuring himself no raiding party lurked in the dark behind Glad, he gestured the boy inside and padlocked the door.

Once his eyes adjusted to the light, Glad saw that he was in a gambling den. There were seven men in the tiny cellar, all crowded around a table. A pile of coins was at each man's elbow. Cards ran down the middle of the table with other cards branching off like tree limbs. This was a fan tan game. He'd seen it played before on small sidewalk tables. But, in those games, no money appeared to change hands.

Even as he surveyed the scene his ears registered the rapid-fire of what his mother would call "jibber jabber" between the men. He couldn't understand but thought their tone was alarmed. He broke in and again said, "Fong Kam Tong", saying the words slowly and with confidence.

The man who answered the door raised a hand, turned to Glad and asked, "Ah! You want Fong Kam Tong?"

Glad nodded his head and said excitely, "Yes! Fong Kam Tong!"

The group seemed to relax as they exchanged a few words. A younger man got up from the table and walked to Glad. He said in careful English, "You want to find Fong Kam Tong?"

"Yes, yes!" Glad insisted, eagerly.

"Okay," the young man said. "We go. Find Fong Kam Tong. You follow."

Glad sighed with relief. Seconds later, he was following the young man up the stairs and through a heavy door at the top. Once through it, Glad noticed that they had exited a false-fronted cupboard. Their way turned stranger with every step and Glad had to fight a growing fear. What was this place? The man was leading him through a labyrinth of hallways, up and down stairs, through sliding panels and always there were six-inch thick doors, sometimes only three feet apart. The doors weren't locked against exiting, only against entering. Glad finally remembered reading about this kind of arrangement in the newspaper. The police were always raiding Chinese gambling dens. To prevent capture and confiscation, the Chinese hid their illegal gambling behind thick, locked doors, secret passageways, trick hallways, and, of course, in cellars that gave them a chance to escape through the underground.

After what seemed like forever, they passed beyond a door. There they found a young Chinese man sitting on a high stool beside a dirty window that filtered pale gray light from outside. His vantage point let him peer out and see who approached. The man leading Glad said something to the scout who jumped off the stool and raised the iron bar that secured the door. Seconds later, Glad and the man stood outside. Glad recognized Second Street, but what he reveled in was dawn's early light. It was the first daylight he'd seen in weeks.

"Hurry, hurry. We go find Fong Kam Tong," urged the young man as he turned and rapidly headed south. Glad trotted to keep up. A few blocks later, they entered a provision store. It looked and smelled like none he'd ever seen. Weeds and other strange things hung from the ceiling on wires. Huge glass jars held mysterious substances and twisted roots. All the labels were written in Chinese squiggles.

A tiny Chinese lady came forward and exchanged bows with the young man who said something that included the magic words, "Fong Kam Tong." The woman broke into a wide smile and turned to Glad. She asked, "You Glad boy? You missing boy?"

Glad nodded only to flush when he realized that her question had sent tears pouring from his eyes.

The woman's face softened and she said, "You safe now. This man go find Fong. Come, have tea. You rest." She gently tugged at his arm, guiding him toward a door at the back of the shop.

"Land sakes, Mae! What are you doing up at the crack of dawn?" Millie Trumbull demanded. She was standing in the doorway of her house, a wrapper tight around her sturdy body, her hair straggling from its nighttime bun. She didn't know it, but the fact Millie answered her own door sent Mae's opinion of her up a notch. Mae knew Millie's husband was a railroad executive which meant they could have afforded a maid. Instead, Millie did for herself.

"Come in, come in. I just finished feeding my husband breakfast and sending him off to work. The poor devil likes getting an early start," she said, swinging the door open.

Inside, Mae saw that the house was well-furnished but not ostentatious—just merely comfortable. She followed Mille into the kitchen and gratefully accepted a cup of coffee. She hadn't slept yet. They'd gone round and round at Hanke's, finally settling on a scheme that they hoped would reveal the man behind all the mayhem and free Lucinda and Glad.

Mae quickly filled Millie in and asked, "If I give you the money, would you be willing to tell Chief Hunt it came from National Committee on

Child Labor? Maybe say the Committee wants the attackers of their photographer arrested and tried?"

"Lord, yes. I suspect, if there's enough time, I could even convince the organization to pay for it."

"Nope. Time's too short. We can't wait. We need those two galoots here now. Sergeant Hanke thinks we can get two Redding police officers to escort them up on the next train, so long as we first wire the money for the officers' wages and four tickets."

Millie stood up. "Well, we better get going if you have the money. It'll take me a few minutes to get presentable."

Mae held up a staying hand. "One more thing, Millie. Do you think Henry Russell will be up to taking a few pictures for us? It could be a bit dangerous."

"Only way to know is to ask him. Lucky for us, he's camped out in my guest room. I'll wake him up and send him down."

TWENTY FIVE

"John, John." Sage jerked awake to find Knute beside his bed in dawn's gray light. Sage struggled into a sitting position. If Knute was still here, on a workday it was either before six a.m. or something bad had happened.

"What is it, Knute? Is something wrong with Ida or Matthew?"

"No, no. They are both just fine," Knute assured him. "Mrs. Clemens is not here. She left about half an hour ago. Ida asked that I come tell you the policeman, Hanke, is waiting for you in the kitchen."

"Have you seen Mr. Fong?" Sage asked.

"I checked. He's asleep in his room at the end of the hall. I did not wake him." Knute's glance toward the window told Sage the man was worried about being late to work.

Sage flipped back the covers. "Let Fong sleep. But, you go on to work, Knute. I'm awake now. Please tell Hanke, I'll be down in a minute. I've just got to get dressed."

Hanke sat in his usual chair, a cup of coffee before him and a glum look on his tired face. Sage wasn't the only one with only a few hours of sleep under his belt.

"Christ! Don't tell me I have to start the day by looking at another dead child," Sage greeted him and immediately felt ashamed of his surliness.

Hanke puffed out some air and shook his head. "Nope, this one's a man. But I remember you said one of the bad guys had a scar on his face. Well, that's what this corpse has."

Despite the heat from Ida's oven and pots, cold washed through Sage. "Let me get Fong. He saw the cabbie better than I did. We need him to come with us."

The three of them walked to Crofton's funeral home in silence. This time the mortician didn't smile a greeting as he said, "Sergeant Hanke, I'm getting more business from the police department than I am from families. I suspect that this will be another body for potter's field."

Dr. Lane's face was also grim though his eyebrows rose when first Sage and then Fong followed Hanke into the basement room. What he said, however, was, "At least, this time, there's no question about what killed him." Lane flipped back the sheet to expose the man's head and the gaping slash across his throat.

"His death was quick. Looks like the killer stood behind him."

Hanke cleared his throat. "No chance he did it to himself?"

Lane's head shake was adamant. "Not likely. A suicide will stretch his neck, throw his head back, making the skin taut. That makes the wound a clean cut. This one's jagged. Also, a suicide's cut tends to be shallow at the beginning, not deep like this wound."

Sage's knees suddenly weakened as his mind superimposed Lucinda's face onto the face of the man on the table. Fong must have sensed Sage's reaction because he stepped forward to grab Sage's elbow.

Lane turned to them. "Mr. Adair, this is the third time I've seen you in as many weeks. Are you becoming the police department's official identifier of bodies?"

Sage cleared his throat. "Believe me, I'm not here by choice. We've been looking for a man with a scarred face like this corpse. My friend here, Mr. Fong, saw the man more than once."

Lane turned to Fong. "So, is this the man you were looking for?"

Fong stepped forward, his face impassive. He quietly said a Chinese phrase, one of the few translations that Sage remembered: "May you now be free from sorrow and the causes of sorrow." He remembered the translation because he'd heard Fong intone the saying too many times in the last few years.

Fong turned and said to Hanke the words that sent a wave of despair washing over Sage, "That is him, the cabbie."

Lucinda was thirsty. The water jug was empty and had been for a long time. She tried to think of things other than her dry mouth and her empty stomach. At least she hadn't needed to use the piss pot for a long time. "Now, now, Lucinda, what have I told you about proper language?" she chided herself aloud, "You should have said, 'toilet facilities.'" She chuckled but it was a bitter chuckle. Soon, her language might make no difference at all.

She forced her thoughts onto more pleasant things. Like the spring rose buds that were just forming. In a few weeks, they'd flower. Portland was famous for its roses. There was even talk of lining city streets with more of them. Of course, if she was in the middle of the ocean or worse, she'd never see those buds bloom or smell their sweet scent. There were many things she loved in the world that she'd miss.

Whoops, back there again. Maybe she should think of Sage and Mae and Fong and Eich and the other friends she'd acquired through knowing Sage. They'd given her affection and her life meaning. For the first time, she felt like she was doing something good and right in the world.

Ah, Sage. Darn his black Irish good looks and kindness and humor and . . . hell, he had so many good parts to him. It was his on-again, off-again, attention that hurt. Mae asked her to be patient but, while she was waiting, who knows what could happen? For sure, if she didn't get herself out of this pickle, it wouldn't matter. She'd never again smell his scent, kiss his lips, snuggle against his chest, feel the rumble of his voice against her ear, or laugh with him.

Damn. Back to gloom again. What had happened to Glad? Help should have been here long before now. If she had to sit in the dark much longer, she was going to start screaming her head off. Why not?

As if triggered by this thought, the door at the top of the stairs squeaked open and footsteps thudded on the stairs. "That'll teach you, Lucinda girl," she muttered to herself. She stood. Damned if anyone was going to slap or knock her down again. The padlock rattled and the door opened. Clark and her henchman stepped into the cellar.

"What? You didn't dig yourself out?" Clark asked. "Maybe all your fine living has made you too fat?"

Lucinda sensed the one thing Clark would hate most was someone stonewalling her insults so she said nothing and kept her face impassive.

"Be that way," Clark finally said. "I was so hoping we'd have a real nice heart-to-heart. This is our last opportunity after all," Clark said, but Lucinda heard a satisfying edge of irritation beneath Clark's mild words. Clark shrugged. "Oh well, it doesn't matter. I'm leaving and will never see you, again, but I wanted you to remember me."

Quick as a snake's tongue, she darted forward and slapped Lucinda's face before jumping back. "Ever since I've known you, I've fought the urge to slap you silly. I find I like doing it," Clark said. "Unfortunately, we've run out of time, so that little tap will have to do."

Clark pulled a tiny gun from her dress pocket and gestured Lucinda to one side. "Willard here is going to open the door to the underground. Then you and he are going to meet the ship captain. He's expecting you. Got a place in the hold all picked out." If there was such a thing as an evil grin, Clark was pulling it off.

"Go ahead Willard, pull out the nails and take her away." Clark turned back to Lucinda, saying. "You better not give Willard any trouble. I've told him to kill you at the first sign of it. He's done me that service once already. Our Willard is handy with a knife. So, you'd best be on good behavior."

Willard got busy with the claw end of a crowbar, yanking out the two big spikes. He unlocked the padlock and swung the door open. A gust of damp, musty air swept into the cellar.

Still, Lucinda remained silent, staring at Clark, keeping her face expressionless though now it felt frozen from the effort. She'd die before giving Clark the satisfaction of hearing her beg. The other woman twitched but she neither spoke nor launched another attack. Too bad really, Lucinda was ready for her this time. Her fists were tight and she wanted nothing more than to punch the smirk off Clark's face.

But the woman wasn't completely stupid. She knew exactly which wounding arrow to shoot because she said, "The boy's been gone long enough. Must be somebody grabbed him. Maybe he's already out to sea. Or could be he's dead—lots of scary things happen in the underground. One thing for sure, he didn't bring back help, did he?"

It took all of Lucinda's willpower to remain mute and unmoving. The fingernails digging into her palm helped her to suppress her fury.

Clark shrugged. "It don't matter what happened to him. Time's run out for you." At those words, Willard tossed the crowbar aside and grinned, showing teeth that were black at the roots..

Clark turned to face Lucinda. "I won't say, 'see you later', because I'll never see you again. I won't say, 'have a nice trip', because I hope it turns into some kind of hell. So long, Lucinda Collins. I'm damn glad to finally see your backside."

She nodded at Willard who grabbed Lucinda's arm and jerked her toward the open door. Clark's shrill laughter followed them as they entered the tunnel into the underground.

❋   ❋   ❋

Sage hadn't strayed from his window. For a few extra under-the-table bucks the surly desk clerk had let him stay behind when he chased the rest of the tenants out and locked the door. In the two hours since, he'd not seen a single customer knock on Clark's front door. Instead, he watched with mounting anxiety as, one after another, her working girls left, suitcases and boxes in hand. It was obvious Clark had closed her brothel down. So, was Lucinda in there?

At this point, he could describe fear in a multitude of ways: A kick in the gut, a hollow stomach, a frantic whirling in his brain. None of the descriptions were big enough to capture how scared he was. What made it worse, was that he'd swear she'd been very near, close enough he'd almost heard her voice indistinctly murmuring in his ear. Maybe he had some of his great aunt Mary's psychic powers. If so, then he was now even more anxious because his sense of Lucinda's presence was abruptly absent. Had she died?

They weren't going to kick off their plan until later that night. Something was telling him that would be too late. They had to make the rats scurry sooner. Suddenly he straightened in his chair and leaned forward. Was that Terry standing at the corner, staring at Clark's house? Yes!

Sage jumped from his chair and ran for the door. Racing across the empty lobby Sage took note that the desk clerk was not at his post. That made sense what with the cribs closed down during the day. Sage opened the outer door, setting its spring bolt in the lock position. That way, the bolt would prevent the door from closing.

Once across the street, Sage softly called Terry's name. The boy whirled around, his face twisting fearfully until he saw Sage.

"Oh, finally," he exclaimed. "Matthew's out looking for you and Mrs. Clemens. I came back here because . . ." he paused, his forehead wrinkling before he shrugged and finished, "I didn't know where else to look."

Sage smiled. "Same with me. But why were you looking for me?"

"Last night, I followed that fellow I think is the boss. Anyway, he didn't look or act like one of Mrs. Clark's customers."

"Where'd he go?"

"The Imperial Hotel. He's staying there."

Terry's words nudged loose a memory. Early on, Sage had followed another man to that hotel who hadn't seemed to be Clark's customer. "Was he wearing a suit and looked kind of posh?" Sage asked.

Terry nodded eagerly. Sage didn't have time to think about what that meant because, over Terry's shoulder, he saw Fong running toward them.

TWENTY SIX

Willard pulled Lucinda through the brick-lined tunnel that led from Clark's basement into the underground. Water seeped from its walls and glistened in the lantern light before flowing into the muddy puddles sucking at her boots. She slowed her steps as best she could.

"Where are we going?" she asked. He didn't reply, just jerked her arm to speed her up. She pretended to stumble and went to her knees in the mud. With a grunt, he yanked her onto her feet as easily as if she were a three-year-old child. She yelped and he growled, "Shut up."

Upon entering the underground itself, the lantern's light shone about ten feet, beyond that she could see only shapes. Willard's boots scuffed through the dust sending it drifting upward into her face. She clamped shut her lips and raised her arm to cover her nose.

"Why are you doing this for her?" she probed. "Vera's probably heading out of town and leaving you behind to face the music for doing what she ordered."

He gave her arm a yank and said, "No, she ain't. This ain't our first rodeo together."

Willard's voice was unexpectedly high-pitched, shrill like an excited juvenile's. Still, she wanted to keep him talking. "You've been with her for some time?" she asked.

"Five years."

"Not here in Portland, then. Vera's only been here two years. Where were the two of you before that?" Lucinda cared nothing about the answer. If they kept talking, someone might hear and wonder why a woman, an American woman, was in the underground. Maybe they'd act on a chivalrous impulse and rescue her. Or, even better, maybe Mr. Fong's cousins were searching for her. Plus, there was the chance a distracted Willard might not notice she'd slowed her steps.

It didn't work. He sped up even as he said, "San Francisco. Stop dragging your heels or I'll yank your arm out of its socket," as he emphasized his declaration with a jerk.

"Ow!" she yelled far louder than the pain justified. "I'm wearing a skirt and I don't have long legs like you, Willard. Slow down. Otherwise, I'll trip."

He said nothing, only grunted, but his pace lessened.

She thought she'd give it one more try. "I bet you that, right now, Vera's finished packing and sending a messenger for a cab. You get back, the place will be empty."

"Nah, I got our train tickets in my wallet." He gave her arm a little twist and said, "You shut up. I don't want to hear no more from you. One more word, I'll stuff a damn kerchief in that yap of yours."

Lucinda stumbled along in silence, taking small steps, slowing him down, not knowing if it would help. She didn't know where she was. The lantern lit only concrete and brick walls, inky corners, and scatterings of rubble everywhere. Poor Glad, he must have been terrified. How could a ten-year-old find his way through this mess without any light?

Willard, though, seemed to know exactly where he was going because his stride didn't falter and soon they entered another tunnel. She tried to recall what direction they'd traveled. If she escaped, she needed to know in what direction to run. They'd exited Clark's heading east. Once through the second tunnel, Willard had turned right. That meant they were under the blocks between Second and First Avenues and heading south. It was the same route she'd told Glad to take.

She peered around, looking for signs of the boy. If he lay in a dark corner, she'd never spot him. Besides, he'd been gone more than a day. Once again, dread filled her at the thought of Glad being forced aboard a sailing ship. Forget it, Lucinda, she chided herself. You can't do anything about Glad now. You've got to figure out how to get away from Willard. Then you can start searching for Glad.

He hauled her through another tunnel. Now they were under the building east and across from Erickson's on Second. They were heading toward Burnside Street. Another two tunnels and they'd be beneath the blocks where many Chinese lived. She trusted Fong's men were still looking for her. That would be where she'd have the best chance of getting away or being rescued.

The next tunnel was the longest yet. It confirmed their location. They were passing under Burnside's wide road with its crowded sidewalks and two trolley tracks. She heard iron wagon wheels rattle over the cobbles and fought the urge to scream. Burnside was too busy and noisy. No one would hear her and Willard would gag her. If he did that, she'd be unable to scream when she needed to. She pressed her lips together, kept breathing through the sleeve across her nose and allowed Willard to haul her into the next basement.

Before Sage could say a word, Fong said, "Glad boy escape, find cousins. He safe."

At those words, Terry sagged to the ground as his knees gave way. Seconds later he was jumping up and down and waving his hands like a demented holy roller.

Sage grabbed the boy, "Shh. Don't draw attention to us. Stay calm. There's still more to do." The admonition worked and the boy settled down except for the joyful sparkling of his eyes.

Fong had more information to share. Glad says Lucinda is in Clark house cellar. Or, maybe in underground on way to ship. Boy hit head, lost track of time."

Now it was Sage who lost control. He whirled to run toward Clark's only to have Fong grab his arm. "We stick to plan. Glad say Willard has gun. Make Miss Lucinda real mad you get killed charging into house."

Sage froze on the spot, undecided. Fong patted his arm. "Eich on his way. I send Matthew to get Hanke and his men. Soon they have house surrounded."

"We need Clark to identify the boss. So, I guess you are right, we'll stick with the plan." Sage said, even as he gritted his teeth in frustration.

He turned to Terry. "Go over to the corner and stay out of sight. A ragpicker and his cart will turn up soon. Once he takes up a position on the side street go over and tell him who you are. We need you to do what he tells you to do, even if it seems peculiar. Okay?"

Terry's eyes widened with surprise and concern but he just nodded his agreement.

Sage turned back to Fong. "I guess that means you're heading below ground and I'm heading to Mozart's.

Fong nodded. "That the plan." For a moment his dark eyes studied Sage's grim face. "Don't worry. Everything go fine."

TWENTY SEVEN

EICH'S CART RATTLED AS HE pushed it down Third Avenue. He stayed close to the street curb, carefully sidestepping the ever-present horse manure. Because the street cleaners couldn't keep up, horse droppings tended to mound, leaving pedestrians to high step across the streets. Of course, cleaning North End streets was never a priority for the City. That same indifference was probably why only rotting, wooden boardwalks fronted the streets north of Burnside.

His floppy hat shadowed his face but Eich's eyes studied everyone. It was when he crossed Couch that he spied the boy he'd been hoping to see. Fong had described him well. Besides, the boy had to be Terry Tobias. No one else would have reason to lurk about on such a chill afternoon.

Eich halted before the center one of three houses that covered the southeast corner of Third and Davis. Dropping the cart's handles to the pavement, Eich pulled a folded sheet of clean white paper from his coat pocket. Mounting the steps he knocked on the door. A frantic woman, hair in wild disarray, threw open the door. "What the hell do you want?" she snarled.

Mutely, he extended the note to her, asking, "You be Miss Vera Clark?"

"Did you read it?" she said as she snatched it from his hand.

"No, Miss. I can't read," he lied. Technically, he hadn't read it but he knew what it said. He'd penned it using the perfect script he'd learned while attending the best of Eastern schools.

After giving a dismissive snort, she read the note slowly, her lips parsing out each word. Reaching the end, she whirled to holler. "Agnes,

I've got to go out. Help me fix my hair and then get me my coat." Eich peered around her and glimpsed travel trunks, with leather straps buckled, filling the dim hallway.

"Why are you still standing there?" Clark demanded. "Get on your way." She waved a shooing hand at him. He tipped his hat and returned to his cart. She watched until he rounded the corner onto Davis Street and disappeared behind her end house. She slammed the door and just missed seeing Terry Tobias jump from his hiding place and race after the ragpicker.

Terry stared dumbfounded at the fine suit of clothes the ragpicker thrust into his hands. A pair of polished shoes sat atop the clothes. "Hurry boy, get these on and get back on Third Street. If Clark comes out and waves down a cab, run to the corner and signal me and then hightail it over to the Imperial Hotel. Mr. Miner and Mrs. Clemens are waiting for you."

Still, Terry didn't move. Eich shoved him gently toward a narrow gap between two buildings. "Do it, boy. We don't have much time," he ordered. "I'll stand in front and make sure no one sees you."

Terry stepped into the gap and hurriedly began disrobing, hopping first on one foot and then the other while yanking off his boots. His canvas pants dropped and he donned trousers that felt silky on his skin. Thin-soled shoes replaced the scuffed boots. Next, his flannel shirt and canvas coat were hurriedly replaced by a white muslin shirt and a fine wool suit coat. The new clothes weren't as warm but that didn't matter. He'd be running.

He stepped over to the ragpicker who straightened his collar, buttoned the coat and nodded his approval. Terry had left his old clothes piled on the ground but Eich snatched them up and shoved them under the cart's tarp, saying, "Waste not, want not." Then he instructed, "If you see me come to the corner and wave it means she's gone out the back door and down to Second. Take off running to the Imperial if you see me do that."

Terry had just disappeared around the corner when Eich saw the woman cautiously slipping from behind the corner house. She hesitated at seeing him so he pretended to be busy tightening the tarp's ropes. Seconds later, she headed east on Davis toward Second Street.

He watched Clark round the corner and then he sped to Third and waved vigorously until a well-dressed young gentleman charged out of a doorway and ran south toward the business district.

Eich returned to his cart. He'd barely reached it when a troop of five policemen rounded the corner and hustled up to him. "Perfect timing," he told their leader. "She just left. Remember, the Willard fellow might be inside with a gun. So, be careful."

Hanke's men didn't hesitate. Two ran behind the houses to block escape that way. The other three ran to the front and charged across the center house's porch. One of them gave a mighty kick that burst the door open. They rushed into the house hollering, "Police!" A single woman's shrieks heralded their invasion. Minutes later, one of the officers returned to the porch and gestured for Eich to enter. Stepping across the threshold, Eich saw an open door and descending stairs.

One of the officers hustled up with a lantern. He and another officer cautiously descended the stairs with Eich trailing behind. An open padlock hung from a door hasp at the staircase's end. The officer quietly lifted the padlock and slowly eased the door open. Pistols raised, they stepped inside and lifted the lantern high.

The air was fetid with the smell of excrement. The lantern light revealed a small cellar containing only an empty wooden crate lying on its side, a jumbled pile of clothing, two metal pails sitting against a wall and some wooden boxes. Across the room, another door stood partially open. Eich crossed and pulled the door wide. On its other side a vaulted, brick tunnel led into blackness.

He turned to the officer holding the lantern and said, "May I have that lantern? I need to set a beacon."

Silently, the man handed it over. Eich sloshed its contents and was gratified to find it full of fuel. He walked to the tunnel's end and into the underground where he turned the lantern mantle to a high burn. After setting it down in the dirt, he retreated to the cellar and followed the men up the stairs.

Terry's feet flew up sidewalks and across streets. Maybe the light-weight shoes made his feet swifter. They certainly helped but, mostly, it was joy. Glad was alive. He was free. He was safe. Terry imagined his mother's face when she first caught sight of her youngest son. And Carrie Lynne, she'd cried buckets over Glad. He bet she'd cry again but she'd be grinning, too. Tomorrow they would go out to the sanatorium. Mr. Miner and that nice Mrs. Clemens would take them, he was certain of that.

Glad was free, Terry rejoiced over and over again as he ran. Then he realized that, if Glad was free, then so was he. No more Speedy Messenger Service. No more Willard. No more disgusting Vera Clark and people like her.

Rain began its cascade from the roiling clouds and he welcomed it even as it drenched his fine clothes and soaked his new shoes. He didn't care. The tears he'd suppressed since hearing Glad was safe could now freely fall. Tears and raindrops. Who could tell the difference? He raced to the Imperial Hotel, oblivious to both the shouts of the drivers he dashed in front of and the scowls of people he brushed by.

TWENTY EIGHT

THE FOUR OF THEM LOOKED toward the door as rain-saturated air gusted into the lobby. A bedraggled and drenched young fellow stood just inside the entrance. Well, thought Sage, at least he is well-dressed. He jumped up and headed for Terry, reaching him the same time as the bellboy. Sage turned to the uniformed young man and said, "Kindly fetch some towels for my son, here, if you will." A silver coin accompanied the request and the bellboy ran off, returning just as Sage and Terry reached the lobby sofa.

Now they were five. Hanke and Trumbull faced the door; Sage, Mae, and Terry faced the elevators. Anyone would think them a gathering of relatives. The hotel manager beamed at their presence. The guest, a man named "Miner" was very well dressed and had just rented a double room for himself and his son. The two women visiting with Miner were proper matrons and escorted by an equally respectable gentleman who looked vaguely familiar. They'd ordered coffee, tea, and pastries and had quietly conversed for the last half hour or so.

Soon they would rise and head into the dining room now that Miner's son had arrived. The silly kid had gone out without his coat. A worry flitted that maybe the boy's wet pants would stain the sofa cushion until he remembered seeing the father lay a towel down before the boy sat. These were decent, upstanding, thoughtful people—exactly who the hotel wanted as guests.

Sage turned to Terry. "So, what we need you to do is identify the man you saw at Clark's. We expect him to come out of the elevator."

Terry's face screwed up. "How do you know he's going to come out of the elevator? We could sit here all night waiting for him. I want to see my brother. I need to see Glad."

"Shh, Terry. The man will be down momentarily. Right after Vera Clark gets here."

Even as he spoke, Hanke and Millie straightened in their chairs as a cold draft hit the back of Sage's neck. "She's here, isn't she?" he said without turning around.

"Right on time, that one," Hanke said. "She's come in from Broadway. She's heading for the reception desk, speaking to the clerk and now he's picking up the house phone." Hanke glanced around, giving an imperceptible nod at a man who stood perusing newspaper headlines at the lobby newsstand and another to the man quietly smoking a cigar near the hotel's Washington Street exit.

Mae and Millie rose to their feet and began wandering the lobby, making a show of admiring the décor, the ceiling's stucco whorls and the various paintings on its walls. Slowly they drifted in Clark's direction. She'd taken a seat near the piano, screened by a row of potted palms. Mae and Millie settled into a conversational seating just beyond the palms where Russell was already waiting, his new camera concealed in a bag.

Sage pulled the boy closer to him. "Get ready, Terry. Lean against me and tuck your face behind my arm so neither one of them will recognize you. We don't want to take any chances." Terry pressed close and Sage felt the boy trembling, though whether from excitement or fear, he couldn't tell.

For seemingly endless moments a breathless stillness filled the lobby, each person having a role in the silent tableau of those who waited and watched. Hanke and Sage stared silently at each other until a soft ping cut through the silence, signaling the arrival of an elevator car. Both men straightened in their chairs as the ornate bronze doors slid open and a well-dressed man stepped out.

Sage stiffened at the same time Terry hissed, "That's him." Sage quickly averted his face because there was a chance the man would find it odd to see Mozart's owner in the lobby.

He needn't have worried. The newcomer didn't glance around as he stalked over to Clark, anger stiff in every line of his body. He loomed over her and quickly spat out something that sent her fishing in her handbag.

Hanke and Sage exchanged a look. This was it. Sage whispered to Terry, "Stay here." Both men moved quickly, Sage heading for the

Broadway door, Hanke to admire a flower arrangement decorating a table in mid-lobby.

Clark thrust a paper at the man who read it, crushed it and threw it in her face. Then he froze as realization washed over him. He slowly turned to survey the lobby. When his eyes met Sage's, Sage winked.

That was all it took. The man exploded into action, running for a door just beyond the piano. He was only a few strides away from it when Russell's camera flashed and he stumbled. Mae stepped out from behind a palm. With a two-handed shove, Sage's mother sent the flash-disoriented felon crashing to the floor.

Vera Clark, meanwhile, jumped up and ran for the Broadway exit, holding her skirts far higher than considered respectable in such an upscale establishment. Sage and the other policeman moved forward to block the door. She halted a few feet away and looked frantically around the lobby for another escape route.

"Don't even think about it, Miss Clark. Every exit is covered," said the officer who moved forward, whirled her around and snapped steel bracelets on her wrists.

Across the lobby, Hanke was pulling a manacled Ambrose Abernathy to his feet. Once everyone was gathered in the lobby's center, the camera's flash popped again and again. Sage cast a look at the reception desk. The arrests had happened so fast that the manager was still immobile, his mouth frozen in a shocked "o".

Though surrounded by three policemen, Mae, Millie, Sage and Terry, the two criminals only had eyes for each other. "You stupid bitch. If not for you, they wouldn't be here," snarled Abernathy.

"Don't think I'm taking the blame for what you ordered done," she snapped back and followed her words with a wad of spit that landed on his chin and dribbled down onto his ornate vest. She turned to Hanke, 'Every single thing was Abernathy's idea. He told us what to do. He ordered the kidnappings and Jasper's murder. I didn't have nothing to do with none of it. He made me do it. And, Willard killed Jasper, not me."

"'Jasper'? Who's Jasper?" Sage had never heard that name.

His question turned her eyes toward him and her mouth fell open in surprise. "Why, you're the messenger. What are you—" Her glance fell on Terry and the fear on her face tightened into anger. "You little shit. You did this, didn't you?" She made as if to charge at him but Terry stood his ground. "You'll pay," he promised. "You'll pay for every single thing you did."

Hanke grinned and turned to his two men. "Take them to the station but keep them separated. I'll be along in a tick."

Once the prisoners were gone, Hanke turned to Mae. "Thanks to your shove, we caught him. I missed covering that door. What did you two ladies hear them say?"

Millie waved a small pocket notebook. "At last, I found a use for that shorthand they made me take." She glanced down and read:

"He said, 'You stupid woman, I told you never to come here. You stick out like a sore thumb.'"

"She said: 'What do you mean? You told me to come here.'"

"He said, 'Ridiculous. That opium crap has you imagining things.'"

"Then Clark dug around in her purse and held out the note," Millie said. "There was silence as he read it and then he said, 'Oh my God, they're on to us.' Then he threw it at her and took off running and so did she."

"You'll testify to all that, Mrs. Trumbull?" Hanke asked.

She gave him a wide smile, her big brown eyes twinkling. "Why, I would be delighted to, Sergeant Hanke."

This exchange came to an abrupt halt as the entrance door flew open and an intent Matthew strode swiftly up to them. He grabbed Sage's elbow and pulled him aside. "Mr. Eich says the Willard fellow must have taken Miss Lucinda into the underground. We need to meet him and Mr. Fong at Clark's house pronto quick."

TWENTY NINE

THEY'D BEEN STANDING IN A basement for at least fifteen minutes when light began glowing in the distance. Willard quickly twisted his lantern off and pulled her into a corner. His arm gripped her around the waist, holding her against him as he pressed a dirty hand tight across her mouth. She began struggling until he moved the meaty hand to cover her nose as well. Only when she'd quieted did he let her breathe again.

Eyes wide, she watched the light brighten. This was it. Her one chance. She prayed those coming were Fong or his cousins. Willard would stand no chance against Fong, she was certain of that. She reached up, pried feebly at Willard's hand and then let her prying hand drift down to her bodice. With trembling fingers, she fished for the hatpin. Once she gripped its steely stem, she held it tight and waited.

This is it. I'll just have one chance, she thought and took a slow, deep breath through her nose. As she did so, Sage's face filled her mind, his dark blue eyes warm with approval. Feeling strong, she tightened her grip and stabbed at the hand across her mouth, trying to drive the pin straight through it.

Willard roared and flung her aside. She caught her balance, lifted her skirts and ran, leaving the pin behind, certain she'd plunged it deep into the brute's hand. "Good, that'll take him a bit to recover," she murmured even as she ran towards the light.

Just as she passed through an arch in a basement wall, Willard roared, "Grab her!" When those words penetrated, Lucinda halted and stared at the two men she could now see. Scruffy, gap-toothed white men, they stared back at her. Realization struck. These were no rescuers. These two were the men Willard had been waiting for. Shanghaiers.

Lucinda whirled and ran back the way she'd come, straight past the corner where Willard stood cursing. The two men must have finally jumped into action because the light behind her bounced and grew, sending her shadow far ahead and lighting up the entrance to the Burnside Street tunnel. Five steps inside and the light vanished. Her fingers groped for the brick sidewall and used its damp surface to guide her forward.

The darkness lasted mere seconds because her three pursuers were close on her heels with their two lanterns held high. She ran faster not thinking about what she'd do when she reached the other end. About midway under the street, she started screaming, "Help, help!" and ran faster.

Suddenly her wall was gone and she stumbled into another basement. Strong hands grabbed her by the waist and jerked her to one side. Startled all she could do was gasp and fill her lungs to let loose another scream. "Shh, you're safe now Lucinda, sweetheart," whispered a familiar voice in her ear.

She froze, not believing what she'd just heard. "Sage?"

The hands turned her around and pressed her against an equally familiar chest. Squeezed tight, surrounded by the smell of him, "Sage," she said again and hugged him back with every bit of strength she had left. For a minute, they just stood there, both awash with relief.

Another familiar voice spoke in the darkness. "Better move out of way. Maybe hug later."

Sage reacted quickly, pulling her against a nearby wall. "Stay right here," he said, "This will be over in a minute, you'll see."

"Sage, that boss is the new lawyer, Abernathy. He's the one I had to throw out of my house so I recognized him when he went into Vera's house," she whispered.

Sage patted her arm. "Hanke's arrested him," he whispered in return.

"Quit your bitching. You ain't gonna be late getting back to the ship," came the muffled voice of a man.

"Willard has a gun in his back pocket," Lucinda whispered.

An advancing light entered the tunnel. In its faint glow, Lucinda saw her rescuers: Sage, Eich, Fong, Hanke, and two of his uniformed officers stood waiting on either side of the tunnel entrance.

Willard's high pitched haranguing came ever nearer and clearer. "Don't blame me. I told you this was a stupid way to deliver her. A carriage would have been better but, oh, no, you wanted me to drag her around down here."

There was a muted answer and Willard responded, "Where the hell can she go with no light? We'll corner her. I saved her hat pin just so's I can return it to her the same way she gave it to me, with interest."

Even knowing she was safe, his threat sent a chill skittering up Lucinda's spine. She held her breath as Willard stepped out of the tunnel and into the basement with the two other men close behind. Ten steps in, just as Willard raised his lantern to search for her, Hanke shouted, "Police! Halt!" and rushed forward.

With remarkable speed, the two shanghaiers turned tail and ran back the way they'd come. Hanke opened his lantern's shutter as he and his men gave chase.

That left Willard who stood rooted, staring at the small Chinese man and the larger white man who were cautiously advancing on him. In an explosive movement, he threw his lantern at them. The basement went black until Eich, standing in front of Lucinda, opened the shutter on his lantern.

In that dim light, the action began. Willard waded forward like a big bear, his arms wide. Fong glanced at Sage. "You want it quick or you want to play?" he asked.

Sage glanced at Lucinda, took in her muddy dress, filthy hair and face and said, "Quick" as he stepped back. Fong grinned and sidled forward.

Now it was Eich who put an arm around Lucinda and pulled her close, as if to shelter her from the sight of violence. She pushed his arm away and stepped so she could watch, "No, no. I don't want to miss a single minute of this. I might learn something," she said.

He chuckled. "No wonder Mae is so fond of you. You could be her daughter." His words instantly blurred her vision.

She blinked rapidly, not wanting to miss seeing the small Chinese man in action. Fong stepped toward the hulking Willard. In a flash, Fong's head and shoulders went down and to the side, even as his foot connected with Willard's chin. The big man staggered back.

Willard snatched up a loose brick and charged forward with the brick raised. Fong stepped in, grabbed the wrist of the hand holding the brick and effortlessly flipped it to the side. The brick flew through the air and landed at Lucinda's feet.

Seconds later Fong sent Willard staggering back again, nearly into Lucinda who shoved him forward with both hands. As Willard flailed for balance, his hand groped for the gun butt sticking up from his waistband.

In an instant, Lucinda had picked up the brick and jumped forward. "Oh, no you don't!" she exclaimed and brought it down on the back of Willard's head. The big man's knees buckled and he collapsed face-first in the dirt, a small gun lying inches from his hand.

Wordlessly, the three men turned to look at her, astonishment on their faces.

"You said you wanted 'quick.' Besides, I owed him," she said. She dropped the brick and dusted her hands together, a smug smile on her face.

They chuckled and Sage stepped forward. Lifting her in his arms he hugged her so tight it hurt. When he set her down, he whispered in her ear, "That's my girl but, whew, you could maybe benefit from a bath."

She responded by punching his arm in the exact spot where Mae always punched him.

Whines and curses echoed from the tunnel down which the two shanghaiers had fled, cutting short their playful exchange. Hanke and his men emerged, the officers tightly gripping two handcuffed men.

"You caught them!" Sage exclaimed.

Hanke shook his head. "Nah, Fong's men caught them and delivered them right to us. Soon as we handcuffed these rapscallions, the Chinamen disappeared." He turned to Fong, "Thank them for us, will you?"

Lucinda looked at Willard who'd begun to stir. "You better cuff him as well. He and Vera Clark are responsible for the death of a little boy named Dougie Spencer. And, he also murdered someone else. I suspect it was the cabbie who drove me around before they locked me in Vera's cellar."

She turned to Sage and asked the question she feared most to ask, "The little boy, Glad?"

He grinned at her. "He's safe and sound. He's the reason we found you." At those words, she burst into tears and he again wrapped his arms around her.

THIRTY

"WHAT DID THEY HOPE TO accomplish? I don't understand it," Mae asked as they sat around a large table in Mozart's empty dining room. It was another traditional wrap up of their adventure. Each time, the group seemed to grow larger. Sage, Mae, Fong and his wife Kum Ho had always attended, but their group had grown to include Eich, Hanke, Lucinda, and Matthew. And tonight, there were two more additions: Millie Trumbull and Meachum.

"Some east coast investors wanted to create a national messenger service to rival and eventually takeover ADT, the American District Telegraph company. Abernathy told them he could make that happen. As it turns out, Portland was their test case," Hanke said.

"He told you that?" Sage was mystified.

Hanke shrugged. "Well, it took some piecing together but Vera Clark's running her mouth off. She's terrified of the noose. When I confronted him with the scheme, he didn't deny it."

"What's going to happen to Vera Clark?" This question came from Lucinda and held no animosity.

"She tried to distance herself from Dougie Spencer's and that cabbie, Jasper's, murders but once that hulk, Willard, realized she was going to abandon him, he talked a blue streak. Like Glad thought, they didn't intend Dougie Spencer's death. The boy just tripped on the stairs and the fall broke his neck. But, they are still are responsible since they tied his hands so that he couldn't catch himself when he fell."

Hanke drank deeply of beer and continued, "The cabbie is a different matter. Your surprise visit to his room unnerved him. He went straight to Abernathy and demanded money to leave town. Evidently, he was too greedy. Abernathy agreed to pay but arranged to meet him on the Couch Street dock. When Jasper got there, Willard met him instead. According to Willard, the order came from Vera. She, of course, claims Abernathy ordered the murder. Still, she might not hang since she's been cooperative about giving evidence against Abernathy and Willard but she'll be a guest in the women's prison for many years to come."

"What about those two fellows they caught in Redding?" Sage asked.

"They're residing at the Portland City jail. They've admitted to being the strong-arm part of Abernathy's takeover plot but they insist and, there's no evidence to the contrary, that they had nothing to do with the kidnappings or murders.

Hanke lifted his glass in a salute to Millie Trumbull. "They do admit to attacking your photographer, Mrs. Trumbull. And they also confessed to engineering those little disturbances outside Jeff Hayes's, Hasty Messenger office. We'll charge them with those crimes. Since they've both agreed to testify against Abernathy, Clark, and Willard, the prosecutor will recommend leniency."

Millie straightened in her chair. "I've spoken to my fellow members on the local Child Labor Committee. We plan to use this incident to push the City into drafting an ordinance forbidding children under sixteen from entering in brothels, saloons, gambling dens, and other disreputable places. If he's willing, I'm hoping Terry Tobias will testify before the Common Council as to what he saw in those places when he worked for Speedy Messenger."

"Speaking of Speedy, what happened to Prang and Kimble, the fellows running Speedy?" Sage asked.

"Other than being all around rascals, we have no evidence they were involved in anything more than running the messenger service so that it undercut every other messenger service in town. To do that, they admitted Abernathy ordered them to illegally hire underage kids. Willard probably strong-armed Tobias and Matthew for them, but we can't prove that happened with their knowledge. They've been advised to leave town and I think they've taken that advice."

Matthew cleared his throat and asked, "What about that Willard fellow? What's going to happen to him? Even though he shoved me around, I don't think he has all that many brains between his ears."

"You're right about that. He's almost childlike. Clark took advantage of his stupidity. But my detectives have discovered that the two of them have left dead bodies behind in every town they've lived in. We're still trying to straighten that out. So, Clark may not hang in Oregon but she might in some other state. Like I said, old Willard's talking."

Lucinda was the first to break the ensuing silence. "And, Glad and his family, what's going to happen with them?"

Millie Trumbull's smile was radiant. "Things are working out wonderfully. When Mae and I took Glad to see his mother, you should have seen that poor woman's face. I've never witnessed such joy. In the past week, her health significantly improved. Dr. Lane is confident she'll be ready to leave the sanatorium in less than six months at the rate she's going."

Mae jumped in, "I saw the children yesterday. Millie's gotten them settled at the Boy's and Girl's Home. The three oldest are going to school with both boys working just two hours every day after school. Glad's still selling newspapers. He's still got those big plans for buying a regular route. Terry's now apprenticed to a carpenter. Come summer, he'll be working full time. Little Carrie Lynne is finally getting a chance to be a child instead of a little mother. And, baby Emma Jane is thriving."

Sage spoke up. "I talked to Stuart Franklin. He needs someone to help around the boarding house. When Mary Tobias is healthy enough she has the job. And, the good news is that the house right next door is being renovated and will be just perfect for the family."

Lucinda grinned at Sage, letting him know she knew exactly who had bought the house and was turning it into a suitable home for the Tobias family. He responded with a slight shrug.

"Those are fine children," Mae said. "Mary Tobias has done a good job raising them."

Sage raised a glass in a silent toast to her comment and added, "Both boys are doing well in school. Glad's started that morning paper route he wanted. Terry is liking carpentry. He says that's what his dad did before the liquor got him. They both insist that we call on them if ever we need help with anything."

"I saw Glad yesterday," Lucinda said. "He couldn't stop talking about how grateful he was."

"I'm sure you buying him that paper route had something to do with his gratitude," Sage said as he sent a tender look in her direction.

Hanke cleared his throat and turned a somber face toward Meachum. "Mr. Meachum, Mr. Adair says you know something about that little boy who died of exposure."

Meachum looked down into his wine glass and sighed before meeting Hanke's gaze. "Well, I found a man who rode the rails west with the lad and tried to look out for him. You were right about those burn scars. He worked in a glass factory but not in Chicago. He traveled here all the way from St. Louis. His name was Johnny Devlin. He was only nine-years-old. He'd worked at the glass furnaces for three years."

Meachum's face stayed glum. "The man said that Johnny'd been bought off one of those orphan trains by a couple who lived on a floating barge in St. Louis. They bought four boys off the same train, including Johnny. The boys were made to work shifts in the glass factory. Since the barge only had two bunks for the kids, two of the kids were always working in the factory. The couple didn't work at all. Just took the kids' wages and drank them up. I'm told a lot of that goes on in St. Louis.

"Both of Johnny's parents died but he remembered hearing them talk about a cousin who lived here in Portland. So, when Johnny ran away, this is where he headed."

Silence lay heavy as they contemplated the life of the dead nine-year-old who'd experienced so little compassion or kindness. As if reading their thoughts, Meachum added. "The fellow who'd traveled with Johnny, and told me all this, was heading for Seattle. He's the one who gave the boy the spare clothes you found with his body and what little money he had. I guess it just wasn't enough to save him." Meachum took a big swallow of wine and looked at them. "At least the poor kid knew some kindness before he died," he said.

Fong stood up and raised his glass. "I give many thanks to Mrs. Trumbull and every person who hears bitter cry of the children." The others joined Fong's toast, the mood lightened, and laughter soon rang out.

Sage caught Lucinda's eye and jerked his head toward the front door. They both got up and soon stood outside in night air that hinted at spring's coming warmth.

Sage draped an arm around Lucinda's shoulders and pulled her close. "I was so worried about losing you. I never, ever, want to worry like that again."

She looked up into his face. "Sage, it was the thought of you that kept me going during the worst moments."

"Lucinda, will you marry me?" Sage asked. He was surprised at the words, hadn't known they were coming until they burst from his lips. He knew he meant them and felt a sweet relief from saying them.

Her eyes filled with tears as she looked at him. "Oh Sage, you don't know how much I've wanted to hear you say those words."

He grinned. "Is that a, 'Yes'?"

She cradled his face in her hands, the tears spilling down her cheeks. "I love you, Sage. I want to always be with you but I can't marry you."

He jerked his face away, feeling shock and pain. "What do you mean?"

She waved a hand at the people they could see through Mozart's front window. The recitation of the adventure over, their faces were alight with good cheer. "Look at them," she said softly.

And Sage looked at the people sitting around the table: Mae and Eich, Hanke, Meachum, Fong and Kum Ho, young Matthew and even Millie Trumbull. "They'd never object. Mother loves you. Everybody loves you."

At those words, her tears increased. "I know, Sage. I have you to thank for giving me the first real family I've ever known. But, what you and they are doing is important. I am proud to be a part of that and it would end if we were to marry."

He shook his head vehemently. "No, it wouldn't have to end."

"Portland's most eligible and wealthy bachelor marrying the city's most notorious brothel owner?" Her arched smile pierced him.

"We don't have to stay here."

"Where could we possibly go that I wouldn't be recognized? My patrons are wealthy men. They all travel extensively. And, what about your work for St. Alban? Sure we could move to some small, out-of-the-way town where maybe I'd go unrecognized. But how could you carry on your work in a place like that? What about the people here who depend on you?"

She gestured again toward those sitting inside the city's second most exclusive restaurant. "How could you bear to leave them and your work behind?"

She placed gentle fingers on his cheek, her expression soft, a teary mix of love and regret. "With all of my heart I thank you for your proposal but I must say, 'No.'" She gave his face one last caress before she turned and went back inside.

Sage stood on the sidewalk, staring sightlessly down the empty street and then up into the drifting overcast. "Well, damn," he said aloud before he turned and followed her back into Mozart's.

The End

Historical Notes

THIS STORY'S TITLE IS TAKEN from John Spargo's book, *The Bitter Cry of the Children,* published in 1906. Spargo provided clear and convincing evidence that thousands of American schoolchildren suffered from starvation and malnourishment. Today, Spargo is best known for the impact he had on the child labor issue although his lifetime focus was on all the negative impacts of childhood poverty.

Rather than adding to historical notes below, I wanted to confirm, here, three historical facts included in *Bitter Cry.* First, at the time this story takes place, funeral parlor directors also served as coroners. Second, the Flying Squadron, with its discipline of brutal railroad bulls, did exist though just a few years later than when this story takes place. And, finally, the gambling den labyrinth described in the story was taken from a news article of the time that was written by a reporter who accompanied the police on an unsuccessful raid. Some of the story's other taken-from-history historical facts are as follows:

Social Agencies

1. There were scores of social service agencies in Portland in the early 1900's. This story mentions just a few of them. Many of these agencies were created through the efforts of progressive women, though written history fixates on the involvement of what was frequently a figurehead male.

2. The Boy's and Girl's Aid Society was incorporated in 1885 as a charitable, nonsectarian organization. It received homeless, neglected and abused children from all parts of the state, from infancy to 16 years. All children of school age in its care attended public schools. Many children were temporarily housed by the Society until their parents were able to care for them.

3. In 1904, "The People's Institute" was established in the heart of the working-class North End. Valentine Pritchard, a kindergarten teacher and trained settlement worker, served as its first director. After visiting homes in the neighborhood, Pritchard saw that the Institute provided services to meet the most pressing needs: kindergarten; laundry and bathing facilities; classes in citizenship, hygiene, sewing, cooking, and mothering; also provided were an employment bureau and a free medical clinic. The Institute is credited with being the origin of the University of Oregon's low-income outpatient clinic. The words spoken by the Pritchard character about the plight of the country's and Portland's poor children were taken directly from reports of the day.

4. The open-air TB sanatorium was located on River Road between Milwaukie and Oak Grove and was the first in the state. It was much as described in the story, with small cabins, tents and an administration building situated on a wooded bluff above the Willamette River. Sister Mary Theresa, formerly Carolyn Glisan, was its first director. She is a featured character in an earlier Sage Adair mystery, *The Mangle*. The Sister is also notable for using sociological data to convince the state legislature of the necessity for minimum wage and maximum hours legislation—the first such enforceable laws in the nation. The Visiting Nurses Association was an important component of the medical care provided to Portland's poor.

5. The Women's Trade Union League (WTUL), one branch being in Seattle, was the first instance of middle-class women joining with working-class women to organize unions and eliminate sweatshop conditions. In the first two decades of the twentieth century, the WTUL played an important role in supporting the massive strikes that established the International Ladies'

Garment Workers' Union and Amalgamated Clothing Workers of America. The organization was also at the forefront of campaigns for women's suffrage and workplace protection. The organization existed until 1950.

Millie Trumbull

6. When I started researching for this story, I'd never heard of Millie Trumbull. Now, I feel something akin to outrage that there is no civic recognition of her contributions—no statue of her, no street named after her. Many of Portland's streets are named after rich white men whose greedy self-interest shaped the city…as it still does today, unfortunately. At last count, Trumbull was a board member of at least in at least fifteen organizations that were dedicated to social improvement and justice. Not only did she sit on these boards, but she usually was the secretary of the organization. In that position, she performed the yeoman's work of the organization—report writing, correspondence, public speaking, etc.

7. Trumbull did everything attributed to her in the story and much more. Among other efforts, she advocated before the legislature for minimum age laws and compulsory education. She served as the Oregon Child Labor Commission's first staff person and inspector. She arm-twisted Portland's Common Council into outlawing underage messengers in saloons, brothels, gambling dens, and other disreputable places. And, some credit must also go to her husband who supported her innumerable unpaid endeavors.

Harry Lane – Poor People's Doctor

8. Harry Lane grew up in Lane County which was named after his grandfather, the first territorial governor and senator of Oregon. Despite being educated in elite Eastern schools, Lane chose to forego the privilege his family's wealth and history offered. Instead, he became a rabble-rouser and doctor to Portland's poor. He was, in fact, known as Portland's "Poor People's Doctor."

9. Considered "witty, unafraid, and pugnacious" Lane fought unsuccessfully for a meat inspection code for local packing houses. He also fought to prevent the use of "night soil" as fertilizer on Portland's commercial truck farms. When that plea fell on deaf ears, he took a gun to the largest truck farm and blew apart all of the clay jugs storing the human waste. There is no record of him being arrested but his action apparently put a halt to the practice.

10. Lane was appointed director of Oregon's hospital for the insane but he only held the position for four years. He immediately took on the rampant corruption and graft at the hospital which earned him strident and effective opposition from contractors, government administrators, and politicians.

11. Disgusted with the City's lack of response to his very accurate and forceful demands for certain social hygiene practices, Lane successfully ran for Portland Mayor in 1905. While in office, he stayed loyal to middle and lower-class Portlanders and attempted improvements—all of which were in the vanguard of the progressive changes being sought nationwide. Of course, his entire tenure was bedeviled with unrelenting opposition from the monied and developer classes.

12. Lane was the first mayor to value the inclusion of women in traditionally male roles. He appointed Dr. Esther Pohl Lovejoy as City Health Officer; Sarah Evans as market inspector; and, Lola Baldwin as the nation's second policewoman.

13. Also as mayor, Lane took on the major corporations, especially the railroads and utilities, by demanding better regulation. He promoted public control of utilities, started the Portland Rose Festival and spent his two terms as mayor battling special interests, fraudulent contractors, prostitution and gambling.

14. Newspapers of the time report an incident where Lane learned of a complaint of fraudulent performance of city contracts. Specifically, he was informed that the new sidewalk curbs were hollow—evidently, it was a way for the contractor to use less concrete while charging for more. Lane took a hammer out to the

construction site and began hitting the new curbs to see if they were hollow. They were. Young boys were watching him so he enlisted them to throw stones at the curbs and put a chalk "X" on all those that rang hollow. Most did. The contractor wasn't paid.

15. Lane's consistent advocacy of progressive change stood him in good stead when he ran for the U.S. Senate because he won the office. He continued to have great support from his constituency until he was confronted by World War I. He was one of only six senators who opposed the war. In Oregon, the response to was a campaign to impeach him. He died on May 23, 1917, while riding the train back to Oregon to face his critics.

16. Lane is also noteworthy for his advocacy on behalf of Native Americans in the U.S. Senate. When he was growing up, he spent a considerable time with the local Native American tribe in Lane County. In the Senate, he honored that experience by proposing numerous pieces of legislation that would have benefitted the people he believed had been cruelly and unjustly treated during the Euro-American invasion of the West.

Henry Russell

17. The character of Henry Russell was inspired by the work and contributions of Lewis Hine who has been called the "Crusader with a Camera". Without a doubt, his photographs of child workers did more to educate and outrage the public about the problem than the reams of studies, articles and opinions being written by progressives at the time.

18. Hine worked for the National Child Labor Committee. He traveled the country sneaking and bluffing his way into workplaces where he obtained beautiful but heartrending pictures of the children producing coal, textiles, glass, artificial flowers, food, shoes, shell fish, as well as those children earning money through child care, selling newspapers and delivering messages. Hine wrote with great feeling about his photo subjects describing, for example, one child subject as: "An emaciated little

elf 50 inches high and weighing perhaps 48 pounds…[who] works from 6 at night to 6 in the morning."

19. Today, Hine's photographs are lauded, both for their ability to touch hearts and for their technical and artistic quality. He is credited with capturing the beauty that resided in every single child he photographed. But this recognition came too late for Hine. He died in abject poverty, his contributions forgotten.

Mother Jones

20. Mary Harris Jones, "Mother Jones" began life as an immigrant who'd fled the Irish potato famine only to lose her husband and all four children to yellow fever. Following those dire circumstances she began fighting for worker rights. Using rousing speeches and theatrical gestures, she forced the American public to notice the cruelty inherent in child labor, working-class poverty and the capitalists' greed.

21. In 1903, to protest the lax enforcement of minimal child labor laws in the Pennsylvania mines and silk mills, Mother Jones organized and led a children's march from Philadelphia to the home of President Theodore Roosevelt in New York. Banners of her Children's Crusade made declarations like: "We want to go to school and not the mines!" Roosevelt refused to meet with the children but her Crusade put child labor firmly on the public agenda and helped to push reform forward.

Child Labor

22. My recent legacy-related thoughts have focused on the long-term impact of textile mills on the white Southern mindset. Post-civil war, the mills in the South grew from a few hundred to thousands. Both northern and southern money funded that explosive growth. The mill owners built houses and towns around their mills and recruited Southern tenant farmers who were starving on land exhausted by tobacco and cotton crops.

These desperate people considered a steady job in the mills, with a house, to be a great leap up the economic ladder.

23. These textile mill towns created two problems. The first problem was that only whites were hired, never blacks. And second, the owners focused on hiring tenant farmers who had lots of children. A condition of the adults' employment was a signed contract stating that their children would also work in the mills as soon as they reached age five or even younger. These children then had to work in the mills ten to twelve hours a day, six days a week. They never went to school.

24. When Southern progressives tried to make schooling compulsory, these white parents were manipulated by the owners to fight those efforts. They also joined with the mill owners to fight minimum age labor laws. They wanted their children working in the mills earning money for the family and they feared losing their own jobs. Ironically, because these turn-of-the-century mills would not hire black adults or children, the black children's parents sent them to school.

25. According to 1900 census data there were 580,000 children in the U.S., between the ages of ten and fourteen, who could neither read nor write. Of these, 570,000 were in the Southern states. The other 10,000 were in the Northern and Western states.

26. The withholding of education from Southern white children, as well as their parent's opposition to laws that would educate and better their children's lives, had to create a mentality and legacy in the South that is still at play today.

Newsboys

27. According to author Hugh Hindman, it is no exaggeration to say that most poor, urban boys worked as newsboys for at least a short period. After buying their papers from the publisher, the "newsies" would hawk the papers on street corners. This arrangement meant that they only profited when they sold a

paper. The situation led to fierce competition between them for the best locations and made established residential routes their preferred way to sell papers.

28. Portland's newsboys started the Newsboys' Benefit Association in 1903. It mostly focused on providing a safe place off the streets for its members and on giving them social opportunities like theater going, fair going and holiday dinners. Later it began to address working conditions and income. Unfortunately, intense lobbying by the large city newspapers caused the legislators to exempt the newsboys from the minimum age legislation.

29. The Chicago superintendent of a boy's home stated that one-third of the newsboys who entered the home were suffering from venereal disease. Another large city educator stated that the newsboys, who infrequently attended school, were fully one-third smaller in stature than boys of the same age.

Messenger Boys

30. The National Child Labor Committee was particularly opposed to night messenger work by children for precisely the reasons set forth in this story. Most of the night messenger work involved going into brothel houses, gambling dens, saloons and other such places. And the danger was real. The statistics from juvenile delinquency homes of the time establish that boys who formerly worked as messengers far outnumbered boys who worked in every other occupation except for newsboys. And, newsboys came in second.

31. Western Union was the single largest employer of child labor at the dawn of the twentieth century. The American District Telegraph (ADT) was the second largest. In Portland, messengers struck the ADT in 1903 to win a 2-cent per message increase. There is no evidence, however, of a Portland area scheme to supplant local area messenger services.

32. Sage's messenger adventures with the cow in the garden, crying baby and missing husband were taken directly from local news

articles of the time. These articles were intended to give readers an understanding of the messenger job.

33. The character of Jeff Hayes in this story is based on a real person. Hayes managed a number of messenger services in town until he began owning and operating the Hasty Messenger Company. He was blind but well-known for exercising strict control over his messengers. Long before the Common Council enacted an ordinance, Hayes declared that his messengers, ". . . are not allowed to enter disreputable houses, drink, smoke cigarettes or use profanity."

34. Idle messengers were blamed for hooliganism at the corner of Third and Stark Streets, in front of the Hasty Messenger Company. This included throwing a Chinese man's laundry onto the street. It created a problem for Hasty Messenger Company with Jeff Hayes defending his messengers and insisting that the miscreants were not from his company. During this time, messengers riding after dark without bicycle taillights were arrested and fined two dollars.

35. Hayes took great pride in the accomplishments of his former messengers, telling a reporter that, "I have employed probably 5000 boys and clerks and out of this small army less than half have turned out bad. One of the brightest men in the last legislature was one of my former messengers, and he had the pleasure of greeting in the Legislative hall, six other former comrades. We have doctors, lawyers, dentists, actors, and businessmen by the score. And I know of four ministers of the gospel who formerly 'donned the cap' in the messenger service."

36. In November 1905, the *Oregonian* announced the formation of the Messenger Boy's Protective Union. Its initial purpose was to provide a safe place for messengers to sleep. In 1906, there was a small walkout staged by the messengers of Portland's Western Union office. It lasted only an afternoon. The widespread installation of telephones doomed the messenger occupation. By the 1920s messenger services had greatly diminished in the country's economic life.

Glass Factories

37. Reports at the turn of the 20th century stated over 7,500 boys under the age of sixteen worked in glass factories, two-thirds of them during the night shift. This number is thought to be grossly under-reported. The work was hard, intensely hot, and required constant heavy lifting. One social statistician recorded that a child glass worker traveled twenty-two miles during a single shift. Glass factory children were frequently ill—especially with rheumatism, TB, and pneumonia. Heavy fumes and dust caused serious respiratory diseases and most children carried scars from burns and cuts. Many became blind.

38. The glass factory experience that led to the death of Johnny Devlin in the story is based on a situation that existed in St. Louis at the turn-of-the-century. Using orphans for factory work began in New England. Some factories were notorious for actually starving and working them to death. In St. Louis, the proliferation of glass factories led to a child worker shortage. Consequently, the glass manufacturers hired "getters" to bring them children. Some of these children were purchased off the orphan trains. The reports of the day noted that some of these glass factory children lived on the river scows of those who'd bought them and essentially turned them into slave labor.

Child Labor and Conditions Today

39. It is estimated that 1 in every 6 American children lives with hunger. More than 12 million children in the United States live in "food insecure" homes. That phrase means that those households don't have enough food for every family member to lead a healthy life. Our country lags behind a number of countries, including some poorer countries, when it comes to feeding school children. Sadly, right-wing politicians have been cutting what little society provides to under-fed families and have been engaged in "food-shaming" schoolchildren who need nutritional support. One school district in New Jersey stated, in August 2019, that it planned to let its students go hungry if the

student owed more than twenty dollars for lunch.

40. While federal law currently prohibits minors from working in non-farm industries until they're 14, for example, that is not true of farm labor. Children as young as 12 can be hired to perform agricultural work for longer hours, and under more hazardous conditions than children in other industries. Many of these children are immigrants and refugees from Latin America's despotic regimes supported by the U.S. government and global mega-corporations.

41. Children working in U.S. tobacco fields face great health risks. When Human Rights Watch interviewed 140 child tobacco workers in North Carolina, Kentucky, Tennessee and Virginia, the majority reported symptoms consistent with acute nicotine poisoning, including nausea, vomiting, headaches, and dizziness. The U.S. is the world's fourth-largest producer of tobacco, yet it has no regulations to protect children in the fields from being poisoned by nicotine exposure. Some tobacco compa-nies are now refusing to purchase tobacco from farms employ-ing children younger than 16, but voluntary policies are not enough.

42. The Koch Brothers' right-wing American Legislative Exchange Council (ALEC) has drafted model child labor legislation. Four states have adopted ALEC legislation that lessens restrictions on child labor. Missouri's Republican speaker of the house pro-posed eliminating all workplace inspectors after learning that they had issued over 1700 citations for child labor violations.

43. In dismantling child labor protections, Wisconsin focused on older students—age 16 and over—but enacted much more sweeping legislation, abolishing all restrictions on the number of hours minors are permitted to work during the school year. Previously, 16- and 17-year-olds could not work more than five hours a day on school days or more than 26 hours per week during the school year or more than six days in a row. Despite substantial evidence that increased workloads make it more difficult for students to concentrate in school, the new

law frees 16- and 17-year-olds to work an unlimited number of hours per week, seven days a week, throughout the school year. Maine, Idaho, and Michigan have followed Wisconsin's backward-steps with somewhat less draconian repeals of child labor protections.

44. Today throughout the world, around 218 million children work, many full-time. They do not attend school and have little or no time to play. Many do not receive proper nutrition or care. They are denied the chance to be children. More than half of them are exposed to the worst forms of child labor such as working in hazardous environments, slavery or other forced labor in illicit activities including drug trafficking and prostitution, as well as involvement in armed conflict. The ten worst countries for child labor are Bangladesh, Chad, Democratic Republic of Congo, Ethiopia, India, Liberia, Myanmar, Nigeria, Pakistan, and Somalia.

And then there are the countless children maimed, killed and traumatized by war. As John Spargo noted, every harm done to a child ultimately has a negative impact on human society. Who knows what their individual contributions would have been had these mistreated children grown up healthy, well-fed, educated, and cherished?

ACKNOWLEDGMENTS

SAGE ADAIR HAS BEEN ENCOURAGED to keep fighting for social and economic justice because of the support so many readers have given to this series. As always, the biggest thank-you goes to them. I especially want to thank those people who have invited me to speak to their reading groups and gatherings. Sage, Mae, Fong, and the other like-minded people resonate with readers of this series. Every time I speak, I hear stories of other families' hardships and unsung triumphs in days gone by.

The series is written for those who are fighting for and, support, progressive change today. Encouragement and inspiration abound in the triumphs and courage of those progressives who fought for economic and social justice one hundred years ago against opposition that was just as strong, powerful and amoral as what progressives face today.

As always I am grateful for the work done by the staff of the Portland City Archives, the Oregon State Archives, and the Oregon Historical Society. All of these people are working to preserve our history and heritage. They deserve our gratitude and support.

I also especially want to thank Michael Munk, author of the valuable *Portland Red Guide*, for introducing me to his neighbors; Kelley Baker, author and screenwriter who wrote the wonderful *Road Dog*; and, Layne Poncy, a hostess of KBOO radio's *Labor Show*. Each of them, in their unique way, has contributed much in order to make all our lives better.

Special thanks go to Christine Webb who painstakingly tried to identify and correct all the errors in the story. If any remain, it's solely on me.

And finally, as always, I must acknowledge my husband, George Slanina. Like Millie Trumbull's husband, his unwavering support, kindness and always pithy observations continue to make this series possible. As I've said before, one can never acknowledge or appreciate wonderful partners too often or too much.

*Thank you for reading **Bitter Cry***

*We invite you to share your thoughts and reactions
with your library and on Goodreads as well as on your
favorite social media and retail platforms.*

We appreciate your support!

Black Drop

In this ripping yarn, President Theodore Roosevelt has left Washington D.C., embarking on his historic train trip through the American West. Little does he know that assassination awaits him in Portland, Oregon. The words of a dying prostitute warn Sage Adair and his allies that they will be blamed for Roosevelt's murder. Since life is never simple, Sage also learns of young boys who need rescuing from a fate worse than death. As the presidential train and the boys' doom rush ever closer, every crucial answer remains elusive. Who is enslaving the boys? Who plans to kill the president? Can either tragedy be stopped?

Dead Line

Sage Adair encounters murder and mayhem midst the sagebrush and pine trees of Central Oregon's high desert. This captivating land of big skies, golden light and deadly secrets is the home of hardy and hard people–some of whom intend to kill him.

The Mangle

During a blistering 1903 summer, Portland's steam laundry women are working ten hellish hours a day. Exhausted and ill, they demand a nine-hour workday. Sage Adair, and his mother, Mae, join their fight until women begin disappearing. Desperately searching for the missing women, Sage and Mae face grave danger midst suffragettes, prostitutes, social workers, white slavers, arsonists and heartless bosses. Inspired by actual historical events, this is the sixth book in the award-winning Sage Adair mystery series.

Slow Burn

Arson, murder, kidnapping and false accusations abound in this seventh book of the Sage Adair Series. What begins as a simple assignment—helping the city's firefighters unionize, catapults Sage onto firefighting's front lines and into solving the deeper mystery of who is burning down the city and why.

Request for Pre-Publication Notice

If you would like to receive notice of the publication dates of the next Sage Adair historical mystery novel, please contact Yamhill Press at *www.yamhillpress.net*.

NOTES